CRITICAL ACCLAIM FOR "ONE OF OUR BRAVEST, STRONGEST, MOST INTELLIGENT AND WITTIEST WRITERS"*

CAROLYN SEE
AND HER LATEST NOVEL, *MAKING HISTORY*

"RADIANT . . . EXCITING AND IMAGINATIVE . . . See's prose refreshes the ear with the dizzy, jazzy cadences of California speech . . . a daring book."
—*The Plain Dealer* (Cleveland)

"Every page of *Making History,* every word, is tinted the bloodred color of disaster, yet the novel as a whole, steeped in the bright, dry colors of southern California and full of the music of Van Morrison, is A LUMINOUS, HOPEFUL WORK. . . . There's no way a movie of *Making History* could be nearly as upsetting and wonderful as the book."
—*New York Woman*

"A NOVEL THAT SHOULD MAKE HER NAME, AN IRONIC, HEART-MELTING VIEW of the randomness of fate. . . . See demonstrates a new complexity and maturity. Clear-eyed, brave and compassionate, the novel transcends the particulars of tragic fate to offer a soaring vision of the human spirit's capacity to survive." —*Publishers Weekly*

"A RICH, RIVETING NOVEL that feels larger than its 276 pages. In the manner of a nineteenth-century meganovelist, Carolyn See creates characters whose daily rounds begin to seem almost as real, and as involving, as your own."
—*The Village Voice Literary Supplement*

*Alice Adams

Please turn the page for more reviews . . .

MAKING HISTORY

CAROLYN S·E·E

For Clara
And in memory of
Maria

A LAUREL TRADE PAPERBACK
Published by
Dell Publishing
a division of
Bantam Doubleday Dell Publishing Group, Inc.
666 Fifth Avenue
New York, New York 10103

ISBN: 0-440-50496-1

Reprinted by arrangement with Houghton Mifflin Company

Printed in the United States of America

Published simultaneously in Canada

November 1992

10 9 8 7 6 5 4 3 2 1

BVG

I am more grateful than I can adequately express to a world of good men for their help on this book: Joe Kanon, Daniel Calder and Joel Conarroe for their consistent moral and professional support; Warren Christopher for access to his privately printed work; Peter Ackerman for allowing me a glimpse into the workings of international trade; William A. Clark for material on the Tokyo Stock Exchange; Asakawa-san for faultless chivalry; Van Morrison and Peter Straub for inspiration and information; and particularly John Espey for his haiku, his encyclopedic knowledge, his infinite capacity for affection.

I would also like to express my thanks to the men and women of the Guggenheim Foundation for their generous grant.

Making History

Part 1

*The scale of Brahma is vast,
as vast as space in the
universe. Why shouldn't our
mission be infinitesimal?
Aren't all lives, viewed that
way, equally small?*

Bharati Mukherjee
Jasmine

*The "Systems view of life" is
not life, in other words, it is
a way of hiding from the
Abyss once again . . .*

Morris Berman
Coming to Our Senses

Robin

Pacific Palisades

NO ONE EVER SAID I was very bright. But I know some stories. I've got a line like every other guy. I hang out at the beach and I wait. That's the story on me, that's what I'm supposed to do. I know something now — the dead watch us with a terrible caring. That's not much to build a *life* on, but some friends of mine would argue, what's a life?

Hang out. Tell jokes. Watch the sun. Wait for the moon. Count the waves. Count the cars. Watch the highway. Check out the edge of the world. My ambitions aren't high enough, my parents are always telling me. But I tell *them,* what's the big deal? You can divide things, *everything,* down into doing errands or having fun. Sometimes they say in school that everyone's on earth for a reason, but I'm clueless on that score.

This is my idea of a perfect day. Eat some Cheerios. Blow

on my mom's neck. Get out of the house before my dad gets started. (Even though he means well.) Get to school early to show off my outfit. Check out all my friends. Doze through my classes. Laugh through rehearsals, if there's a play going on. Either that or put on my new Hawaiian trunks. Get my flippers out of the garage. Head down to my own favorite beach, north of the Santa Monica pier, and south of Topanga Canyon. That's a five-mile stretch, but I like all of it. I can't settle on what's the best part. Right by the pier, there's a circus that comes every autumn and sets up on the parking lot. No animals, just acrobats and clowns. The Cirque du Soleil. Circus of the Sun. You can rent bicycles there and ride along the strand, north, to Temescal Canyon. (You can turn inland right there up to the Pacific Palisades, where my family lives. It's a great town — small and neat. A girl got shot there a few summers ago, by a security guard, but that's an exception. Everybody loves the Palisades.)

What I like best is the ocean end of town, the side toward the beach, the cliffs that break off like a cookie so you can see what the earth is like, before the highway takes over at the bottom. And then the bike path, and then the sand, and then the water.

All this is my favorite part. Staying at the beach, counting cars. Counting the flags that fly over the circus tent. Waiting for the moon. Taking a dip. Teasing the girls. Coming home late at night, when my parents and my sister are asleep. Looking in the fridge for a snack, even though I'm already filled to the top with the sun and the moon.

I run into new people every day and pick up all the information I can. But no one ever gave me the Intelligence Medal and I never asked for it anyway. That's the *last* thing I wanted. I'm in it for the laughs, cap and bells. Trying to figure out what's important, trying to separate what's an errand from what's having fun.

Jerry

**Pacific Palisades
January 13**

HE WOKE AT FIVE in the morning and his bed was almost always empty. Wynn got up in the night with the kids: Tina needed changing, Josh woke once or twice a night with screaming dreams. As often as not Wynn ended up in Josh's bed, so hard was he to calm down, and so sure had their doctor been about the crime of bringing the children into bed with *them*. Jerry woke alone, not thinking about it, suffocating, because in getting up Wynn doubled the quilt back on him.

Or maybe he had done it to himself.

He had a schedule to adhere to and did, not from vanity but because he had to. Straight from the bed to the rowing machine, which he took slow at first, favoring his back, then, by the end of fifteen minutes, loving the pure feel of blood as it pushed up through his arms, neck, into his brain.

Waking up.

Get the upper body going first.

Then up off the sweat-damp mat, over to the stationary bike placed just to the side of the TV, this bike a constant source of irritation to Wynn. "If you'd just get *up* on it once in a while, you wouldn't mind it so much," Jerry'd say to her, but she kept thin in other ways.

So he biked in the morning, when she was asleep, or still in with Tina or Josh. He turned on the CBS morning show, screwed the earphones into his ears, set up a whir for twenty minutes, but that whir was barely a sound at this hour, no more than the refrigerator downstairs. The kids, after staying up most of the night, tried to log a little shut-eye between four and seven in the morning.

The bedroom here, renovated, faced the ocean, not the inevitable curling surf but — two blocks back from the cliffs which overlooked Santa Monica beach — just the thin horizon line, blue against blue. After seven years Jerry hardly saw it.

Now he kept his eyes from the ocean, looked at the television, watched the news as a participant. Now that he had begun to do so much more international work, he knew that — just the way Palisades High School had been one small world, and prestigious Stanford an intimidating, but still one small world, — so was the *world* just one small world. Watching the news in the morning was like going with Wynn to the opera. By now, he was bound to see two or three people he knew. Countries, too — they were no more than clubs or relay teams. (Some countries were jocks and some were geeks.)

Then, his legs warmed up, his whole body humming, Jerry hit the shower. I am the only one, he thought. I am the only one who's thinking now. I am *up* now. He used a stiff brush to scrub his skin; rubbed himself dry with a rough towel. Looked at his face in the mirror. Worried. Did any country have a redheaded leader? Not that he knew about. His face, despite freckles, despite the fact that his youthful body had placed fifty-second out of a field of thousands in the last L.A. marathon, and despite his lucky, lucky personal life, looked sad.

Just keep it here. In the bathroom. That hypothetical sadness.

Downstairs, breakfast waited for him. Melon, sliced in a pleasing fan of crescents. Lime and pepper on the side. Two bran muffins. Strawberry jam. The paper, unfolded, divided in half: at his place, the Front Page and the Business section; over at Wynn's, for when she woke up, the Calendar section and View. Nothing for Tina and Josh. Well, of course not.

Nothing for Whitney.

He opened the Business section first. Yesterday he'd been summoned down to the *Times* for one of those off-the-record sessions that the paper was famous for. There, in the Tamayo Room, middle level in the Times Mirror Building, he'd tried to keep his mind off the ego of the matter, *I am the one,* and concentrated instead on two things: the giant Tamayo-painted watermelons themselves, and under them the terrierlike curiosity of the brilliant editor of a mighty newspaper who, like any good journalist, Jerry supposed, wanted no more from the world than simply to understand it. Once encompassed, once understood, it might get fixed.

A science staff writer yesterday had remarked, off the wall, that what was the point of going into space when we were ignorant about the world we spring from? He had begun to talk about the impulse to go *out,* as opposed to the impulse to stay *in,* but was frozen midsentence by a look from his boss. Jerry felt of both minds. This *was* a small world. There was hardly a night, if you were the kind to tune to public television, that you couldn't see Asian elephants decked out in electric lights, carrying somebody's sacred tooth from here to there. Alternately, on the six o'clock news, you saw familiar atrocities in any one of a dozen third world countries. Sometimes that third world was East L.A. Maybe the "third world" was everywhere.

A movement from his right. Serve from the left. Remove from the right.

"Buenos días, Carmela."

"Good morning, Mr. Bridges."

"Los muffins está muy bueno."

"Gracias."

She, knowing he liked calm, kept her big body out of his sight, moving in the remodeled, perfect kitchen on the inland side of this perfect California bungalow with its two stories, its screened veranda, its vegetable and flower gardens, its double garage topped off with an architecturally correct cupola for Whitney.

Lightly, lightly, Carmela poured him more coffee. Strong, black, marvelous, with a pitcher of fresh sweet cream. To which he was entitled, because of his fifty minutes of predawn exercise, and because he was a good person, and because he worked so hard in the day, and because there were only the two of them up at this hour, and Carmela treated him to it.

Jerry took his breakfast at the advantageous seat in the breakfast room. Behind him, the kitchen — commodious, with gleaming pots and fresh fruit and alphabet snacks for the kids, and a pasta machine. A pretty room, done in blues, like an inland lake. This breakfast room had glass doors that opened out onto a perfect side garden.

Wynn had seen to it.

When he looked up from his paper — five minutes, he could give himself, if he played the time correctly — he felt and saw the mechanics of his house. He saw places set for the family: Josh's booster chair to his right, and next to that, Tina's high chair (never quite clean, despite Carmela's best efforts). Across from him, on Sunday mornings, sometimes Saturdays, he saw the handsome, intelligent Wynn, but on weekdays, only the garden itself, constructed in layers to comfort his eyes. Because it was January in Los Angeles he lucked out in this one comforting glance: great puffy beds of purple and white sweet alyssum pushing out of grass margins, and cornflowers, and early blooming daffodils, and birds of paradise and a bundle of things he didn't know the name of, but above all that, their Australian acacia was blooming early. The morning sun, filtering through the million golden blossoms, offered him an enclosed world of perfect peace and safety. And *there*! An Audubon's warbler in winter plumage. And then another one.

How could he admit to Wynn that he was grateful she slept in, kept everyone away? Still, before he left, he took count, from the top down: Whitney, respected stepdaughter, asleep up in the cupola across the backyard. More than a stepdaughter, really. There was everything he wanted to tell her: all the things he'd never get to tell his selfish first wife or his dutiful second one either: Look! One summer I lived in Chicago. I had a girlfriend I went to see over in Bloomington. I used to run on a relay team. I was really pretty good! Have you ever noticed — well, you wouldn't have, you've always been so good about giving your mother and me our privacy — that when I sleep, I sleep all over the bed with my arms stretched out? I read somewhere that means that you think of yourself as a king. I don't think that, exactly. I think it means you know the world will give things to you, and because of that, it does. Did you know that I spent a summer in Athens once when I was still at Stanford, just a couple of years older than you are now? That I've seen the Acropolis in the moonlight? Listened to the music they play there on some old Victrola?

Well, she probably knew that. The family had talked about all that before, listened to him tell those stories. But there were things he hadn't told Whitney, hadn't told anyone. Now, in his forties, how could he stop all this *event,* the job, the house, the kids, his clothes, his car, *Malaysia,* for God's sake, *Japan,* and say, "I walked in the Parthenon"? But if he had precious stories he'd never told, it stood to reason so did everyone — the whole world, everybody else.

Whitney, asleep in the cupola she'd claimed within days after they'd decided on the house. Whitney. And upstairs, his gentle Wynn.

At work, between deals, men he knew talked briefly of "hot numbers" they ordered up in Singapore hotels, Manila hotels, the very best on the other side of the Pacific Rim. They cut down on their fooling around at home: it was a matter of money and face and common sense. Nobody at Bartch, Bridges, Freed wanted his marriage to fall apart because of some pushy MBA or pretty paralegal. Nobody wanted to repeat his own father's mistakes. Financially divorce had become an enormous five-year project — planning ahead so you wouldn't be skinned by California law. To do that planning branded you as an asshole in the community, and it cut down on the deals you *should* be making. So Jerry's colleagues ordered up babes in the luxe resorts of Kuala Lumpur; safeguarded their homes, their bank accounts, their reputations, their health, and so on. But Jerry knew, after the disastrous Delia, who had cared about nothing but her *hair* in the whole wide world, that the only other woman in his life was Wynn. He had hung it up for good and all. He could concentrate on business because none of those musky, sandalwood "almond-eyed damsels," as his partner, Loring Freed, called them, spoke to his soul. Jerry's body and mind were perfectly happy with this house, life, lovely wife. He would just like to be able to say to Whitney, *once* (though God knew, she wouldn't take it in, or care), that once his cousin had run into a deer by mistake out on a highway somewhere in Indiana. His family hadn't been poor, but his uncle had roots in the Depression and said that the least his cousin could do in return for busting the car was to go back and butcher the deer. So he and his cousin went back and found it, pulled it off the highway, skinned it, hacked it up. They brought home meat enough for three months to his aunt and uncle. He wanted to tell Whitney, Wynn, he wanted to tell them *all*, that he knew — had firsthand knowledge of — what it meant to cut open something with a knife, put your hand down into the guts of something that had been beautiful. He wanted to put into words his knowledge of how beauty could turn into something else. Of course, he *had* told Wynn: she understood; she loved him, she "heard" him. After his talk (*very* inarticulate), she took him with her strong tanned arms and pretty much hauled him on top of her, so that on clean sheets, with smells of Chanel and fresh flowers and that other fresh, salty smell, he rolled, from the effort to speak, into lust, and then into sleep. And he couldn't tell Josh and Tina yet, but he'd try. They'd see why he felt so strongly that the combining of prudent laws and the imaginative use of money was the best safeguard against the taking of life, which is why he didn't spend as much time at home as he should.

Again Jerry made his count. Starting at the top, asleep across the lawn in the cupola, Whitney. In the east wing, inland and upstairs, Josh, logging shut-eye; by day sunny and sweet, tormented by night. In the room next door, three-year-old Tina, his wacky darling, who went nuts if you said that one word to her: the moon, the *moon*! When he took her out at night to see it, she raised her arms to it and wailed, her teeth chattering, but she loved it — loved that moon. In Josh's narrow bed, in damp silk pajamas, Wynn, who had turned her life over to caring for him and his family. Behind him, quiet and large, Carmela, who had two boys at her home over on L.A.'s East Side, cared for by an *abuela*, so that she, Carmela, could keep it all running. Yes, he saw the injustice, was giving his life to change the injustice — beginning, as he saw it, from the other end of the chain.

He was careful to break down his charitable giving on the computer: a third to his own good life as he saw it (concerts, museums, the opera), a third to AIDS, and a third to the miscellaneous unfortunate (hospitals in Honduras, orphanages in Thailand or Kampuchea). He had bought rough-cut rubies for Wynn in the highlands miles north of Bangkok, where the peddler polished the gems with a grindstone pushed by his own calloused foot — then spurned the currency of the country and asked for a MasterCard. To make that buy was a kind of tithing, a salute to the possible good life everywhere.

Here was the garden: he had only to open this side door and he was in it. Yet — how often had he seen it on his own travels — the world was in fact a mostly hellish place. Jerry believed, as strongly as he believed anything, that the trick to improving the world lay with fixing what was broken. In that he was democratic, even left wing. He believed just as strongly that if something had reached a working perfection, like the '67 Jaguar sedan he drove each day to work, like his second marriage, his wife, his wife's safe gray Volvo, his children, his *count,* then the equally adroit trick was not to mess with what worked. Not to stain its perfection.

He was familiar with financiers — some of them his colleagues — whose ideas of "perfection" were as excessive as, say, an elephant blanketed with hundreds of wires and thousands sof linking electric lights. That was too much. And it implied worlds of peasants who still had no light at all. The point was not to subtract, not to exploit, but to add, to multiply.

Late at night, when Wynn slept, before Josh woke up with his dreams, Jerry liked to get up and stroll, naked and pleased with himself, into his study. He still owned the large table globe his parents had given him when he was in his senior year at Stanford hesitating between law and business (and when he got *really* drunk, a career in broadcast journalism). The globe was as big as a medicine ball and lit up from within. There was electricity inside: you turned it on by pulling an antique metal chain, a series of tiny ball bearings. The globe turned on its axis: he looked and looked. He would make the whole damn thing his home. But he loved the Pacific. Wallis and Fortuna! New Ireland! Pulo Auna! The Willis Islets! New Britain! Sonsorol! Faisi!

When people say Pacific Rim they think of the ocean as a plate. You could skate across that plate, and perch upon the rim. It was a blue plate, of course, and bordered in gold. He lived in gold here in L.A., and looked across to gold: Hong Kong, Tokyo, Australia's Gold Coast; Cairns with its easy antique wealth, the billion-dollar Sheraton just outside of Port Douglas. But along the plate, within the plate, *on* the plate, you found morsels, tidbits, left two hundred years ago by Europeans who had scurried around the plate before it *was* one, imposing their views, making new worlds, influencing the course of history. Those Sandwich Islands, for instance: from savagery to Mother Hubbards on all the girls, to tourist hotels and Japanese tourists herded on floral carpets in ugly lobbies taking bad pictures of each other.

But it didn't have to be that way — he knew it. Jerry Bridges had read Joseph Conrad's *Victory*: Jerry stayed up late next to sleeping Wynn. In his mind Conrad's all-girl band, with their damp, bared arms, played their violins eternally in some South Sea island. Some moral victory had indeed been gained: Jerry forgot what the victory was, but in his mind the girls would play until the day he died.

The ancient supported the old: the Dutch came to Java and traded, and hammered together "Dutch wives," wooden frames they took to bed to keep themselves from sweating to death. In the Malaysian peninsula the town of Penang had a double name; it was George Town too, just as other ports bore a European imprint: Port Moresby, Port Douglas, Port Arthur. The Solomon Islands were flecked with European ambitions: Bougainville, Santa Cruz, San Cristobal. But on the island of Yap, the Yapese still preferred to be paid in their own stone money, made from those great boulders that dotted the island, because, in the end, World War II notwithstanding, those boulders would stay. They were worth something.

What *was* worth something? Jerry'd studied that, in his youth, not wanting to make wrong choices. He'd fallen in love with the Far East, and with money. He'd remained a bachelor for years and years, way up into his thirties. Well, *sure*, he'd had that two-year Delia-marriage. A woman whose affections extended no farther than the unsplit ends of her own hair. But, what the hell, everyone was entitled to one detour, one wrong turn. He didn't hold a grudge, and she had her own talk show now.

But not until Wynn had he realized that there was drama, courage, on his side of the Rim. Wynn was his own treasure, his dear one. His White Queen, with a silver princess that she'd brought along with her. He had every kind of wealth.

He got ready to go, ducking into the downstairs bathroom to floss, brush his teeth, shit, rewash his face and rub it roughly with a fresh guest towel Carmela kept there for the last of his morning rituals.

At 6:45, he left the house without saying goodbye to Carmela or anyone else. He cuddled down into the cracked good leather of his old and perfect Jag and his mind went directly into numbers. Who he needed to call. In Hong Kong, in Singapore, in Cairns, it was tomorrow, but eight, nine hours earlier. So, tomorrow night. He would work while his colleagues played.

After all his youthful ambitions he had landed, come down

hard, as a financier. He was the Bridges in Bartch, Bridges, Freed, a fast-growing firm with interests all over the Pacific. Without their knowing it, schoolteachers and social workers from the whole western half of the country had given their pensions over to the keeping of *him,* Jerry, and his two partners. The money couldn't be in better hands. Mike Bartch spoke and looked like any salesman, but his knowledge of international currencies was frightening in what it encompassed: he was a genius. Loring Freed had spent upward of thirty years in the diplomatic service and "retired" into this bed of money. Freed expected little. Jerry suspected that he was motivated by pure curiosity. Now that they had this money, how should they invest it — was it possible for them actually to change the world?

Jerry knew it was. It was he who had jerked both his partners out of their inward-looking, purely American investments. "If you're going to deal, then *deal!*" he'd scolded Mike Bartch, and at his words a million five shored up an Australian newspaper, a textile factory in Singapore. Freed went along. The world's economy was expanding; to invest in Asia counteracted Japan's inroads in California. Jerry — he knew it, was proud of it — took his place in the trio because of his vision. If the worlds across the sea were inchoate, unformed, then *fix* them.

And Jerry's idea, his turn, was coming up. A Pacific Rim consortium had been formed. An artificial community about to be constructed, the fruit of all those solitary nights of globe spinning. Not just a resort, not just a workplace, but a new city — hotels, factories, affordable housing for the native work force, golf courses to lure Asian executives, stores (but no chains!) — where people might start up from the beginning under perfect conditions. An American-Japanese co-venture, jacked up by the World Bank.

Today would be a short day at work. After intensive briefings and meetings, he and Loring Freed would take the five o'clock plane to Tokyo. Bartch would stay behind, to scare up extra, glittering Hollywood money. Today, Jerry would point to places on the map where he'd like to see cities rise up. God! His luck was good. He knew it.

He would make the consortium choose New Guinea, because he wanted to go there. To construct a perfect world, you needed beach. As a Californian, Jerry knew that absolutely. No one wanted Africa: the fear of AIDS was too strong. But all whites needed a black shadow, something to be white *against*. Again, the Pacific had to be it, he was sure of it. Southern beaches, fronting on the Java Sea, the Flores Sea, the Banda Sea, the Timor Arafura Sea. No places more beautiful existed in the world, he knew; he had it down pat. As a representative of Bartch, Bridges, Freed, he had speculated carefully in Micronesian patches for mines, for hemp, for solid little trusts. He knew where the beaches were; he knew their beauty.

Some of his colleagues downtown were all for selling off these long-held South Sea assets, putting them into something *safe*, like Belgian lace or Czech crystal, or even some American baseball club, but Jerry wouldn't let them do it. (He whizzed through a red light, and only another driver's reverence for his perfect Jag left him unscathed.) He turned now, left from the horizontal Santa Monica Freeway north to the Harbor Freeway, which brought him within stone-throwing distance of new, fabulously wealthy downtown L.A.

Jerry cut off on Sixth, and north again on Hope, parking in a cave below one of the very biggest Southern Skyscrapers, where the firm occupied the thirtieth through the thirty-second floors. In the elevator, he confessed to himself some fear. He knew parts of the Rim but not enough about the rest. Heavy money hung in the balance. It might indeed be true, as some nervous Nellies on their board of directors said, that radicals (Montagnards who lived in trees? was that the story?) might even now be planning to declare their so-called independence and render null and void any foreign investment.

He walked briskly past the receptionist and several lovely secretaries. His executive assistant was a black woman, Patty. He'd hired her on a dull morning when it had seemed that he might never again be busy, and after she'd told him she was supporting twin daughters with no help. Now he was swamped with work and shamefacedly farmed it out behind Patty's back, gave her a trio of underlings who understood the drill. If she knew, she gave no sign. He knew she did the best she could. And she was already in this morning, dressed in lemon yellow, a linen imitation whose cheapness shamed him, though she was as highly paid as any of the others.

Then, in his office, he prepared for his morning meeting, a pre-Tokyo briefing. First, he twirled his office globe. Took a look. He prepared a positive strategy and a negative one. Positively, they were ready to finance not just a hotel or a factory, but a twenty-first-century city-state. With money and vision they could, not to overstate things, be the next wave of Americans to create a new world — and a better one. Negatively, where *else* was there to put their funds? Again, to look at Africa was to see a giant infirmary: men and women dying, out of control. The only bright side to *that* was to consider that within two hundred years all those endangered species would no longer be endangered. Elephants and rhino would roam the continent unencumbered, while a few last black men and women recapitulated the origins of the human race. Jerry had no doubts about this. He had said as much to men he knew at the UCLA Medical Center: "AIDS will cost a great deal in the next few decades, but not enough for the government to decide to do one damn thing about it. By the time they decide, you can cross off Africa." Jerry considered for an instant a life spent pumping sperm and laughing: dancing the night through, working or not working, making the rounds in — Tanzania, maybe, drinking homemade beer, fucking the day away. Too weird for him! He cast the thought aside.

Europe? Too boring. No real means of return. Every product within those borders bought and sold and bought again. Even the stodgiest men in the firm saw that; even the most conservative and shrill career women saw that. Spanish wine? Resort hotels along the Italian Riviera? Baltic bickering forever and ever? Selling cars to Poles? Never!

The Middle East? Too damn tricky. Though he had clients who loved the sound and name and lore of oil the way he loved . . . New Guinea. Their whole world was at war. And would be forever. Jerry had, over the years, given away more than thirty privately printed, leather-bound and stamped-in-gold-leaf copies of *The Seven Pillars of Wisdom* to clients whose investments with BBF climbed to over a million. He understood the infatuation. But it was too damn tricky.

And a sorry no to South America. Jerry had spoken about it more than once to his colleagues. He'd insisted that all their overseas investment be morally sound, financially above-board. Above reproach! They'd made fun of him, but the years had proven him more than right; had proven him almost infallible.

"Look," he'd said on more than one occasion, "we live in Los Angeles, right? The sun *shines* here, we all agree to that. So, our client goes into the Los Angeles Country Club, or the Riviera or the Brentwood or the Hillcrest. He's going to play golf and have lunch. His wife is into any number of good causes — he can't keep track of them! Even his secretary won't eat red meat anymore. So our client goes into the club. He's with some business guys. By now maybe he's known them for years. They ask him, 'So, what are you investing in? What's your portfolio *looking* like right now?' What's he going to say, 'I'm heavily into Ecuadorean *cemetery* plots? Argentine *shrouds?* I'm shaving the Amazon rain forest faster than my wife's organization can save it'? Come *on!* The guy's got to play golf with these people until they all die! They've got to sit through the opera together! Sit through their kids' school plays!"

Over the years he'd gotten Mike Bartch and Loring Freed and the whole board to see that the moral high ground held a sweetness, a turn-of-the-new-century glamour. The world needed a new race of men, raised well, smart as dollars; men who might change the course of history by living both generously and well. Thus, investments in Colombia were not only bad business but bad conversation.

China. Well. The firm already had it aced and covered. Windbreakers, microwave ovens, filtered cigarettes, CDs. He had no quarrel with any of it. Russia — Russia was for the midwestern dollar. Those people looked alike, withstood extreme winters.

Negligently he gave his office globe another spin. "Nowhere else to *go,* boys! Sure, you've got western Australia but the outback's like the road from here to Vegas, and the waves are great, but Chrissake, *our* waves are great!" Jerry sat back in his chair, rolled his head on his neck muscles, made a stab at touching his elbows behind his back. (Patty saw this gesture through glass, smiled, lowered her head, shrugged into her word processor.)

He surveyed his desk; counted his wealth; again. His silver-framed photos. So, OK. He and Wynn on the slopes of Aspen with the kids. In another, Josh grinned. Tina, arms out to a huge full moon. A prom photograph of Whitney floating in strapless white chiffon, her blond hair flying out from her remote face, transfigured just this once by sly and goofy delight as she and her girlfriend — Tracie? — ignored their tuxedoed dates and fought over a runaway bouquet of Mylar balloons. All of youth encapsulated in one random *click,* blown up and then blown up again so that the edges blurred and they stayed static in a pastel heaven. That was why he knew it was better to invest in beach property than in cemetery plots in Ecuador.

But next to his family photos, he kept two others, framed and prominent. The cover of the February 1989 issue of *Ranger Rick,* a boys' magazine. A colleague had torn off the cover and left it on his blotter. The picture of a Huli Highlander from Papua New Guinea: all done up in lemon yellow face paint and red circles around his eyes and some amazing wig with wool and hair and feathers, and *almost* a smile on those fierce and sullen lips.

Jerry had framed it. While he was at it, he found another photo, copied and framed it too: Another pair of Highland warriors dressed to kill. Black beyond words, their noses painted matching candy-apple red, breastplates hanging from their necks to their waists, leaf fringes poking out from every side, and those leaves creeping up their necks until they mingled, more or less, with a couple of opulent graying mustaches, and nose rings to beat the band, and headdresses that drooped down over foreheads in layering chains of mother of pearl. Their hair, if indeed that *was* their hair, seemed constricted in boxes made of red and blue tree bark, and then poufed out in brassy dyed orange curls, the same, the *exact* same color as the tasteful bronze that certain California Jewish ladies dyed their silver hair. The more Jerry looked at these guys the better dressed they seemed. These men must know what fun was! Forget the Rockefeller son: that was a long time ago, he'd probably pulled some East Coast gaffe — a silver foot in his mouth, wasn't that the phrase?

When new clients came in then, for a simple meeting, they'd eye the beautiful wife and adorable kids, pass over the teenage girls batting balloons, sweetly squandering their youth, but the Highlanders always got a rise. "Oh my *God*! Who *are* they?"

And Jerry always answered, through his freckle-faced smile, "Those guys are my buddies." Leave it at that.

How could he say that he cherished the idea of a place in dark jungles where lovers rubbed their faces together (*turnim head* they called it) until their cheeks bled, before they finally got around to having sex, or where courting couples, befeathered and necklaced, lolled around in grass houses with the girl's legs covering one leg of her male friend, who might be painted kelly green above the nose, and red below. *Carry leg!* A way to spend an evening, a way of saying hi: a time and place to get to know each other. And if, when they married, the groom shot an arrow into the wife's thigh to seal the deal, that was the kind of thing Jerry thought he might be interested in changing, moderating. To take the pain out of things.

But keep the intensity! Dress up in feathers! Rub faces with your beloved (was that even the term?) until you bled and cried out from all that pleasing pain. He could not connect any of that with the floral lust he felt for Wynn, the tenderness he felt for Whitney, the sore concern he carried for his own two kids.

He had the negative argument (nowhere *else* in the world to put money like that where we can diversify as completely!). And he had the narrative to carry his positive argument. My God, he had Melville and Conrad and the South Seas and free love and whaling ships and convicts and mutinies and Macao silks, and the whole Western/Eastern thrust of white men who wanted adventure but needed to hold up their heads at the Riviera Country Club as well. He and Loring Freed had their tickets and their passports and their reservations at the Tokyo Hilton. And the first Tokyo meetings were set up for tomorrow.

So Jerry knew what he was going to say, and he knew that this morning he looked especially good as at 9:28 he got up with a small sheaf of papers that carried all the information he was going to need. He took the Southwest route to the thirtieth-floor conference room, barely looking out of the corner of his eye at the city that spread out before him through transparent glass walls like a whole other crowded dinner plate. Only this time, the Pacific itself was the blue porcelain rim. He averted his eyes because he knew exactly the point of reflected light that was the glassed-in cupola of his own house, and 9:30 at the end of this winter school break was just about the time she'd be getting up and going down to breakfast.

So he turned his head away.

Wynn

Pacific Palisades
January 13

HER HUSBAND was extricating his pants from the pants press, one of those gadgets — like the automatic rower and the treadmill and the stationary bike and the computerized weights and even his pedometer — that he bought and used for a while and tired of but never threw out, so that their bedroom looked, to her eyes, more like a branch of Hammacher Schlemmer than a symbol of affluent ease, or even a place to sleep. When the phone rang, Wynn had to step over him, which only added to her exasperation. The phone was always ringing and she was always answering. She was a *slave* to the thing! They had the answering machine, and behind the machine, a service that would always pick up the call. But he liked her to pick up the phone. When he had calls coming in, seven days a week, at every hour of the day or night!

All this he acknowledged, in a sidelong glance, a suppressed sigh, a good-natured grin, even, as he yanked on the metal press, and yanked again. Packing for his Tokyo plane trip. Almost ready to roll.

"Is this Mrs. Geffin?"

"No. Wynn Bridges. Mr. Geffin is out of the country. In Mexicali. Unitarian Outreach." She relented. "Al Geffin's my former husband. We've been separated for ten years." Like, why do I have to keep track of *everything*?

"Are you related to . . . ?" A silence, as the person read the name, went over it to be sure. "Whitney Geffin?"

A wave of bright light crossed her vision. A migraine in both eyes. "Who are you? Where is she? What's happened?"

Across the room, Jerry looked up from the press. Got to his feet, came over to her. His open garment bags and briefcase lay across the bed.

"She's all right. There was an automobile accident. She's sustained minor injuries. But we'll need you to come down to St. John's Hospital, here in Santa Monica. We need you to bring your insurance card. We'll need you to sign a few forms."

"Of course. St. John's? Shall I . . . Shall I bring anything?" She knew there was another thing to ask. "There had to have been someone else in the car. She doesn't own a car yet. So it had to have been someone else's car."

"Someone else?" The voice grew dim and distant. "I'm afraid I don't know anything about anyone else." The person hung up. Wynn looked around, the room bright in the afternoon sun, her husband's face close and concerned. "Whitney's been in an accident. They say it's not serious. They said it's minor. But I have to go down there."

"What happened?"

"I forgot to ask."

"Honey, they said it was minor, didn't they? If it was serious they would have said so. Listen! This is what you'll do. Stan's coming in a couple of minutes, you know Stan. He should be here already. The hospital's on the way to the airport and I can drop you off. Then I'll have him come back by for you after he drops *me* off. By that time Whitney'll be ready to come home and Stan can drive you back. Because I can see by looking at you, you're in no condition to drive."

Would he have been so casual, so *organized,* if it were his own daughter? But it was true. She had started to shake. "They didn't know there was anyone else in the car. But it had to be someone else's car."

"I don't think it's anything to worry about. Do you have insurance cards in your wallet? Do you want to borrow mine?"

"Yes."

He bent over the bed, folding up and strapping his excellent leather luggage. From their bedroom window they could both see Stan's Beemer pull up. He ran a good service, halfway between the inefficient cabs you couldn't count on and limos, which were the province of hookers and rock stars out here. Wynn watched, her elbows on the sill, the way she had a hundred times before, when Jerry went off on a trip. She watched Stan come up the brick path, heard him knock, heard Jerry's voice. "My wife will be coming with us part way. We'll be dropping her off at St. John's in Santa Monica. Her daughter's been in an accident."

"Gee! Too bad! Anything serious?"

"They say not."

Wynn walked over to the dresser to pick up her purse, looked quickly in the mirror. What she saw made her turn away. She went to the shelf where she kept the old paperbacks she read for comfort when she was sick, picked up Graham Greene's *Orient Express.* She rummaged around for her address book in case she'd have to make any phone calls, and took in the room in its cluttered brightness. She walked downstairs. She remembered to look in the kitchen and tell Carmela that Whitney was in the hospital, had had an accident, and would she mind keeping an eye on the little kids? Tina was still taking her nap upstairs. Josh would be home around six. Before Carmela could say anything, Wynn turned and went down the hall to the open door where Jerry stood quietly waiting. He was patient, really, really patient and kind, she thought, until she remembered that Jerry always factored an extra forty-five minutes into every travel transaction. In theory, he was always forty-five minutes early. In practice, he was always on time. This would be just one more example of how his prudence worked.

"We'll have you there in no time, Mrs. B," Stan said. "She's going to be fine, I know it. Ah, kids! Is it worth the worry, is what I ask myself sometimes."

Wynn nodded. She was beginning to be angry. She'd seen the way Whitney's friends drove down at that school. She'd made the regular, usual noises to her daughter about being careful, driving carefully, and gotten the usual contemptuous response: the chilly gaze, or the toss of that straight blond hair like Al's, or a shrug, or a laugh. Woven into all that was an unspoken message: Who was having the nerve to tell someone else how to live? Who was living in bad faith here? Who had turned the definitive trick, had leased out her body and her agreeable disposition to some rich man for a roof, a car, an income and two more kids? Not *Whitney*! If Whitney wanted to drive fast with her friends in the night, or dance on the end of the Santa Monica pier during all of last summer, or stay up all night in her cupola room, laughing inanely with her pretty friends, or *any* of that stuff, she'd never had to sell herself in any way to get these privileges. She had said as much to her mother, many times.

Spoiled, Wynn thought tiredly. They just don't get it. They have all this *stuff*, that someone's worked hard for, somewhere, but they don't see any of that. They don't see *anything*. She thought of a party a couple of months ago, right after Thanksgiving, when Whitney had friends up over the garage, and the kids had been smoking stuff and drinking stuff and Jerry had ended up calling Stan, who spent the rest of the night driving them all home. The next morning she'd had to endure motherly phone calls from the kind of woman she most detested, asking why she and her husband had permitted "that kind of a party" in the first place, and only her own gutlessness had kept her from saying that they'd ended up having "that kind of a party" because of the Golden Oaks law that said if ever there was a student gathering of over six kids, then the whole class, including the most sociopathic misfits, had to be invited, so that no one in the class would end up feeling "left out." That's what you got from a private school where you ended up paying thousands and thousands of dollars. Every semester. For a total of six years. And that was before you even thought about college.

She'd been trying not to think of the accident, although the spectacle, the thought, the image of another accident, a few years before, kept floating in her mind. Some poor boy with a car full of classmates had pulled a U-turn on San Vicente, the sweetest, safest street in the whole city. He misjudged the distance and ended up dead against one of those beautiful trees with the red blossoms that city fathers long ago had planted down the center islands where men and women jogged day and night. How many dead? Five? Six? All dead. Their friends and acquaintances had sung, and grieved, and pinned notes on the maimed tree. For several weeks, the tree became a shrine. Then the flowers had faded, and gardeners had taken down the notes, so now, as you drove San Vicente from the beach into downtown Westwood — to a movie or some class at UCLA, whatever — you had trouble remembering exactly which tree it had been.

So she hoped it hadn't been a tree.

Jerry had the kindness not to try to say anything to her. He sat quietly, slumped back, and loosely held her hand. He had big, strong, freckled hands with red hairs growing out along the tops of his fingers. No point in being worried. Nothing to worry about. They'd said it was minor. They'd said it was minor and not until they found the hospital and pulled up by the yellow windows of the emergency room itself did Wynn clench with total fear.

"Hey!" Jerry said. "Cool it. We're here. We'll find out right away what's going on." Just inside the window, on one of the plastic orange chairs, bent double, his head to his knees, a kid from Golden Oaks was sobbing, his identity shimmering across his back on an old-fashioned gold satin jacket.

Jerry held her hand tight as they went to the window. A nurse asked, "Mr. and Mrs. Geffin?" Jerry shook his head. Wynn said, "Yes. I am. Is my daughter all right?"

"She's in the back. She's OK. She's fine."

Jerry said, "We'd both better check before I go." He looked at his watch.

"No," Wynn said, "You go on. If they say she's OK, she's OK."

"I'll call you, then," Jerry said. "Call you from Japan. Take care, honey. Tell Whitney to take care! I've got to go."

Wynn called out through the window, for a nurse, for someone, then pushed through swing doors that said No Admittance.

She went down a hall, and down another hall. She passed clusters of worried families and friends, standing against walls, their faces drained by blue fluorescent light. Finding a nurse, Wynn asked, "Whitney Geffin? I'm her mother."

The nurse patted her shoulder. What a strange thing to do!

"She's back in the corner. She's conscious. She looks worse than she is."

Six beds in this room, separated by what looked like white cotton shower curtains. Wynn walked back into the brightly lit corner stall. Whitney smiled at her — a red, moist, gaping smile, crushed tongue, lips split a hundred different ways, one tooth still gleaming in the dead center of her mouth. Her white-blond hair was caked with blood. Her head and her neck were held in some kind of brace. Blood clotted on unwashed cuts along her hairline. The bones around her eyes were horribly bruised. Someone had cut off her clothes and covered her body with a blue and white hospital gown. Her left arm lay splayed out at an angle not meant to be, wrapped haphazardly in gauze and cotton strips. An IV went into her other arm. She lay alone, in a place that seemed horrible to Wynn.

The girl flicked her eyes in her bleeding, seeping head. "Ma! I don't have any *teeth,* Ma!" Her mouth moved like something separate. A sea urchin without spines. Something purple. Something blue. "I don't think they brought my purse. Do you think you could find my purse? Could you find out about Robin? Do you think you could find where Robin is? Could you get them to give me a pain pill? Ah! *Boy! God!*"

Wynn moved to the other side of the bed, took hold of the good hand. "You're all right, Whitney. You're lucky."

"Because I didn't die? I *guess.* Yeah."

They stayed in silence for a minute. From the bed next to them a Latin voice shouted, "I demand! I demand a doctor! I'm dressed for the evening."

"Oh, please," the wet red and blue mouth said. "Can't you get him to quit? He's been doing that forever."

Wynn stole a look behind the curtain. A young Mexican guy twisted on a gurney. He wore a tuxedo jacket and tie but no shirt, and only a pair of bikini shorts. Cigarette burns made a circle on his stomach and lines up the sides of his calves. Some of them looked infected. An intern, struggling with his IV, looked up in irritation. "I'll get back to you in a minute, as soon as I'm through here."

But a nurse came first. She took insurance information on

a clipboard, checked Whitney's blood pressure, monitored the IV, took her pulse and asked briskly, "*So?* What are you going to do?"

"What do you mean?" Wynn asked.

"I'm thinking," the blue mouth said. "Can I have a pain pill? Can I have my purse? Can I see Robin?"

"We're looking at a possible dislocation of the left shoulder, a compound fracture of the arm, possible injury to the spine, possible concussion, and we have twenty minutes to go on this — if you can get a dentist down here in under twenty minutes, there's still a chance you can get those teeth replanted."

The nurse pointed at a hospital table, where several bloody teeth clustered in a dish. "You've still got twenty minutes. It'll save you plenty of money in the long run if you can get those teeth back in. You need to find a shoulder specialist, a spine specialist, someone to look at those head X-rays . . . Someone to sew . . ."

A doctor came into the cubicle. He looked tired, but shook Wynn's hand before he slipped on rubber gloves. "So. Whitney!" he boomed. "What day is it?"

"Tuesday. Can I have a pain pill? *Please?* Can I see *Robin?*"

"As soon as we see what we're going to do about that arm and shoulder of yours. What's your middle name? Do you happen to remember?"

"Louise. Can I have a drink?"

"As soon as we figure out what to do with those teeth. Now listen to me, Whitney. This is important. Were you drinking? What drugs were you doing? Are you sexually active? We have to know *now.*"

Whitney looked at the ceiling. "We were at the Santa Monica Cafe. We had coffee. Where's Robin? Where's my purse?"

"What about drugs? Your blood's already being tested. We'll know sooner or later. Tell us now, so we'll know how to treat Robin."

"She doesn't do drugs," Wynn said, and the doctor gave her a pitying glance.

"Parents know nothing," he said. "That's the thing we *do* know. Why don't you wait outside? Make some phone calls. Find some doctors. If you want me to, I'll sew up her mouth later. I'm pretty good at that. You don't want a plastic surgeon until we find out what else is going on here. Now, Whitney! Did I remember to ask you who the president is?"

"I don't know," the blue mouth whispered. "I don't think I remember that one. Some dumbo would be my guess. Do you have my purse? Can't somebody tell me?"

Wynn stepped outside of the curtained alcove. She paced up and down the length of the emergency room wing. The six beds were full. On one, at the other end, a woman her own age, dressed in expensive slacks and blouse, wept.

As the doctor came out from behind the curtain, Wynn took his arm. "It's *true*. She doesn't do drugs. Her friends do but she doesn't. It's because her father and I, we smoked a lot in the seventies. She hates all that."

"I wanted to know for the boy. On the chance there was anything we could do."

"Robin?" Now that she had his name back, she saw him in her mind's eye, perfect in every detail. Medium height, pale complexion, hazel eyes, long black lashes, curly black hair, delicate frame.

"How is he?"

The doctor sucked on his upper lip. "Do you know him well?"

"Not really."

He decided to tell her anyway. "Critical."

Then he walked away, and into the next cubicle. "So. Frederico! Did I remember to ask you who the president is? How'd you get those burns? Your boyfriend throw you out? Threw you downstairs, did he? Want to press charges on that? We can call the cops if you want."

Wynn went back to the waiting room, where the Golden Oaks boy still cried. She put an arm across his shoulder and asked him urgently, what happened? As hideously strange as it seemed, the sun was only just now going down. The parking lot and its cars blushed pink, then violet. She pulled out a Kleenex from her purse, gave it to him, went across the room to a shelf where she mixed them both Styrofoam cups of instant chocolate. The sugar had to do them both good.

The kid dried his eyes and wiped his nose. He'd been sitting at the counter at the Santa Monica Cafe, eating alone. His folks had been having a fight and he needed to get out of the house. He sat at the counter so that he could watch people come in. When he saw Robin come in with Whitney he was surprised because he knew there were rehearsals going on for a play from two to six that afternoon. Because it was one thing to cut classes, but cutting rehearsals was —

"Hurry up! Tell me what happened!"

They'd asked him to come over and sit with them. They'd sneaked off early because they were hungry and their scenes weren't scheduled until . . . about right now.

Wynn registered it.

The three of them had ordered hamburgers and coffee. Then they ordered one chocolate milkshake and split it with three straws. The three of them stayed in a booth and watched people come in and go out. At first he kept watching Robin and Whitney to see if they were, like, an item, but he couldn't tell. One minute it would seem like they were, the next minute they'd just be laughing like friends. They'd stayed there for about an hour and a half. Then Robin and Whitney said they had to get back to school. They asked him to come back and watch rehearsals.

"They knew I didn't have any place to go. They said I could run their lines with them or maybe I could help in the sound booth. They knew I couldn't go home, but they didn't make a big deal about it. So, I thought I'd go along."

He burst into tears again, the futile crying of a child. "You know the parking lot there at that cafe? It's hard to get out of. So instead of him *backing* out of the lot and trying to pull a hughie in that street right by the cafe, Whitney made him go all around the block and make a right turn back onto Santa Monica. I was in the back seat. And I saw the truck just *barreling along,* when Robin made that right turn!"

The kid put his head on her shoulder and fastened his strong arms around her neck. He cried uncontrollably. The smell of his sweat was almost unbearably strong. Wynn felt that she couldn't push him away, and remained for some minutes, patting the back of his shirt. Finally, when he calmed down a little, she asked him, "Shouldn't we call your parents? Shouldn't we get you home!"

"No, *I can't.* I can't go home!"

"What about Robin's parents? Has somebody called them? Do you know if they're here?"

The boy had pulled away, and scrubbed at his face with a Kleenex. "He's dead. He has to be. I saw what happened to his head. So, he's dead. But I think they called his parents, yes. I don't know."

What was Robin's name? Wynn thought, I don't even know anyone's last name. She looked at the boy beside her. There was something she had to do. A lot of things she had to do. I wish I could *get* it, she thought vaguely. I wish I could *get* it. Fifteen years ago, when she was still married to Whitney's dad, an asshole, the world, though terrible, was easy to define and easy to move around in. Whitney's dad would either be out with some bimbette, or in his "study" not writing a sermon and having a tantrum about it. (Or — be fair! — they'd both be lolling on a raggedy couch, drinking cheap wine and watching bad TV, their daughter asleep across their knees.) And Wynn always had her close girlfriends too. Her own mother, a difficult worrywart, had still been alive. Her father, always quiet as the tomb, was in the tomb now. It was as though her recent happiness had erased any support she needed in adversity.

"I'm going to make some phone calls," she told the Golden Oaks boy, and got up stiffly. "I'll come back in a while."

First she went back to see Whitney. It was worse this time. Whitney held on to her arm, begging for her purse, her pain pill, and, finally, her dad. "I'm going to call him now," Wynn said. "And I'll find your purse. I promise."

She went back to the lost boy in the waiting room and sent him on an errand. They must have taken the car to a towing yard. Could he call a friend and get a ride over there, see if Whitney's purse was still in the car, maybe take some pictures of the car with a Polaroid for insurance purposes? With a terrible eagerness, the kid said sure. For the next half hour, as she made her own calls across the room at a pay phone, she heard him jerkily rehearse the details over another: "I was sitting at the counter when they came in. I didn't know if they were an item or not . . . He's dead. I saw what happened to his head. He *has* to be dead. *She's* all right. Lucky. Boy! Was she lucky!"

Wynn thanked God for her telephone credit card, for a life that in so many ways was easier than it used to be. She knew the Mexicali number by heart — she'd called Whitney's father so many times since he'd been living down there: called him to remind him to call his daughter on her birthday, to wrangle with him over the minimal child support she insisted he pay (even though Jerry said repeatedly she didn't have to worry about it). Al's whole impulse had been to go away from her, from Whitney, from America, from *it*, whatever *it* was. In the real world, she had been unbearably lucky, marrying upward with a vengeance, finding a man both kind and rich. In the real world Al had fallen on hard times, even losing his parish at the crummy church where he'd preached for a while. His job now, though he still liked to be described as a minister, was as a middle-level bureaucrat for an international organization that helped orphans. She had gone to the trouble of looking up his job description and its salary down at the Santa Monica library one boring afternoon. About twenty-eight thousand a year, and the guy was forty-five years old. After going out with twenty-eight thousand females for about five years after their divorce, he'd settled on one with brown hair and glasses who spoke fluent Spanish, and who, evidently, bought every mean tale Al had ever told anyone about his hard-to-please wife.

Wynn dialed the Mexicali number. Al's wife answered. The line was perfectly clear but an electronic delay meant that their sentences would overlap.

"Teresa? This is Wynn. I need to speak to Al."

A pause. An electronic one? "Al's asleep. He was up all night. He can't come to the phone right now."

"But he has to! Whitney's been in a car crash. A bad car accident. I have to speak to him right now!"

The line clicked. "Hello?" Wynn cried. "*Hello?*"

". . . How bad is it? How badly is she hurt?"

"Bad. Bad. She's got . . . She doesn't have any teeth left, and she's got a concussion, and a broken arm and a broken shoulder and something might be wrong with her spine . . ." As she spoke, named those body pieces, she remembered them in Al. He was stingy, mingy, even in his physical self. You could always feel his ribs in his sunken chest. But his teeth were straight and strong: she remembered bits of light falling from his teeth onto his chest during a time they'd both taken acid. So long ago. She could remember, with the tips of her fingers, the feel of his shoulder blades, his spine. "It's his *daughter,* Teresa!"

". . . Can she move her feet? Her toes?"

"Yes."

". . . It's reparable then. I'm not going to wake him up for that. He's been working very hard."

"Well" — and rage and hate that she should have saved for her first husband spilled over to a distant woman who had no part in this — "do you think you might give him the message that *his child is in the hospital*?"

"I'll tell him when he wakes up. But there's nothing we can do about it down here anyway." A click, and she had hung up.

A few other people had come into this public room. They were worried. An old man had a fish bone stuck in his throat and couldn't swallow. He kept spitting into a paper cup as his family looked away. The Golden Oaks boy repeated on the phone, "He's dead, I know he's dead. I saw his head." Wynn looked in her address book under I for internist and O for orthopedist and left messages with their answering services. Both these guys kept their investments safe with Jerry. She knew they'd be here in twenty minutes or less, wherever they were. She'd sat next to one of their wives at a dinner party and been told that the doctor's beeper ruled their sex lives and every other part of their lives. So they'd be here soon. Who else should she call? She didn't know anyone else to call, now that it was seven o'clock on a Tuesday night. People would be with their families.

A car pulled up outside the waiting room and the Golden Oaks boy sprinted in that direction. "Don't worry, Mrs. Geffin! We found out where they're holding the car. We're going over there right now. I'll bring back Whitney's purse, and we'll get some Polaroids!"

I'm not Mrs. Geffin, she thought of saying, but in a way she was. Not married to Al but still her daughter's mother. Like everybody fucking else at that fucking school! But that wasn't right. It wasn't the school's fault. And the boy had gone all the way around the block to make a safe right turn. But what about the *truck*?

What about the truck? What about the driver of the truck? "In the accident that came in here a couple of hours ago? Is the truck driver here?"

A nurse, behind the desk now and preoccupied, looked up. "You'll have to ask a police officer. They'll have a report on this."

Only forty minutes. Only an hour had gone by since she'd come through those doors. Only an hour and a half, two hours, since she'd picked up the phone. Oh, if she had Al here, she'd kill him. She'd take her hands and clamp them around his neck and nothing he could do would ever make her let go. She'd squeeze his neck and squeeze his neck and his hands would flutter and then he'd die. But he wasn't here.

She walked back through the room with the six curtained cubicles. An intern questioned the well-dressed woman in the first cubicle. "What made you do it?"

"I was having a bad day, I guess. But I did call 911, didn't I?"

The boy in the tuxedo jacket had passed out and begun to snore. His bow tie twisted halfway around his neck.

Whitney's eyes were worse than before. Her mouth had puffed up. The doctor was there, questioning her again about drugs. "No, *asshole*!" her daughter said, but she pronounced it *ash-ho*.

"When are you going to sew up her lips? I've called Dr. Goldschmidt for her arm and Ron Fishback for her spine. So can you do something about her mouth? Can you do something about the *blood* and *dirt*? I don't want them to see her like that."

The doctor pointed at a bowl of soapy water. "Why don't you have a go at it? We're shorthanded tonight. Listen, *Whitney*? Do you know why I work in an emergency room?" As he spoke he threaded a needle with a gleaming length of nylon.

"No."

"When I was twenty-six, outside of Omaha, my wife and I

37

were driving home from a party. I won't lie to you. We'd had a few beers."

"Yeah?"

"So we ran into a cow. Don't laugh! That can be a fatal collision. Have you ever heard of the golden hour?"

"No."

"That's the *hour* . . ." He placed his rubber-gloved little finger just under Whitney's left nostril, pressed and pulled so that her upper lip pushed upward and out. The flesh hung in shreds. Delicately, seemingly at random, he ran the needle through skin and membrane, reached through pulp to catch at another edge of skin, drew them together over the pulp. He nodded to a nurse who had drifted in and stood now, with tiny scissors. She waited until he'd pulled the thread into a knot, then snipped the thread. "The hour you have until you croak."

"*Ah*," Whitney muttered. "You're hurting my hand." Wynn loosened her grip.

"Sorry."

Another puncture, pull, knot, snip. And another. Another. Another. Another.

Another. Wynn held the hand, so little, frail tendons, little chicken bones for bones. Her daughter's eyes were shut. The doctor kept talking. The nurse held her scissors ready, ready to go snip.

Into this zone of pain, steps thudded down the length of the emergency room. The boy from Golden Oaks appeared, flushed and out of breath, holding a big tan leather Missoni bag. "I found it, Whitney! Right where you left it. Boy! You should see the *car*! I opened the passenger door and reached in and the whole windshield fell in on me! It's a miracle we aren't all dead!"

The boy had been covered in shatterproof glass. It still fell from him like hail, rolling and banging across the floor.

"You can't be in here," the nurse said. "Put the purse down in the corner and wait outside."

"I took pictures of the car too. Boy! You should *see* that thing! It looks like somebody put it into a blender. Jesus, *Whitney*! My *God,* girl! You —"

"Out," the nurse said. "You can't be in here."

But by this time the cubicle had begun to fill up. A man from the insurance wanted Wynn to sign something else. The two doctors, whom Wynn had only known from dinner parties, blew in. With their white coats thrown carelessly over meticulously chosen shirts and pants, they brought a hearty assurance that, hey! No problem! Patients get banged up all the time!

They held up the X-rays like family snapshots, deciding that the spine was bruised but OK, that the shoulder was broken and so was the arm, but after three months, six at the most, she'd be out of a cast and good as new.

"This isn't bad," Dr. Fishback said. "This isn't bad at all, Whitney-Babes. You know what's *bad*? They're going to close down the Car Wash at Wilshire and Centinela!" Everyone laughed. The boy from Golden Oaks shook more glass out of his hair. The doctor who had kept at his lip-job through all this, primly, looked up and said, "Did any of you happen to notice what this kid did when our backs were turned? Wanted to save on dental bills, I guess."

Each person there peered at the girl, whose lips were studded now with dozens of nylon knots.

"Look," the doctor said. "Take a look inside there."

Whitney gripped her mother's hand a little harder. "*Hah!*" The syllable was a blast of triumph and contempt. Inside the mass of blue and purple flesh where her sweet mouth had been, her own teeth twinkled, uneven, but each in its right place.

"She picked them up when we were out of here and jammed them back in by herself." The sewing doctor placed her lower lip against her upper one and began sewing up a bad cut on her chin. If even fifty percent of them stay, that'll save you thousands of bucks on dental bills. Good going, Whitney!"

"Some dentist won't be able to get his car washed," Dr. Fishback said sadly, mournfully. "Car wash won't be there anyway."

They would be operating at eight the next morning. The nurse washed down Whitney's left side. "We can do this now that they know what they're *doing*," she said confidentially to Wynn. "They don't like you to put a finger on a patient until they've had their *look*." Wynn washed down the side of her daughter's body that wasn't very hurt. One nasty flap of skin lay open and Wynn squeezed soapy water over it and over it, remembering skinned knees, the cuts of childhood that required stitches, and how when Whitney was little, she had loved to watch the way peroxide bubbled over open cuts.

Another nurse came with the news that the head X-rays were OK and both doctors agreed the patient should get some sleep before the morning. The nurse turned Whitney on her side, finally gave her a shot for the pain, and slapped her on her haunch, before and after. "That's it, Kidree. You held up real well. I heard what you did with your teeth. That's good going!"

Suddenly, the place, the time, the scene, died down. "I *demand*," the man next door repeated one last time, and Whitney murmured, "Oh, shut up."

The doctors left. Two orderlies came in. "We're taking her up to the fifth floor. You can come up in about twenty minutes to say good night to her."

"You did real well for a mom," the nurse told Wynn. "Do you think you can drive home OK? We can give you two pills to help you sleep when you get home. We can do that much."

"I'm fine. Thank you. Thank you for everything."

She left the room, taking a last look at the poor boy who'd been burned and beaten for somebody's pleasure. A new man lay in one cubicle. The nurses, the sewing doctor, were busy cutting off his Levi's and his leather jacket. The man looked about as close to dead as he could get. In the cubicle closest to the door the woman who had tried to kill herself was sitting up to smoke a cigarette. Wynn hurried out.

The parents of the other boy waited in the outside room, Robin. The parents of Robin. The boy from Golden Oaks spoke to them excitedly, telling about the hamburger, the malted, Robin's cautiousness about going all around the block to make the right hand turn back onto Santa Monica.

Wynn had to go up to them. "My daughter was in your son's car. How is he?"

"We don't know," the mother said. But she did.

Wynn went out into the parking lot. Only then did she remember. Whitney, on the fifth floor. She walked around the hospital and in through the front door of the building. Someone was swabbing down the linoleum floor. She took the elevator and walked around the square tower of the fifth floor. Most patients still had visitors. Everyone seemed to be watching television. The second time around she realized that there were two people in a darkened room that she had thought was empty. On the side by the door, a very ill woman; on the side by the window, Whitney. Looking out the window, Wynn could see the modest neon lights of the Santa Monica Cafe. No question of any "golden hour." They probably didn't even need an ambulance. The hospital was across the street. Absolutely across the street.

In this light, and seen in this way, Whitney looked about eight years old. Wynn remembered something her own father had once said. "Life has a way of kicking the shit out of you." Wynn thought about it. "I'll see you tomorrow," she whispered. But Whitney was asleep.

On the way home, Stan kept quiet and turned on the news. As Wynn listened to KNX roll out the regular weeknight disasters, the gang killings, gang wars, domestic murders, she remembered with a rush of relief that this really *was* minor. A dislocated shoulder, a busted arm. And a boy she didn't know was dead.

At home, Carmela snored peacefully. Wynn poured herself a brandy and went upstairs. Josh and Tina were sound asleep, their nightlights glowing, their rooms smelling of soap.

Carmela had turned down the bed and put out a nightgown. Nice. Nice of her. Wynn crossed to a French escritoire that they'd had refurbished to hold a television set, took off her clothes, crossed to the bureau to pick up the remote control before she fell into bed. She checked out the pants press, a pair of dark gray slacks jammed half in, half out of the machine. The voice of her ex-husband's wife came to her. "Reparable." She ran her fingers on the remote until she came to the twenty-four-hour news, and watched until she fell asleep.

J e r r y

T o k y o
J a n u a r y 1 5

IT WAS A STRETCH, but Jerry made the plane, even had time to change his dollars to yen before he showed his passport, had a chance to rest two minutes before he boarded. The plane left at 5:00 P.M., perfect businessman's choice, giving tired men a chance to sleep across the Pacific, arriving in Tokyo at 8:30 the next night, just in time to party. He saw Loring Freed in the VIP departure lounge reading, predictably, the *Wall Street Journal*, the overhead lights catching his bald spot. All around him, serious men bent to their reading materials.

Plenty of Japanese! All of them impeccably tailored, none of them talking much. Some American tourists, grave with the idea of pleasure to come. Jerry hadn't taken this flight since Tina was two. A year since he'd crossed the Pacific. It wasn't

43

because of family — that was only a way of marking time. The reason he'd stayed home for so long was that in order to stake out major claims eight thousand miles away you had to strengthen your own home base.

He and Mike Bartch and Loring Freed had made big money for their clients. Bartch kept his sleeves rolled up, called every client by his first name, imported and exported products nobody knew they wanted until they saw them. Mike, against the whole current of the American economy, kept their own balance of trade in perfect line: he knew that the Japanese could not resist Texas barbecue sauce to go with the great quantities of second-line American beef they were importing, so while Loring, for instance, might spend six months finding the right Wyoming cattle ranch for a consortium of Japanese buyers, Mike would fly out to Cheyenne, interview *cowboys,* auditioning cheekbones as well as lariat rolls, lining up hundreds of personal merchandising appearances in the four Japanese islands. There were a million ways to turn a profit. The trick was to hold everyone's interest.

When told that the Japanese weren't into buying (unless it was U.S. real estate), Bartch might reply, indifferently, "So! What do they plan to *do* with our American beef? This isn't pussy *Jap* beef! This Wyoming product has *texture.* They're going to have to exercise their jaws!" And though he didn't say these things in front of Asians, word got back. Mike let it be known that to eat this beef they would need barbecue sauce, and paper plates with cowboy boots embossed on them. They would need Texan cookbooks translated into Japanese. They would need long forks to turn this tough and flavorful marinated beef on colored metal barbecues, so different from the dull Japanese hibachis.

In small, steady, lucrative sales, Southern California–based businesses, merchants of glass jars and bar-b-que sauce and long forks and hot mustard and pretty soon, American chili, found themselves accomplishing the impossible: doing business with Japan through one transpacific organization which had early on grasped the transcendent principle of trade: you have to sell them what *they don't have*. Stop whining about silicon chips and transistor radios and sell them a chef's apron, one for every family in Japan, not a joke apron, but a piece of clothing that looks more like armor than an apron, with the pale outline of a cowboy on it, and on that piece of rough cloth, see if you can embody the image of what they *really* don't have — wide-open spaces.

Those images, those ideas — they came into Jerry's purview. For every architect who designed interlocking communities of the future, he knew dozens of researchers who tracked down the executors of the Frederic Remington estate for the use of his cowboy images. Young zealots who found paper companies owned by BBF clients for the cookbooks, plates, napkins, labels. The very best graphic designer — a woman in Glendale who had space in her *eyes*; she knew what the Japanese craved. Jerry had climbed Ayers Rock a year ago, out in the center of Australia. For twenty minutes, he had been able to see as much land as any human eye could see, or ever want to see. A lot of it! And it meant perfect freedom. Without being grandiose, Jerry knew that while Loring was statesman of the outfit, and Mike was the money man (his happiest days spent out in the badlands of the Valley, *turning out product*), he, Jerry, was the dream man. In charge of the future.

They invited first-class passengers to board. As Jerry got to his feet Loring met his eyes from across the room, an intimate agreement to pretend they hadn't seen each other until now. They stood in line together. Loring grimaced as a flock of sumo wrestlers were encouraged to cut in front of them. The biggest came with them into first class. The other six turned into business, where they took up two seats apiece.

The hostess, doll-like in a traditional kimono, brought

Jerry and Loring their own bottles of champagne. An hour later, she beamed proudly when they ordered the Japanese dinner, which came to them in a box as elaborate as a hand-tooled suitcase. They opened theirs, and found mountains of room-temperature green noodles. Jerry watched as Loring opened one of his many little plastic jars and slung its contents across those noodles, which lay across a set of wooden slats.

The noodles tasted like the wood itself. The tastes were so strange, so strange. Across the aisle the sumo wrestler gobbled up coq au vin. So simple. People wanted to be somewhere else. That was the beauty of his plan. This Japanese trip, just a foray, to talk money, industry and land. Testing for money, testing for dreams.

The hostess cleared their food away. Tom Cruise appeared on the screen. Loring and Jerry opened up their laptops. Loring had a set of yellow legal pads, and he transcribed numbers from them into the secret jive of his PC. Then considered. Then tore up the yellow paper into small squares and stuffed them into an airsickness bag. Jerry's PC had color as an adjunct and he turned the whole screen red, the Day-Glo red he'd seen in some pictures of natives getting ready for a sing-sing in the Highlands. He opened a New Guinea travel guide — the kind written for the last remaining refugees of the counterculture. He began to read: "*Banz* and *Minj*: Sadly, the provincial high school at Minj was closed at the end of 1987 after a series of deliberate fires and the murder of the school cook. . . . There is very little to attract the traveler now, although there is an excellent golf course at Minj."

But that was in the western Highlands. Beaches at the end of the earth. *Somewhere else.* Lae, on the northeastern coast, a javelin's throw from Los Angeles to the east and Tokyo to the west, might be the spot. "*Lae*: A green, attractive place. Unfortunately, it now has a very bad reputation for Rascals. The paranoia on the part of the locals is intense. Even more unfortunately, the reputation and the paranoia are largely deserved. In happier days Lae had a reputation as a garden city and there was no better place to appreciate the reasons for this than at the Botanical Gardens. Today, the gardens are still beautiful but you would be most unwise to visit them other than in broad daylight, in a large group, and preferably with a local guide." Just above the Lae listing, a story of the Anga, those midget natives who for so many years had been called by the wrong name, Kukukuku: "When the first white man arrived in an Anga village, many of those otherwise fearless people literally fainted."

Jerry flipped through the guidebook, to pictures of deserted beaches and lagoons, visions of total beauty, total authenticity. He shut his book, slid back his seat — but not too far, that was rudeness to the passenger behind him — turned off his overhead light, took up his glass of champagne. Across the aisle, the sumo wrestler softly snored. Jerry focused on the ordered square of his laptop, deep deep red, and considered the ways of a people who mixed Wesson oil with pigment, or used straight spray paint to turn their faces glistening red. *Why* was that adventure? Because it was. Toward the back of the plane, vacationers buzzed excitedly as the movie ended and the lights went up for another meal. Up here in first class dark and quiet ruled. Tycoons and celebrities, their shined shoes kicked off, snuggled down on silk-covered pillows and caught their zees. He glanced aft, to the telephone. Wynn and Whitney should be home by now. But the line to the phone was six deep.

Hours, hours later, they were awakened by their hostess, who carried platters of steaming, perfumed towels. Behind them, in business class, men brought out their pocket shavers, shaving shamelessly where they sat, before they got up in twos and threes to hit the head, to splash on cologne and then breakfast on strong coffee and good scrambled eggs. Loring pointed to his open laptop, where he had pecked in one of the haiku he was famous in the firm for composing:

> *Free movie, free booze,*
> *Free legroom from LAX to TYO:*
> *Executive class.*

The feeling of jet lag — some people didn't like it, tried to get out of it, but the thing to do was catch it like the perfect wave. Take it as a drug.

The airport was even more gadget filled than it had been a year ago. One-minute massage parlors, cubicles to steam your pores open ("For a healthier, ruddier complexion"), pretzel vendors, fast-food curries. All around him (and Loring, who looked, now, as if he could use a one-minute massage for his sagging, tired face), Asian men were running — running in three-piece suits with briefcases in their hands. How could they get off a plane from Singapore, the PRC, Taiwan, the USA, go through customs, get their papers stamped, and then *run* like that?

A limo driver waited for Loring and Jerry — a lank teenager holding a nicely lettered sign: BARTCH, BRIDGES, FREED. The kid stacked up their suitcases and led them through what now seemed to be hordes of desperate people. Nine at night, still the rush hour in Tokyo. A million times worse than anything on the eastern side of the Pacific. Jerry felt dejected suddenly, out of it. His whole belief system revolved around going west, toward the setting sun, stretching out the day, going *west*! But now, after hours of chasing the sun, he and Loring had become the Easterners, the fogies.

Jerry heaved himself into the limo with a sigh. The driver turned out into the traffic and stopped. They moved perhaps fifteen feet in as many minutes. Beside him Loring turned on the Japanese evening news (which in this limo came with Eng-

lish-language summaries on a whole separate video attach-
ment), opened the bar, poured them both a scotch (single malt
that retailed at home for $139.95 a bottle. Jerry slid it around
his mouth — it was like drinking money). "Tell me this, Loring. If this is as fast as we go, why was everybody running?"

"The subway, remember? The only way to go in this town.
But we can't afford to take it. Bad for the image, Big Guy."

Jerry looked out the window to see how the city had
changed in the year since he'd been here. Like New York. Like
a *New* New York. Middle-level buildings, twenty stories high,
packed in to each other and next to the highway. When they
passed Disneyland, from a distance, even it looked overbuilt,
a *city* of amusements, not a park.

And yet . . . things looked great here! Every window of
every office building revealed three or four men in white shirtsleeves, conferring, talking on the phone, bending over computers, getting work done. Jerry knew they came in at seven in
the morning, usually stayed until the last hour the subway was
open. But they *played* too: they took life like strong drink;
there was something swell in that.

They hate us, he reminded himself. But, what the hell, we
hate them too. We can evolve out of that. Forget our reptilian
selves. Keep our eyes on the larger picture. The Rim for one
thing: the pretty blue plate, with the thick gold rim.

The Hilton made him forget that the Japanese hated him
or anybody. The lobby, many-tiered, many-gardened, many-
fountained, made him forget. The wonderfully polite women
and men behind the counter made him forget. He remembered, with joy, that this was a country where the taxis provided immaculate antimacassars for everyone's head, where, if
you lost your room keys in any part of town, they had ways
of tracking those keys down and jamming them personally
back into your hand, then refusing, adamantly, to take a tip.

A set of pretty girls in silly uniforms with white gloves

clustered around the elevators, pressed the button of their floor for them, then bowed them onto the elevator. A bellman took them to their suite, two separate bedrooms opening onto a perfectly furnished living room — Oriental simplicity, together with the comfort of Western couches and chairs, two courtesy computers, a copier, a fax, phones everywhere. (He'd have to call Wynn! But they'd be asleep by now.) And by an enormous picture window, a formal Western dining room table big enough to seat six.

"This is the good side of the hotel," the bellman said in excellent English. "In the foreground, MacDonald's, in the background, Mount Fuji. Six months, two weeks and three days since we have seen it, however." Outside, miles of neon beckoned. Time to party!

"I'm getting a massage," Loring said. "Want one?"

Sure, Jerry wanted one! And as he checked through their messages he saw they had a late dinner scheduled at eleven thirty with Yakamoto-san. Their opposite number in Tokyo. A bigwig. Ten o'clock now.

Eleven P.M., fresh as a washed baby, Jerry was ready to go, ready to roll. Loring looked good. The limo waited. The drive was short this time, no more than a mile away.

Again, as a courtesy to the guests, the setting was Western style, cocktail lounge format, hundred-dollar steaks, a menu in Japanese and American, a piano, a Japanese chanteuse bathed in a pink spotlight singing "My Funny Valentine." Men in business suits, hundreds of them, packed into red leather booths, their ties loosened, their heads thrown back in raucous laughter. In the corners of the enormous room the smoke was so thick Jerry couldn't see. But he could hear — a rough, guttural racket of Japanese, English, and a little Spanish, a little Tagalog, throw in some French. Everybody on their seventh scotch. Sometimes you got to be in the exact right place. Jerry took it in, smelled the smoke, absorbed the audio,

50

the waves of energy coming off these guys, men of accomplishment, making the world, kicking back after a sixteen-hour day, having fun. This was *it* for him, his reward for months of careful planning; his place, his happiness.

Two young men came toward them from the back of the restaurant, through smoke, shouting over the din.

"Blidge-san! Roring-san!"

Did they do it on purpose by now, as part of their ferocious courtesy, mix up their *l*'s and *r*'s because it was expected of them? Or was it a feint, merely, a neat little slip of the ball on the court: Magic and Kareem working together, and the other team left blinking and bewildered?

Loring fluently responded in a sentence of nicely rehearsed Japanese. His father had been stationed here in the years after the Real War and his Japanese was more than adequate — one of a hundred reasons he was an asset to the firm.

Already the four of them were bowing, smiling, bowing, smiling, bowing even more deeply. They had all *night* to do this! They were young guys, these Japanese, but in the gloom their older partner waited back at the booth, far too august to come out in this public arena for a couple of mere Americans.

Then came the exchange of bilingual business cards. But these guys didn't want to be called by their Japanese names. They were "Gus," with rimless glasses and a winning, guileless grin, and "Mac." When they finally got around to an American handshake, their fingers and palms were delicate, mouse-like, flaccid. How did this square with the bruiser back at the hotel, who'd pounded the jet lag out of him? Or those sumo wrestlers who took up two seats at a time in business class?

Chill out and *listen*! You don't have to know how the engine works when you learn how to drive a car. Jerry had said that to someone; or had someone said it to him? His dad, maybe? Back at the table they met Yakamoto-san, silver-haired, outfitted in immaculate pinstripes. More bows, cut gruffly short by this elegant lion who ordered them to sit down, pick up their drinks. More single-malt scotch, a hundred and forty a bottle, *at home.*

"Yakamoto-san apologizes for his lack of English. But he welcomes you and hopes you are not as *henpecked* as the three of us!" Gus laughed and shrugged.

Jerry looked at Loring. *Hand packed? Handicapped? In a wreck?* But no, they meant *henpecked.* Mac put his head in his hands and comically shrugged. By now the five of them were seated, a fresh new bottle just opened, displayed like an icon in the center of the table. Jerry remembered that he'd always trained himself to *fly out of the problem.* He *saw them from above,* as if he were a camera in a ceiling. At the center of the red leather booth, the silver hair of the grand old man, who must have his own, real, memories of the war Jerry only knew from the movies. To Yakamoto's immediate right, Loring Freed, banker and sometime poet, courtly and bilingual, his mind faster than the fastest computer, and to *his* right, on the aisle, Mac, with his head in his hands, about to entertain them with an anecdote, shoring up their booth, a line of demarcation between this booth and the smoky bedlam beyond. To the old man's left, Gus, guileless and bespectacled, his English *spectacular,* after that first false greeting. And, to the aisle, another border, another line, *him,* Jerry. The dream man. The way to know was to fly out of the problem, observe from above.

"Since Friday night, this is already seventy-two hours, Mac has not been allowed into his house. His wife is a general in her house, and she is giving the enemy a beating!"

"Since Friday night. That is when it started. I missed the last train to my suburb. I had to sleep in a capsule. You know these capsules, Blidge-san?"

"Jerry. Call me Jerry. Sure, I know them. A great idea!" He didn't know if they were a great idea or not — these stacks of plastic bullets, billets, in every downtown subway station, built expressly to accommodate businessmen who got caught when the iron gates to the city had clanged down behind them, and the last trains had already left. For a moderate chunk of money you could rent a capsule, with maybe nine inches between your face and the ceiling, and sleep in science fiction comfort until the morning, when you could rent a shower, purchase a shave, get your shoes shined, buy some fast food, and hurtle out again onto the frantic Tokyo streets.

"The next night, when I come home, the door to my house is locked. The lights are on, but the door is locked."

"What time was *this,* Mac?" The question came from Gus, the straight man tonight, leading him on.

"I took the last train. I always do. I work very *hard.*"

Yakamoto snorted, a powerful, explosive grunt. The young men giggled, almost girlishly.

"I called to my wife, Foumi. 'Foumiko,' I called, 'let me in! It's late. I work hard for you and the boys.' You must understand that although we live in a suburb, we have a crowded street. Houses go all along our river. The lights turn on in our street. I hear women all around me. 'Don't let him in, Foumiko! He is worthless!'"

"But," Jerry interrupted — he couldn't help it — "why didn't you use your own key?"

All the men laughed. "In Japan," Mac explained, "men own the streets. Women own their house. Oh, they have a voice, and they like to use it. I called out to my father-in-law, but even he would not answer. I slept in the street that night. The next morning, I called out again, asking only for tea and a little cold rice. But no. All the houses in the street were closed against me."

The men laughed, no one was sorry.

Mac went on. "Last night, I went home again. *Early.* Ten o'clock. I needed shirts. There is a mulberry tree outside my

53

wall. I climbed it, calling on the way, 'Foumi! Foumiko! Enough strife in our house for now.' One soft light is all I see. I think, I will surprise my wife. I will be romantic."

"Like Jurin Sorlel," Gus observed ironically, and Jerry marveled. *You don't have to know how the car runs to be able to drive it.*

"But as I swing my way over to the window, she opens it and throws perfume on me. 'Go back to your fancy women,' she says, so unfair. 'I am new woman now, and vote!' So, here I am, in the same suit for three days."

Their steaks arrived. Had they ordered? No. It must have been Yakamoto. Red meat, a sin in America. Japanese beef, soft as flesh, human flesh. Jerry took a first bite, then a huge second one. "So," he said, swallowing and reaching for his scotch, "what will happen? When do you get to go home?"

"Tomorrow," Gus said beside him, "Yakamoto-san will call Foumi's father. He will be the one to remind her of her duty. But we will send flowers, to soothe her feelings, because we work so hard. *That*," he cried out, "is not so bad as what *I* went through when my sister was jilted by a student who failed his exams. He should have killed himself, his grades were that bad, but he was a modern man, so he broke off his engagement as a sign of mourning. It was my sister who mourned. Day and night, in a very high voice. We were told we could not intrude upon her sorrow. Finally, when my sister began to tear apart the fine linen for her trousseau . . ."

Jerry tried to look at all of this from above. *Trousseau?* How often had this story been trotted out? What was its meaning? Loring Freed had pulled out his pipe, and with deliberation, lit it. "I have a story of love, of two cultures colliding. When I was at my university, the war was still close enough to us all to infuse American hearts with daydreams of Japanese wives."

Infuse? Jerry thought, *infuse*? Jet lag overwhelmed him. It would be so easy just to lie down. What could they do with me, if I just put my head down in my plate? People must do that here. Because they work so hard. He thought of loosening his tie. But he couldn't. He pulled at his scotch instead.

"A Chinese friend of mine — not a foolish American, but the son of hardheaded Chinese-American merchants — was sent on a buying trip to the Orient . . ."

Beside Jerry, Gus filled his own glass, passed the scotch around. Yakamoto-san listened, his face grim. Dread swept through Jerry. Was Loring bungling the deal, right now, in this moment? They said the Orient was inscrutable, and — they were right. Maybe Jerry was just drunk. In California, with all that white wine, all those glasses of mineral water, you lost the knack of this kind of drinking. What if he puked? What if, instead of sleeping in his plate, he puked in it?

"He traveled through Singapore, staying at the old Raffles. He voyaged the length of the Malayan peninsula, staying in Penang, where Russel's vipers waited for him, curled up in bolts of old silk."

"Oh yes," Gus said appreciatively, "snakes in grass."

"He acquitted himself well in Macao, stayed away from fancy girls and gambling houses, taking only a few shiny gold ingots from before the war. He swallowed two —"

"Swallow two," Mac interrupted, "shit out three. A lucky man!"

Yakamoto sat, not even lifting his glass to his lips. God, he must get bored, Jerry thought, with stupid, predictable American stories. Did he even understand English? Maybe Yakamoto would be the one to go to sleep. But then, what would happen to the deal? They needed his money; they had to influence his imagination. On the surface, from California, the deal looked — not easy, but feasible. But what if it was a mirage, pure and simple? When had a Japanese company ever offered, of its own volition, to put in with an American firm? Spend real money for an *idea*?

"In China, the relatives his grandfather had left behind

welcomed him. They gave feasts for him, but their feasts were meager. Not much meat. They made him understand that they needed transistor radios and Walkmen, and even Nintendos, in order to hold up their heads in the home village."

"*Nintendos!*" Gus and Mac giggled. Jerry finished his glass. His lips were numb. He hadn't been this drunk since college.

"But my friend honored his family obligations. He had brought a trunk of television sets, steam irons, transistors, and, yes, a Nintendo for the public hall of the Home Village. When he left, he took with him only a few worthless pieces of village trash — a few splintered wall sculptures, a few household gods that his relatives had put away during the beginning of the cultural revolution."

"Family possessions," Mac said quietly. "He didn't have to buy them, and he didn't have to show receipts, isn't that right?"

"Not 'antiques'?" It was Gus, now.

Loring puffed on his pipe, blew out smoke unashamedly, something you could never do in America now. "Antiques? Hardly. This was *junk,* souvenirs of an old life, something for his Americanized parents to remember *their* parents by. In San Francisco, customs might have known what they were looking at, but in Los Angeles, at the Bradley Airport — my friend apologized for bringing in such junk, taking up their time. It was only for his mother, my friend said. His markup was over a thousand percent."

"What about Japan?" Yakamoto asked the question, his first English words.

"What happened in Japan? My friend journeyed to Japan. He went to Kyoto, that beautiful city, staggered by all that he saw, the dignity amidst the commerce. He had planned to stay at a Japanese inn, but he was met at the airport by a man his grandfather had bought from many years before. This man took my friend on a long ride out into the country, to his own family retreat. There, his wife served him a meal with her own hands."

Gus leaned forward. "His *wife* served?"

"Oh yes," Loring said, nodding appreciatively. "Even before that, his daughter, a silent, modest maiden, had been commanded by her father to perform the tea ceremony for their Chinese-American friend. She blushed and trembled, but, to my friend's eye, at least, she did it perfectly."

Jerry felt Gus's body heave beside him. He was laughing. Across the table Mac hid his face. He could see what was coming. What was it? What was going on? Jerry peered through the smoke, first at Loring, then at Yakamoto. Something was happening to the old man's face. His eyes had narrowed. His lips turned down, as if he had tasted something fetid.

"During the meal, which was served Japanese style, only the men ate. The mother and her daughter scuttled across the floor in that movement which only the women of your country have mastered — that feathery motion which mimics the flight of wounded birds.

"That night, my friend was put to sleep in the daughter's room. There was no inconvenience. She would sleep at the feet of her parents."

Yakamoto's head moved from side to side. It was as startling, in its own way, as if a statue had begun, of its own accord, to move.

"My friend lay awake that night. The sounds of the countryside came in through his fragile windows. Toads, and crickets, and the wet *plink* of a crane as he carefully set his feet among the lily pads of the pond hidden somewhere in the garden."

Gus couldn't control his laughter. "Oh dear," he said. "Oh *dear*!"

"Finally, he slept. When he woke, at dawn, his suit waited

for him, freshly pressed. His shirt, fresher than the day it had been bought, waited as well, its sleeves crossed and joined in an attitude of Christian prayer. His shorts were folded into a spotless, seemly square. But his socks — his socks had been done as origami, fashioned into the ornamental shape of butterflies. Of course he married her."

Yakamoto opened his mouth, showed his teeth. "*Ha! Ha! Ha!*" Then he asked a long question in Japanese.

Loring answered, "What do *you* think, Yakamoto-san?"

"What is it?" Jerry asked. "What are they saying?"

"Yakamoto-san says, 'And now what happens? Does this wounded bird let her husband into her American home when he comes late from work? Does she pour hot cooking oil on him when he sleeps? Does he often see a pair of origami socks now?'" Gus took his glasses off and cleaned them with his handkerchief. He had laughed until his tears came, and he wiped them away now, off fresh young cheeks.

Loring spoke, in careful Japanese. And provoked another avalanche of mirth.

"Roring-san sum up. He says, *one* buying trip, *one* mistake. Is that so *bad*? He says, what merchants have *not* been fooled by Japanese businessmen? He says his friend is in very good company."

Yakamoto gestured. The waiter came immediately. The two older men argued briefly about the matter of the check. Shouldn't they wait to finish the scotch? But the empty bottle stood as evidence that they already had.

"Time to go see our beautiful city. Fill our chests with fresh air. Oh! I never see Yakamoto-san so amused!"

Outside, cold air bit into Jerry's face and lungs. What a world they had here! Spotless, nervy, exotic! The five of them walked single file, following Yakamoto. All along these streets, men in suits had bedded down neatly on the sidewalks. It took too much time to go home. Some of them lay under

Japanese quilts, some fitted themselves into Western sleeping bags. Some of them propped themselves up against marble walls to read paperback books, battery-operated tensor lamps casting light on the pages. One man, setting two ghetto blasters up as a kind of wall between himself and the rest of the street, caught Jerry's eye and waved.

Then a door, marked only by a bronze Japanese lantern, opened. Another square of dull gold light lit the black street. Inside, the five men paused to take off their shoes. Girls in kimonos removed their coats. One woman led them to a private room, all tatami mats, paper partitions and, on a low polished teak table, a stark arrangement of peonies. The men sat. More drink waited — sake in small cups. A woman came in very quietly, her eyes cast down, her makeup careful but modern, not geisha. She wore a vermilion kimono, held in place by a gold-worked obi. She had brought a koto with her. She bowed, once, preoccupied, it seemed, with the music she was about to make, scarcely noticing the men she was to play for. She tuned her instrument, placed her bright red nails along the strings, began to sing. Soon the room began to fade, the light played tricks. Lights appeared all around this woman, who sang and sang. The only sound was her high-pitched singing. Jerry drank his sake, heated so that it seemed less liquid than aromatic air, and saw his cup filled by someone beside him, a Japanese girl, her eyes cast down, the dewy skin of her face and neck as fresh as a child's. Jerry looked away.

The woman finished one song, bowed her head. Yakamoto commanded another. This one seemed mournful and was soon over. Then another song, spirited, crazy. When the woman had finished this, she panted a little. Part of her glistening, lacquered hair came loose.

Yakamoto ordered sake for the woman. She took it from a servant girl, asked for more. Her kimono had slid a little to the side, just a little, so that the upper part of her right breast showed. The men stared, greedily. She met their stare and bared her teeth in a sloppy kind of grin, blood red lipstick on her teeth. She began to sing and play again. Another song, a song of scorn. At the bottom rim of his peripheral vision Jerry watched a girl's hand fill his cup. Was it his mind only, or did he feel her other hand on the back of his neck? Fingertips? Fingernails? One fingernail? He kept his eyes on the koto player's breast. The woman was not young, the breast had sag and pull to it. Her hair loosened, strand by strand. Her made-up face glistened with trapped sweat.

In the breathing, glowing drabness that came from nothing more than keeping his eyes focused too long on one place, or drinking too much, Jerry saw Mac bow deeply from his knees, in front of Yakamoto, who responded with a grunt. *What is this,* Jerry thought for one lucid millisecond, *a fucking Toshiro Mifune* movie? Why can't these people get up on their feet and walk and talk like human beings? But his eyes, his gaze, went back to the musician, who bent, then arched her back and allowed, with each moment, a little more of her milky, hanging flesh to be seen. Mac and a girl went to another room, or no, just behind a screen, a flimsy screen, where his groans and her shrill yips added to the cat cries of the musician, who paid no attention.

Loring, in the company of an absurdly young girl, left. But *how*? How did they leave? They didn't stand up, they didn't crawl. It didn't matter. You thought yourself to be in another place — and then you were. Gus took off his rimless glasses. He raised his arm as if to cuff a slithering woman away from him, but pushed his hands into her elaborate hairdo instead. Hers was not made to come undone: it was, in fact, a wig, and rolled across the tatami. Her real hair, shiny and golden, fell across her narrow shoulders. She was a Western girl. Gus took her whole ear in his hand and pulled her, mewing, to a corner of the room. Someone had turned down the lamps, so that light shone only on the woman with the koto, who kept playing.

Jerry heard a voice in his ear, soft as sake, an insect in his mind. Cumbersomely he got up to follow her, but turned at the last second. The koto player's breasts were bare, the nipples rouged and huge. Yakamoto stood. A young girl scuttled out and took him away. The woman put her koto aside.

His own girl tugged at his hand, pulled him behind a screen. One shaded light lit her body. She was very young. Fourteen? Her pubic hair had been waxed away. Rhinestone posts pierced each nipple. Teeth marks, someone else's teeth marks, on her hipbone. Wait, wait! But that was useless now. She knelt in front of him, irritably batting his numb, clumsy arms away as he tried to touch her. He was ready to come in thirty seconds, less, so she stopped, let her jaw hang slack, as if there was nothing, no one, there. He was standing, as Yakamoto had stood, and he needed a nap now, needed to lie down and close his eyes and forget all of this. And as he thought that, and began to droop, she worked on him again, bringing him back to that same point, then going slack again. Soreness and pleasure contested in his body. His stomach lurched, he wasn't used to this. And he knew, from other times, when he got like this he could never come, never come, never come. There would just be this joyless pulling. He heaved a sigh and opened his mouth to tell her to stop, forget it, this wasn't happening. She took his dick out of her mouth, laid it across her cheek, rolled her eyes up at him, found that place along that rim which his foreskin might have protected if it still had been there. She showed her teeth, then found the sixteenth of an inch of his skin where he was most sensitive and bit down, hard. His knees shook from the pain, he boxed her ear and shouted. Then, irrevocably, amazingly, he came, and came. She held him clamped in both her hands, hard as a vise, squeezing the last, the last, out of him, not into her mouth, but all over her face. When he had finished, she used her palms to wipe it across her cheeks, her neck, and down her smooth flat breasts to her twinkling nipples. "*Dozo!*" she murmured, bowed her head, and held up her hand, palm out. Dazed, he stood there until her waggling fingers finally brought him back to the world. His dick still hanging, limp and out there, he reached into his inside jacket pocket where he kept his passport, his credit cards, his money. No way in the world he could figure how many yen! He pulled out half his cash, a hefty handful, stuffed it into her hand, zipped himself up, tried desperately to *get a grip*. As he turned he saw Loring, standing against the wall, waiting.

He followed his partner into the more brightly lit hall, bowed, along with Loring, to the woman at the door, and like Loring, pressed more bills into her hand. Then they were outside on the cold, black street. Loring waved into blackness and a parked taxi turned up its lights to pick them up.

"Hilton Hoteru!" But Jerry had to have the cab stop twice so he could puke in the gutters. It was close to dawn when they hit the suite. Their message machine was blinking, a swirl of faxes awaited their attention. Loring disappeared into his room and shut the door. Jerry pulled the paper windows of his own room shut, went to his private refrigerator and pulled out all the mineral water he could find. He got his dop kit, found the vitamin B, took a handful, along with three aspirin. The trick was to get all this down and keep it down. Then add a Valium to sleep.

He woke up with an enormous hard-on, thinking only of the girl with the rhinestone tits. He couldn't jack off because of the bite on his dick. The fear of AIDS kicked in, and then, finally, he allowed himself to think of Wynn, he had to; and thought of how, when she lay on her side away from him, her breasts pushed fully down on top of each other, and her stomach, from having three kids, lay out beyond her ribs and hips — even though she exercised — along the crisp sheets which Carmela changed every two or three days and which always smelled of sunshine and Clorox, because Wynn insisted on hanging out sheets in the sun. The thought of that clean, strong smell made his stomach heave. He remembered the hospital he'd left only the afternoon before, the terrified face of his wife, and his stomach heaved again. He barely made it to the bathroom.

Now that he was in here he realized a shower had to be the best, the only thing. It was one of those round-the-world showers with six spigots. He turned it on full blast and hot, not flinching when the water battered his cut. There wasn't any point in thinking about it. He'd have to take his fucking chances, just like everybody else in the world. But wasn't she taking a chance too? Beyond his hangover terror, another voice made every effort to reassure him: she dealt with straight men, AIDS was almost unknown in Japan, it was just a nick, not a real cut. What was the big deal? He would always see to all of his responsibilities. So what if he lost it once or twice? He got out, rubbed himself down, shaved, threw on cologne, sat down to take a shit, put his head in his hands. He let himself remember how he'd left the hospital. And that he hadn't put in a call, not from the plane, not even from the Hilton.

He was sure it wasn't serious with the kid, or they would have said so right away. But he knew, he let the thought wash over him because it was going to anyway, that he didn't want to hear about any of it. There was no way he would have put off this trip. Let people think what they liked. The trick, *somewhere else,* was to party all night and work all day. He was ready for the deal. As neatly as changing a cassette in the dashboard of a car, another set of worries clicked in. He reached in the refrigerator, found a Classic Coke, chugalugged it for the sugar. He combed back his wet hair, reached for a terrycloth robe with the Hilton logo stamped on it, pushed his feet into thongs, and went into the living room.

Loring was up and already dressed. His face shone bluish in the gray smog of the city. The table held a service with an extensive continental breakfast.

"Have a croissant. I've been working on a haiku. About the view."

"Was that a geisha place last night?"

"Whorehouse is more like it."

"Any messages?" Jerry turned away from the older man as he poured out his coffee. Why should he be embarrassed?

"An invitation from the Indonesian Embassy to tea this afternoon. They think something along their archipelago might be the place for us. They argue it has no World War II associations. And no wreckage either."

"How do you know?" The question, boyish, naive, burst from him.

"Talked to Yakamoto last night." (Last night? *When?*) "And again this morning."

Jerry forced a laugh. "I thought, after last night, the deal might be off."

"The deal is on." Loring sat in a swivel chair next to the fax, but he looked out the windows to the dreary scene below. He reached for a croissant, spread it with extra butter, plenty of jam, and took a sizable bite. Crumbs spilled on his shirt.

"I wrote another one. Get this.

> 'Good harmony view
> Makudonuorudu
> In front of Fuji.'"

Jerry crossed to the window. The gray air that hung over Tokyo seemed even more poisonous than what he saw from the office in downtown L.A. There was no Mount Fuji out there. No more than you could ever see the San Gabriels from the east side of their own building. Miserable, he scanned the horizon, looking for a mountain. Just to drive him crazy, the sun broke through for a second and caught the reflection of one faraway window.

Wynn, Kathy
Whitney, Tracie
Baby Jonathan

Pacific Palisades
January 17–April 15

WYNN FITTED OUT the back veranda as a place for Whitney to recover. Veranda? Really what her own mother might have called a screen porch; it *had* been a screen porch when they'd moved into this house on Georgina. They'd sorted out rooms with a combination of brutality and tact. The family, "the *real* family" as Jerry had once carelessly named it, lived in a nucleus upstairs: master bedroom with that southwest-facing greenhouse window, that look at the ribbon of the Pacific, for Jerry and Wynn; two bedrooms across the hall for Josh and Tina. Before the accident, Whitney had lived in the cupola over the double garage. She had heard the "real family" remark, and it had clung to her like a birthmark; no favor or natural kindness that Jerry (or Wynn) could ever perform would smudge it out. She lived out across the lawn, and *up* — a stranger to the rest of them.

During those early years, when they were making decisions about this house, Jerry had taken the front library for his own office, with locks that fastened from the inside. Whitney made her move across the yard, up over the garage, aggressively lonely: *You may not want me, but you can't have me either*!

Wynn, not really noticing at first, because her peace of mind and her whole future depended on not noticing, decided that she would take the screen porch for herself. Wynn bought wicker and chintz and made a solarium. Late at night, before she'd had the little kids, after Jerry had finished dinner and closed the library doors behind him and Whitney had excused herself with spiteful manners and gone out across the garden to be by herself, Wynn, restless, fretful — despite all this furniture, this smell of new glazed chintz — would come down here late at night. She sat in the dark, looked at the blocks of artificial light above the garage, and yearned after her daughter. At those times she understood why some parents made a raging-hell fuss about kids on liquor or drugs — it was a way to reclaim their children, to hold on, to have a conversation. But Wynn could never do that.

Sometimes, nine or ten at night, she'd see kids hotfooting it darkly down the driveway and disappearing up the outside stairs and into the soft yellow of . . . where Whitney lived. A million times had Wynn wanted to mosey on out on those stepping stones she'd had embedded through the garden for just that purpose. Go on up and say hi. But Whitney was nacreous. Inanimate. Unattainable. When she came inside the house, for dinner, or to pick up laundry, she still remained out of reach, but Wynn knew at least she was there, under the roof. None of this was talked about, none of this mentioned; not by Whitney, because she was too fragile, maybe, under that aloof shell, and never mentioned by Jerry because he was too damned dense.

In the first days, first years, it had been a lot harder than Wynn would have expected. She would say that sometimes to, oh, women at the park, where she took Tina or Josh. She might even have talked about it sometimes at a Firm dinner, when she was alone for a while with some of the wives, the older ones — whose conditions might not have been all that different from hers.

But now in Wynn's screen porch, Wynn's "veranda," there was a hospital bed from Abbey Rents, and a hospital table that slid across the bed. Her daughter was here, in the heart of the house, Wynn's heart of the house. She'd positioned the bed, almost without noticing, so that at night, through the sliding glass windows and old-fashioned screens, they could see the dark squares of Whitney's apartment over the garage. *So many nights,* Wynn wanted to tell her daughter, *I came down here and looked up at your windows*! Could Whitney *see* that — that no matter the hard things that had happened between them, during Wynn's seven years with Jerry, and the two new kids, at least they were back together?

Because the truth was, in spite of the terrible, terrible accident, Wynn woke up at night happy. Even though she prayed, unevenly, for the soul of that poor boy who died, she was assaulted by waves of happiness. The first night that Whitney came home from the hospital, she, Wynn, lay on a wicker couch not six feet away from her, and even as she was wakened out of a light sleep by Whitney's sobs and cries, she remembered older days and nights when it was just the two of them in a room, against the world. But they'd done OK! When, out on the veranda, Wynn heard Whitney cry in the night, she felt the anguish that was appropriate, sure, but there was that other wave of calm, of union, the sense that some way, some terrible way, things had gone right, and that for a while she had her daughter, her dear heart, back again.

Because, for one thing, sickness was something everyone knew exactly what to do with. Dozens of family friends and school friends came by. They sat in those wicker chairs with the flowered chintz and chatted along to Whitney and to Wynn, as if this was the most natural thing in the world — as if mother and daughter had never been in the least estranged. They brought puzzles and X-rated comics, and had enough sense not to talk about Robin although several times a day, Whitney cried for her lost friend. (Wynn had gone, alone, to the funeral, and watched the searing grief of the mother, and seen these same people over there in church, sobbing, transported by grief.) The school would be doing a memorial service later, in another month or so, to "put it in perspective" for the student body.

One day in April, when Wynn was in the kitchen, putting a tray together for her daughter — chicken soup from a can, and chocolate pudding, and some herring on crackers, since last night her daughter had mentioned herring, and how they used to eat herring — she heard the sound of laughter. Real laughter, Whitney's and somebody else's.

She carried the tray out to the porch and saw Whitney's bed shaking, heard her daughter's voice: "*Please*. Don't! It's killing me to *laugh*, Trace!" Wynn saw Whitney's best friend, Tracie, who for years had only nodded or mumbled to Wynn, never talking directly to the hated parent, keeping her distance, looking either cautious or hostile, focusing her glance on the floor, or those stepping stones, as she bounded through the back garden to the garage apartment. But disaster had humanized the kid so that she looked up from the wicker chair she was clinging to like a spider monkey and called out, "So, Mrs. Bridges! She's looking better, don't you think?"

"Wynn. Call me Wynn, for heaven's sake. Can I get you some lunch?"

But Tracie was fiddling with the TV at the foot of Whitney's bed. "Time for the G.H. break," the girl explained, and Whitney gave her mother a furtive look. What if all those long afternoons, when Whitney had closeted herself upstairs above the garage, with her exotically dressed friends — what if, instead of doing dangerous drugs, or planning to run off and live in the street, or at the very least playing perverted sexual games, they had only been watching "General Hospital," and, maybe, Oprah?

Wynn sat on her wicker couch with her feet up on the flowered cushions, watching as well. When Carmela brought Josh and Tina home, Wynn let them crawl all over her, and observed with amazed contentment as, after banging up against Whitney's bed a few times so she could say "*Ouch! Cut that out!*" and make it clear that she was ignoring them and all they stood for, Josh went over to Tracie, who did nothing overt to entice him but simply bent her long, tan body down toward the floor from her waist, so that her big fluff of blond hair, part frizz, part braids, full of beads and barrettes and bits of torn silk, was at a level for Josh to survey and tangle his hands into. And he did. Tracie whooped obligingly. "Someone's got ahold of my *hair*," she cried. "Who could it *be*? Who could it *be*, Whit? Do *you* know who could it be?"

And even with a broken arm with a new, uncomfortable cast, and a bum shoulder, and a very bad headache, and maybe still something wrong with her spine, Whitney answered like the sport she was, "It looks like Tina to me," so that Tina, climbing up on their mother's lap, got to yell out, "*No!* It's Josh!" And Josh, with his hands still buried in that inviting mop, twisted his body around to explain to his half sister, "It's *me*."

"You're shittin' me, babes," Tracie remarked. Whitney sent out silent vibes from her bed of pain — watch the language, Trace, that's my *mother* we've got sitting here — but

Wynn focused in on the world of "General Hospital."

Tracie said engagingly to Wynn, "Mrs. Bridges! I just became a sister. My mom had a baby about two minutes ago! How do you like *that*?"

Meanwhile Josh shouted, at the top of his voice, "I'm not *shittin'* you! I'm Josh. *See?*"

And Tracie explained, with perfect calm, "Well, how should I know? *I* can't see anybody. I can only see the floor from where *I'm* sitting," which made Josh let go of her hair and run around to the other side of the chair, where he could see Tracie face to face. "You look upside down to me," Tracie said soberly, and Whitney, her face washed pale with pain, had to smile. Tina, quick and bright, saw that this was a good chance to cleave to her mom and settled in so securely and quietly next to Wynn that it seemed their whole life might now be given up to watching daytime soaps.

Two hours passed — a "General Hospital" hour, an "Oprah" hour — where Wynn had all three of her children with her, and this other great kid, Tracie. Whitney allowed herself to be brought herb tea and rocky road ice cream, and was dosed with something Tracie's mom had sent over, queen bee jelly, which tasted dreadful but everybody swore by it. Wynn knew that around six P.M. the inexorable pain that had plagued her daughter for the last three months would catch up with her, and that she would begin to cry tears that would last until eleven at night, or until she slept. (The receptionist at the doctor's office said Wynn shouldn't think of it as pain exactly — rather that the body itself was crying. Not Whitney, but Whitney's body — the unexpected spinal complications, the lesions in the shoulder that would not heal — mourning its trauma as it went about the business of repairing itself.) The doctor never talked about any of this at all. The orthopedist was more distant than the mechanic who fixed her car. The orthopedist talked about this bruised flesh and these dislocated bones in much the same way as the insurance adjusters, on that first day after the accident, spoke dispassionately about the destroyed car. Wynn tried to remember Robin's parents and their friends and their own set of doctors.

An image, a memory, of the boy's doctor coming out and shrugging and dusting off his hands and saying, "The kid is totaled, he's *unfixable*," came to Wynn, although she knew the "unfixable" part had to have been from when she got a flat tire a few weeks before any of this had happened.

Tina slept, sweating lightly against her. Oprah took the high road this afternoon. Several couples discussed the question of unemployed husbands, who staunchly insisted they did their part around the house. Tracie had pulled a chair up to Whitney's bed. Josh too had drowsed off, his feet on Whitney's bed, his body lodged in Tracie's lap. The couples on "Oprah" would never get anywhere, if they went on bickering like that. Wynn stole a glance at her daughter's face. What she saw was the effort to stay tranced out, to stave off the pain by total and complete concentration on these unhappy couples who couldn't even come to an agreement about making the bed in the mornings. You'll never get anywhere taking turns! Wynn wanted to advise them. Somebody's always going to forget or pretend to forget, isn't that right? And then you'll have another fight. The thing to do is make the bed *together* . . .

But what did she know about it? She hadn't made a bed in over seven years. She always let Carmela do it, and never even offered to help.

Unfixable. What had that doctor said to Robin's parents? She'd seen it. She'd seen them. She'd seen the mother, and the father and a brother. She and Jerry had gone over to the house after Robin's funeral. The two couples had embraced, shed some tears. Then she and Jerry had gone home, where Whitney, so soon after the accident, was twisted in agony.

By the time Whitney got out of the hospital, Jerry was

home from Japan. At night, Jerry slept right there beside Wynn. Before he slept, though, he opened up his briefcase. He turned on the tensor lamp over his head. He was always reading a prospectus — or was it a profit and loss sheet? It was double-sided, the left-hand pages printed out on a bilingual computer: Japanese characters, with the reassurance of numbers. For a few minutes a night, Wynn allowed herself to read them over his shoulder. She let her eyes stray from her bestseller over to the papers propped up on Jerry's knees, illuminated with perfect clarity by that tensor lamp . . .

For one year, still married to Al, she'd gone to graduate school. Philosophy. A few of the women had kids. They dealt with them somehow. In the seventies you could do anything. She'd had a couple of friends with kids Whitney's age. They'd never gone "to the park" — they were all studying too hard for that, but sometimes they'd go shopping together, carrying each other's kids, or bringing them to school and watching them run around outside, on wide campus lawns. As a baby, Whitney had marched in some of the last of the demonstrations. She'd gone, as a baby or a tot, to a whole collection of parties, where she'd been danced around, but that hadn't been any way to raise a child. There had certainly been drugs, but no harm had come to any of them, except maybe to Al himself. The truth was that when Wynn tried to remember that part of her life, she got such faded stuff, such trippy stuff, that it looked like a seventies rerun: Earl Holliman, Angie Dickinson running around in "Police Woman." When they talked about communism happening in a *cell*? Well, there were all kinds of cells. She'd broken out of one cell, the cell of the past, where everything was dark and smoky, and nobody really *gave* a shit about you, except as it pertained to exams or sex or ideology. She'd decided, when she met Jerry, to go west with him — west to the beach; west to the bank.

And if she and Whitney didn't speak as much as they used

to, maybe it wasn't mother-daughter conflict or that scourge of Golden Oaks, the prospect of drugs, but that they couldn't really, in the midst of this homespun affluence, sit down and say, "So! You remember those cockroaches?" Or "Do you remember that time when we all came home from the beach, and it was so hot, and we had to take turns for the shower, and that guy Leo got so mad at his wife he knocked her unconscious? And your father preached a sermon on the efficacy of righteous violence the very next Sunday?"

She'd been friends with Leo's wife but walked away from her, stopped returning her calls.

Her own mother would barely speak to her since she'd married a kind and rich man. Her sister wouldn't speak to her at all. Just moved away and out on her, because, to her sister and mother, breaking out of the cell of poverty and sadness was the worst kind of betrayal.

Her first husband had walked out on *her*, although no one seemed to believe that now. Al had said he needed to see the Amazon jungle before they shaved it down to the nub, and she and the kid were welcome to come along. But she'd already had to quit school while Al decided to pee or get off the pot; to find a new ministry or help the poor, as he was always and forever promising to do; either that or turn his fondness for plain wholesome marijuana into some kind of export-import career: *anything*! It didn't matter to Wynn, just something to give their gray life a direction, because the sixties and the seventies — her childhood, her young adulthood — had *had* it.

When Al went south to Mexicali, then, she'd stayed home with Whitney. And kept her friends for a while. But her first husband, her friends, her past, all had lived in a place where the cosmic light had come in at about a twenty-five-watt level. And that was really *true*; there weren't any windows in those early San Fernando Valley apartments and bungalows where she and Al lived. The print from the L.A. *Weekly* and *Reader* was dark and hard to read and came off in her hands. It was dark, dark.

But now, as she listened to women her own age, in her current station in life, she thought, Jeez! the worst thing that happened to them was that they got the *family car* for their sixteenth birthday, instead of the sport car they *really* wanted? Or that they can't find their own best *foot* surgeon? And she remembered Whitney, three years old, on a couch somewhere in dark Van Nuys, with an ear infection, and Al saying, "Isn't that just supposed to *burst*? Isn't that the way you deal with this? Because I can't afford this! We're certainly not spending the money to take her to any doctor! Not with other people needing treatment so much more!"

And the funny thing was, locked in the light now, a white cell as opposed to a gray cell, Wynn grieved that she couldn't talk to Whitney about old days, old ways.

At five in the morning after Whitney and Robin's accident, two hours, really three hours before the operation, when grim dawn tinted the parking lot outside the hospital, Wynn drove back in. She saw, as she waited in traffic, hordes of exhausted workers going off to hard jobs (even here in Santa Monica), stopping their cars under the drive-in part of the Jack-in-the-Box down the street from the emergency waiting room. Wynn cursed her gray, careless friends who let her go out of their lives so quickly. She couldn't call them now. She'd have to go through this alone. No, *Whitney* would have to go through this alone, with no father, just a mother, and, eventually, this stranger and his tensor lamp, who signed the checks. He knew as much about suffering as what she knew about the computerized Japanese characters on the left side of his rustling printouts.

She had thought hard during the morning of the operation. *This is my fault.* But I don't know how I could have avoided it. She didn't worry about losing Whitney during the operation because seven years before, when she'd married Jerry, she'd lost Whitney then. Cell division. Unfixable. Not reparable.

But who would have known that pain might heal that? That, for these few weeks at least, she and all her children could live under the same roof, and spend these hours together? Wynn lived through these days cautiously, not thinking about them at all, that was the point. When Robin's funeral came she sent flowers and, besides going to the service, a short note, so that her real thoughts wouldn't shine through: *I'm so lucky*!

Wynn's dad, a Texas dude long gone out of everybody's life, had earlier delighted in driving everyone around him crazy with senseless platitudes: "What's bad for you's good for you. What's good for you's bad for you." Finally, after thirty years, Wynn got it. No up without a down. No down, no up. Besides giving her a daughter back on loan, some goddess of chaos had taken pity on her and given her an extra gift.

Tracie came by every afternoon now. She and Wynn had an unspoken agreement to do one thing, stretch out those afternoon hours when Whitney was without tears, stretch them out, out, just a little longer. Because the tears were unbearable, and Whitney's big sleeping pill couldn't come until ten at night. When the tears came, Tracie left, and those were the bad hours in between, where Whitney looked into hell. And her mother could only sit by her and clench her fists, because any touch to Whitney's body only increased the pain.

But one afternoon, when "Oprah" had slid into the local news, and Whitney had begun the restless thrashing that preceded her terrible tears, Tracie, getting ready to go home as she collected school books and papers and cosmetics to stash in her huge tote bag — the mirror image of Whitney's — said casually, "So, Mrs. Bridges! Remember that baby my mom had? She's going crazy hanging around the house! Do you think I might bring her over some day?"

A full three months after the accident, Whitney wasn't doing too well, restless and sad, saying with perfect sense and rationality, "There's no reason why it shouldn't have been me who died. Why wasn't it me? I was in the passenger seat, isn't that supposed to be the death seat?" Wynn answered, with the same kind of platitude that used to drive her crazy when she heard it instead of said it, "You're so lucky. You don't know how lucky you are. When you take a look at that car! Your back's OK. And thank God you're right-handed. And remember, even the doctor says the left hand didn't suffer any real damage."

"*Damage?*" Whitney's eyes filled with tears.

In the silence after this exchange, Wynn heard voices, one of them Tracie's, heard a familiar scuffing up the driveway, followed by a second tread, and there was Tracie coming in the back door followed by a woman Wynn's age — looking forty right in the face, but not too upset about it. How often do you meet a friend — more than a friend, a soulmate? Wynn could remember two other times. Once, in a restaurant when she was seventeen, working as a waitress, and required to wear a uniform with a starched Dutch hat. A girl rounded the bend around station twenty-eight, a girl named Margie. Wynn still thought of her. The kind of girl with whom no explanations at all were necessary or appropriate: you sat down in the employees' dining room over free pieces of coconut cream pie and began. Margie married a navy man, went to a state in the East and disappeared. The second time: in her one year of graduate school, Judy, perfect "answer woman," sidled over to Wynn at a teaching assistants' meeting. "Does this mean we're in with the in-crowd?" she'd asked. They'd talked three, four times a day during those dark seventies times, and — when anything was possible — had fallen in love with the same low type. Part of the stuff Wynn didn't want to remember, and so she didn't. But she would always remember Judy's watchful, amused, intelligent, scrubbed face as she sidled up:

"Does this mean we're in with the in-crowd?" A love at first sight far scarcer than the other kind. Friendship. Far more important than love.

The woman who came through the door looked like Tracie, only older. *Naturally!* She wore 501 jeans and a blue T-shirt the color of a bruise. Her eyes were made up heavily and her frizzy brown hair went all over the place. She carried a kid in a high-tech knapsack slung across her back, and she looked strung out. "My name's Kathy," she said. "This one here is Jonathan. How you doing, cupcake?" She meant Whitney, who had to smile. And Wynn thought, This isn't a Golden Oaks parent any more than I am! Later she would consider that Whitney loved Kathy — and Tracie too — because Kathy was an emissary, a freed slave, from the dark past that had to do with dishes in the sink and husbands who drank too much and flat tires on the freeway and patchwork quilts made from scraps, because "you kept your clothes, you didn't throw them out!"

The women's eyes met, asking and answering a silent question. *So tell me: Are we finally in with the in-crowd? What do you think?*

The baby, Jonathan, was asleep, cute little generic baby. Kathy said that the backpack was going to kill her off once and for all, but that she had to wear it because her new sister-in-law had given it to her. "It's like carrying around a chrome chair, like it's not enough you have to carry the *baby*?" But her hands were gentle and patient as she extracted her infant from its flying buttress contraption and laid him out on a couch. "Do you know I have to *hide* every pacifier when my in-laws come over? It's hard. Don't you think it's hard?" As she chatted along, her eyes moved across the porch, a smile wandering across her rouged lips. Is this a hoot, or *what*? She overlooked the sick and teary girl — something that will pass, she silently commented. Just an excuse for us to get acquainted. I'm dying for someone to talk to. I'm going nuts for someone to talk to.

Kathy accepted some herb tea, ironically. (Don't we both remember when, in the afternoon, we could open a beer, as we chopped up lettuce and fried cheap hamburger for a taco dinner?) She said, "So, the *second* Jonathan was born, well, the morning after he was born, I called up Golden Oaks and put him on the waiting list. And you know what? They *put* him on the waiting list!"

Kathy's second husband was an older man, an attorney, head of the western branch of an East Coast firm. "This week I've got to go to a firm dinner and it's got to be a long dress but the only things I've got are strapless, and I'm not getting any younger. I'm not doing *that* anymore, so just for the hell of it I went over to Giorgio's and Chanel, and *I'm sorry*! They had a dress at Giorgio's that looked really good but you know what? Six thousand dollars *marked down from eleven*! You could buy a car for that."

"Chanel," Wynn said, and unexpected tears stung her eyes. "I went in there before all this happened. I thought, at last I'm going to get to wear a real Chanel dress. And you know what they had? About forty-eight yards of black chiffon with real cheap gold chains, and —"

"That medal. I know. Like you're a French general. Or you're wearing a charm bracelet."

"Three thousand!"

"Marked down to —"

"*Fifteen hundred!*"

Over by the bed, the girls observed, protective, parental.

In a sudden, peaceful quiet, Kathy stretched, looked down at the baby. "You have two little ones, right?"

"Tina and Josh, three and six. Golden Oaks. Of course."

They smiled tiredly. Together.

"And mine's Jonathan. What is it" Kathy queried the universe, "with these J names? Did I ever *think* I was going to have a kid named Jonathan?"

"I'll tell you one thing," Wynn said solemnly, and they said

the next sentence in unison, "*It sure does change your life!*"
And then they laughed so raucously that their girls, one well,
one in real pain, looked at them, offended.

When Carmela brought in Josh and Tina, they poked at
baby Jonathan so much that he woke up and began to wail.
Carmela tried to coax the kids away, and reported that someone had dented the Volvo in the parking lot of the grocery.
Whitney decided that she had to go to the bathroom. Tracie
helped her to swing her legs cautiously over the bed, get her
bearings. Then wincing, Whitney lay her uninjured arm across
her friend's shoulders. They disappeared together into the
downstairs maid's bathroom. Josh and Tina scammed some
Popsicles and went outside. Kathy changed the baby and fed
it four ounces of juice, which disappeared in an instant. Whitney came back, pale and close to tears. Tracie was helping her
back onto the bed when Kathy said, "Wait! Want to hold the
baby, Whit? Before you lie back down? With your good arm?
Why not give it a shot? With your good arm?"

Whitney sat, listless and teary, her bare feet dangling, her
bare legs frail, their muscle tone gone. Her hair, though
washed, drooped, dull and toneless. "I don't know, I'm afraid
I —"

The baby, as if in apprehension, set up a series of little
barks of protest, a squeaky-wheel cry, not loud.

"Come on, Whit. You held him when he was a week old,
remember? He liked you. You liked him! He only weighs
twelve pounds."

Kathy got up, carrying Jonathan. He wore regular baby
clothes, white shirt, white diaper. He was one of those *little*
babies. Tracie sat on the bed next to her friend's bad arm.
Nothing's coming at you from this direction! Kathy dropped
the baby into the curve of Whitney's right arm, not lying
down, but with his butt on her forearm, his head on her neck.
Jonathan stopped crying, just like that.

"See?" Kathy said. "He always liked you. Didn't I say so? Isn't it true?"

Whitney's body bent to the task of holding the baby. Her legs tensed a little, some color came to her face. Her good arm held firm. "Hi, kiddo," she whispered. "How you doing, J.B.?"

"Jonathan Bradshaw," Kathy explained. "His middle name is my maiden name."

Whitney's body swayed. Outside, Tina and Josh chased each other, the sun catching their hair. Tracie held still, watchful. Imperceptibly at first, then with automatic confidence, Whitney's left hand, extending from a turquoise fiberglass cast, began to move, the bluish, bruised fingers patting the baby, who took it for a minute, two minutes, his head held back so that he could survey the scene, the moment happening. Then he flopped forward again, onto Whitney's shoulder and neck. His own left arm, about as big as a cigar, began to pat Whitney's back, comforting his holder.

"I've never seen that before," Wynn whispered. "*Never*."

The sun dipped a little more and caught them there. Watchful Tracie, Whitney smiling with her eyes closed, grave baby.

It was almost too much. It *was* too much.

"Come on," Wynn said in a low voice to Kathy. "They'll be OK. Let's you and me commit a sin. How about a blender margarita?"

"Fine with me."

Ice cubes and tequila and lemon and salt. And not a peep from the back veranda.

Jerry

West Los Angeles
May 11

JERRY AND WYNN had trouble parking the car for Robin's "last, light" memorial service, but then they always did, coming to productions at Golden Oaks's Little Theater. All the industries up and down this street had complained from the beginning of time about parents parking, students parking, faculty parking. Jerry remembered dropping his wife off by the door to the theater, more than once, while he said, with false consideration, "You go on in. Save me a seat. No use *you* being late . . ." Remembered it all so clearly, like a scene from his own childhood, the hard, tolerant look Wynn shot him as she got lightly out of the car without a protest. *Yes, she's my kid, not yours. But I'm a Golden Oaks parent, even if Whitney was a scholarship child — and I bring that to Tina and*

Josh. Other wives piled out of other cars, with the same iron social will.

The memory happened in an instant. He'd thought he'd filed all that stuff in his mind under U for unimportant; F for forgettable. The look of the women as they stood on the sidewalk, tucking silk blouses into linen pants, appraising the crowd, making sure there were enough souls there; tallying the ratio of adults to kids, and were the kids the right ones? Remembering as well the covert and shit-eating glances of the husbands (never his friends, just guys whose first names he was conscientious enough to remember, and to click into what made them distinctive: Lee and his passion for billiards, Mike who liked the Dodgers, Bob who worked for CAA and loved his children with an embarrassing passion). These guys, out of a thousand things to do on a weekend night, would put a high school theater production far down in the four hundreds. But they were there, gathering on the sidewalk, sentenced to an extra forty minutes of this, while he, having managed to be fifteen minutes late, got to escape, to park the car, far away.

Usually he had to walk six or seven blocks and managed to miss the first act of whatever it was, standing outside by sawhorses covered with boards and paper tablecloths and pots of marigolds and plates of cookies from Paris Pastries. He spent that time in the company of an anonymous wife who doled out glasses of white wine, whose name, thankfully, he didn't have to remember. He always managed, during intermission, to strike the right note of interest and detached pride; to talk about the play, even if he hadn't seen it. Then he went inside with Wynn, where he sat, in an auditorium painted arty black, high up in bleachers, and caught some shrill lines from Pinter, Brecht, sometimes Shakespeare. Fifteen minutes, usually, until he dozed off. But he woke easily and effortlessly, clapped heartily; enjoyed the fresh, young, flushed faces as they stood on the sunken stage, bowing, bowing again, soaking up applause, affection, love. Enjoy it while you can, he might have thought sourly, knowing that most of the kids — for all their privilege — were headed for medium schools in the Ivy League, or middle management positions in their fathers' businesses. Some of them would end on dirty beaches, on second-rate islands, doing drugs, "finding" themselves, soaking up sun and family money. Privilege choked the kids today, he'd told Wynn when he thought about it, but she'd rewarded him with her hard and tolerant glance: *I wouldn't have happened to have cast my lot with a skinflint, would I?*

If he'd planned so hard to forget, how come Jerry remembered? They parked and walked together past the Mexican restaurants, the low office buildings, greeting other well-dressed couples, moving quietly toward the school. This Sunday afternoon, it seemed like they were going to church. This deliberately modest campus was dotted with sad monuments. A building named after a teacher dead from AIDS. A piece of outdoor art that he knew pertained to some friend of Whitney's, a girl he didn't remember — ruddy, athletic legs, long blond hair like Whitney's, always dressed in sweatshirts, always carrying pompoms. Always laughing. Hazel eyes with long lashes. Something had happened to her. You never knew about the particulars of anyone's life.

The Japanese were wise about that as in so much else. Never let anyone into your home! Never let them see your wife and kids. Take them to a geisha. Drink scotch, tell jokes. Get drunk. Keep it clean and clear and joking and free. That was the way to build things. Because walking past a piece of alabaster with a dead girl's name on it didn't serve anyone.

He knew some parents by now, after seven years as Whitney's stepfather. Their first names and their last; their kids. Some he knew from the elementary school where Josh was in kindergarten and Tina still hung out with the toddlers. T-ball and soccer. That was OK. Out in the air. *Straight!* It really did teach you what you had to know. Hit the ball. Laugh when you strike out. Hit it again.

So he knew these men he saw, bleak and sad, their pace measured and slow, their wives — in some cases their ex-wives — together for this sad occasion.

He and Wynn stopped for a glass of wine, and then another. The woman — that same woman behind the table at all the plays he'd seen at this good school — had been crying.

They sat where they almost always did, about ten rows up in the theater bleachers, surrounded by people he knew. During these last seven years, the parents had changed not at all. Was this Jerry's wishful delusion, or the wonderful ministrations of the medical profession in this city, and good health, and fitness? But there were other adults, single people, young couples, he had a hard time recognizing. They called him "Mr. Bridges." Wynn knew them, reached out her hand to some of them. When a stocky young man whispered "Hi, Mom" to Wynn it clicked in. They were Whitney's schoolmates. High school seniors. Graduation in a month. On their way to college. They had been *kids*. Well. People grew.

The mourning family came in, the grandmother (he supposed) in a wheelchair. He stifled a blast of resentment. How could this foolish memorial service, a full four months after the boy's death, help anything, change anything at all? He felt Wynn take his arm as the lights went down. He felt the sorrow off her body, calm and stoic and controlled.

He didn't remember the kid, that Robin, at all, thank God.

The lights went down and a video tape went on, grainy and small. One of the old plays — no, something *around* one of the old plays — two boys, no more than fourteen, hurling themselves across the floor of this same theater, tumbling, turning cartwheels that broke in the middle. First one, then the other. Awkward, flinging their bodies like beanbags across blue plastic mats.

Sobs began around him. Wynn kept steady and calm. A girl's stern voice came from the video: "Come *on*, you guys! Come *on*, you guys! Will you cut that out? Can't we get started? We've got to get *started*." He recognized the voice from a dozen of their playlets, and, taken off guard, laughed. Half the audience laughed. Then stopped. In attention balanced between grief and recognition, the audience watched the tape to the end, two gawky boys fooling around, not particularly joyful, not very profound. Engaged merely in irritating the female voice behind the camera, not knowing, not knowing, what the future held.

The lights went up. There was the stage he'd seen / not seen so often, cluttered with this or that lovingly accomplished special effect. Bare, today, with only four risers. Maybe six, seven young men and women reclining, sitting, standing, motionless. Their faces were set in determined smiles. He didn't recognize any of them. A young man, *young* man, called conversationally up to the booth where the camera, the sound, the technical effects came from. "I think we'd like to see that tape again. Roll it again, will you?"

This time, with the lights up, and with the smiling adults onstage turned from the audience to focus on the tape, it was OK to laugh. Even the family laughed. The young man waited for the waves of laughter to wash away. The lights went down again. The spotlight focused on his young face.

"That was Robin, all right. What a *brat* he could be!"

Then Jerry remembered Robin. For a whole semester Robin had hung around the house, he and Whitney jabbering nonstop to each other without listening to each other. He remembered asking Wynn, "Doesn't that kid have a *house* he can go to?" Remembered. Going into the den, shutting the door, turning out the light, turning on the globe so that he could concentrate.

Another young man talked now, about going on some

camping trip where Robin faked a sprained ankle so that he could spend the night in a Fresno hotel. But Jerry remembered the kid rehearsing a scene with Whitney in that same den, with Whitney as a boy king from Shakespeare: "Will you put out mine *eyes*?" Whitney asking over and over, "These eyes that never did nor never have so much as frown on you?" And this same guy, his voice changing back then, his hand recklessly waving a poker he'd picked up from the den fireplace, repeating, "Indeed, I have sworn to, and I must."

So he knew these people. Remembered Whitney sneaking down their driveway with clusters of them, taking them upstairs over the garage to her room. Something in Jerry's chest shifted.

"What happened to me and Robin," a pretty blonde said, "was that we ditched out on an afternoon rehearsal. It was right after school, broad daylight. We knew that once we left, we'd be late getting back. Robin and I would be late for rehearsal. But Robin was *always* late for rehearsal!" She waited, again, for familial laughter to subside — didn't they all know it? Hadn't they all waited for Robin, or covered for him, or gotten mad at him, or gone into the den and shut the door and turned on the globe to get away from his presence and his pranks? Jerry remembered. "Doesn't that kid have a *house* he can go to?" And his wife torn up about it, and those kids going, one more time, out of the main house, up over the garage. That was better. That was the best thing for everybody.

"Robin had just got his driver's license and he had this bright red Audi . . ."

The girl wore pale, often washed loose jeans and a loose white silk blouse, with a boy's jacket slung over her shoulders. Her pale thick blond hair washed over her eyes. You could see she resisted the urge to push it back.

"He loved to make left turns in traffic. Some of us think that's a male characteristic, like growing a beard." She paused to let the laughter fade away. "All of you know what happened that day. The truck came out of nowhere." She paused to take a deep, shaky breath. "I don't think Robin would want us to think that he left the planet making a careful right turn. I think I'm wrecking his reputation. I do know my mom would never let me drive anywhere with Kevin Seidenbaum because she saw him do a U-turn in front of our house once, but Kevin's right here, across the stage."

With severe formality five performers bowed to a kid who reclined on a riser. Kevin smiled an even smile.

"Kevin's with us today. Robin is too, some way. I know it. When the truck came, Robin was in the middle of a joke. He was laughing. When he left the earth, he was laughing."

The spot moved from the girl. Jerry saw now, the girl was Whitney. The boy's jacket covered the cast on her left arm. Kevin Seidenbaum began a story about Robin and baseball — how he always ended up playing shortstop and what that meant to him. But Jerry tried to see Whitney's story from the top. Because he hadn't heard it before. Couldn't the Audi have cut up onto the sidewalk? Or maybe there were pedestrians. How about the kid in the back seat? Didn't he survive? How about seat belts? That must have been the problem. How did Whitney live? And how could she, so young, have already seen a person die? Because Jerry had never seen a person die. Anything he could ever tell her or show her — that would be stupid, now. And he had made her leave his house. Go live across the yard! But that was the best thing, wasn't it?

A round of applause — the baseball story was over. Kevin had said something about Robin's character; that it was generous and funny and good. But wait a minute! Wasn't it irresponsible to let kids drive a car like that at all? Couldn't the parents somehow be at fault? He remembered one of a dozen times during the last three school years when Whitney had been really late coming home. Wynn had paced and panted like a dog; had blasted Whitney, when she came in, with full force, her voice, her gestures, her body. Jerry remembered a couple of times when the cops had actually come to the door, Whitney one of a flock of kids messed up from a party. Wynn had lost it entirely with her kid and had actually hit her a couple of times — not on the face, but along her shoulders, across her collarbone. Whitney, half laughing, half crying, had let herself be pummeled and pushed across the hall and then the den, half tripping on beige throw rugs. Then she went out across the yard to her own place. Jerry had tried to stay out of it, not unhappy to see Wynn ragging on her daughter, since it only meant that Wynn was happy with *him*. She'd never try that stuff with Tina or Josh. She'd better not even try.

In the dark — they'd turned down the lights and switched on the video again. The sounds of young voices with the audio on too loud filled the place. A tape of one of those plays. Pinter or Brecht. But Wynn was next to him and this whole damn thing would soon be over. His mind sneaked over to Japan, the development deal. New Guinea. Day-Glo faces. Perfect beaches. But then he remembered once again the truck plowing into the Audi. The driver laughing. The passenger watching. The kid in the back seat, where was *he* today? Thought how his first wife would have taken it — one high-pitched scream for hours. But Wynn! She'd be able to handle it.

He gave her arm a squeeze. She tensed her other fist around his own arm so hard he almost said something out loud. Chrissake! Quit it! Looking over in the dark he saw her face locked shut, tears streaming down it. She was straining to see, fighting those tears. He looked toward the stage again. The videotaped play had stopped. The lights came on, low. The kids weren't looking at the video now, but out at their audience with iron smiles on their faces. *See what we were then? they queried silently. How beautiful we were? You were in it with us, all the way.*

He took the chance to look at Whitney: blond, frail, fine-boned, not glamorous, not cheap. Aristocratic. She'd looked at death. She set her teeth and smiled it down. He remembered other, furious nights, the way she was a few years ago, her blond hair shingled far up the back, red earrings, was that it? Sent whirling by her mother's blow across the den like a spinning top. He'd dismissed the whole thing, forgotten it.

He was a one-woman man. The whole world knew that about him. And Wynn was his woman. And he might still — God help him — still be married to his first, shrill wife, if she hadn't gone out on him, and set her hair in big curlers, and waked him up at night, and cried in the morning when he'd gone to work, and cried when they'd gone on camping trips, and told him she hated sex and *God! All of it!* She had left and he'd paid up and he was happy now, living with a woman who held him in regard and loved him, and he had his own children, Tina and Josh. "Write a poem, plant a tree, write a book!" That was what the proverb said. His poem, his tree, his book, would be his children, and a better world.

But in the dark, and to himself, because he was an honest man and he prided himself on that, he acknowledged that if there were ever to be another woman in his life, it would have been the young woman facing him directly in the half dark. A woman stronger than her mother. Stronger than he was. Reckless and controlled. In a wave of grief he covered his eyes. That's what the globe had been about, his tirades, the closed doors, Whitney's banishment across the strip of backyard grass. He could not allow himself to remember any of this, and when the lights went up, he had managed to forget. He embraced one by one, each member of the mourning family and the excellent cast of this affectionate memorial. When Whitney's body came into his arms, he held her carefully, with the tenderness of a "real" father, with the chasteness of an honest stranger.

■
▬▬▬
▬▬▬
■

Donny and Thea

Simi Valley
January-May

STANDING OUT BACK behind his house, Donny could look two ways. It was Thea who first turned him on to it. "Pay attention," she'd said. "Look what you've got here." The view to his left — just over the leaning fence — was trucks and jacks and tires and windshields. Cans of paint spilled over into dead grass, in puddles of lavender and turquoise and chartreuse — all those colors people bought at certain times in their lives, when they painted the kids' rooms, then threw out the rest. Every month or so, a biker would ride through the yard, browsing, looking for a cap for his gas tank, budge those cans, flatten them, bang them, tip them; there went the paint. Donny liked the look. He squinted his eyes, looked at gas cans, rag piles; sniffing things he knew were bad for you but smelled so good anyway — carbon tet, benzine, plain old gas. He breathed deep, saw a map — ever changing, a new splotch, new wreckage, a few friendly rats.

Nice. He liked it.

But, early mornings, he also liked to take a step or two in the other direction and look at the land to his right — as it might have been, had been, still was. A silvery green-gray carpet that caught dawn light and looked like pure Eden, and in the foggy mornings disappeared into eternal mist.

This tract, this Simi Valley "track," had been thrown up after the war — raggedy stucco, rust stains under the wooden windowsills every time a nail went in. Donny's house marked an edge. Out back there on his right was a break in the world, a yawning acreage of unused land: pale green rye grass kept mown with a power mower. The woman who lived there pruned and clipped and planted. When a man came back into her life to run the mower, she'd throw a neighborhood supper, building a barbecue fire at the end of the double lot.

The next morning, the fog would be in again, the barbecue embers lost in mist, and the last of the smoke wafting — he could barely see all of that. Just as, after a biker party on his left side, he might go outside with coffee in one hand and a Pop Tart in the other, and the only evidence he'd see of past events might be one sleeping biker, still in his leathers, his big beer gut spread out on the crushed weeds, and from his mouth, another island on this world, a tidy vomit mountain: Chef Boyardee and beer.

Donny rented out his garage, to make ends meet. The garage fronted on the street — a style favored by the postwar builder of this street in 1947. The house itself was big — five bedrooms, a playroom, a wet bar, a laundry room. Poor deserted Donny, when he first rented to Thea — would that have been only this January? — had offered her first the master bedroom and then the whole upstairs, so desperate had he been for human company. But Thea turned him down, meanwhile suggesting that Donny, deserted, his children having either run away or chosen to live with their mother, didn't need to keep the games, the old trikes, the sewing machine, the tool inventory, the Winnebago, the newspapers for recycling — all that junk in the garage.

Sometime in January with Thea's prodding, Donny held a sale. Before the sun passed noon, it was all gone — tricycles to young mothers, clothes to thrift shop owners who kept track of those things. The Winnebago got bought by the guy next door, who drove it out to his backyard and told Donny he could borrow it anytime.

By three in the afternoon, Donny, bummed out, took the last cartons of family photos and jammed them into a line of trash cans in front of the house. Thea ate a grape or two and watched. The cartons could have gone in one of the kids' rooms upstairs, but events must take their course. By sunset the garage was empty. Thea said she'd rent it. That night she slept outside. The next morning she walked to Standard Brands and came home with a broom, a brush and the first of many gallons of white paint. Donny kept her company as she painted.

"*Why?*" Donny groaned during those first days, as Thea painted the double garage — walls, ceiling, floor — with five coats of pure white paint, *why* did he, Donny, honest all his life, pick the poisonous women, who looked so good and told you they'd "be there for you," and then, just after you got used to them and their four kids, *they* just left, leaving Donny to pay the bills? *Again!*

Why, Donny asked, as Thea painted, with the doors to the garage still open at that time, and neighbors stopping to gape, as they pushed tots who baked in the California heat. All of them knew it was just a double garage. But at certain times in the late afternoon it began to look deeper than that, weirder than that. The kids across the street might put off watching TV when they came home from school, and kneel up together on the battered old couch in their own living rooms, pushing aside dirty net curtains as they watched the gleaming shell get brighter and brighter and stay that way as the rest of the dirty world turned gray, and pretty soon their own tired mom or dad would call them into their own cluttered, lemon-yellow kitchen for another round of Swanson frozen dinners, dark meat chicken, frozen brownie in the middle.

"So why do you think it *is,* Thea?" Donny would ask: Donny, a poor laid-off guy stuck with that big house he couldn't sell, and hard-faced women who still came and went, hardly even staying for a second-run movie at the mall. Why *was* that? Donny, perched on the lip of a filled trash can, half in, half out of the garage, would tell Thea stories of his sad life and ask the question, not expecting an answer. Asking had driven away those poison-wives and girlfriends, driven away too his no-account, low-down children, since as far as they could see, their wrinkled old dad was *born* to be left. How had he even managed to buy this house, even though it *had* just been $250 down in the days after the war, $250 down again, after it had been repossessed by the bank, and repossessed again, and $89 a month for thirty years after that?

Donny asked the question of his new tenant, who, by the first two weeks of February had cut a space for, and hung, a door in an outside wall of the garage.

"Thea, can you answer me that, why they think they can walk all over me, use me up and leave me for a piece of trash when they feel like it and never, not one of them, make a bed or cook a meal or give me a kind word? They take me for everything I've got, and I don't get one kind word! They treat me like a savage, not a man."

"Of course they would do that." Thea dressed meticulously, her bleach-blond curls tied up tight in a white polyester bandanna, her nylon jumpsuit spotless, dithering with shiny-light emanations.

"Come again," Donny said. "How's that?"

"Of course they would treat you that way." Thea was coming to the end. She was working with a small brush now, drawing down along the four corners of the garage with white paint tinged with the palest blue, the blue of outer space.

"Of course they would." Thea spoke again.

Donny peered into the garage. Everything shimmered. The woman he'd rented to yanked off her white scarf. Bright yellow chemical curls sprang to life like a metal scrubbing pad.

"Donny. You might think of that name as meaning 'darling,' and you couldn't be faulted for that, but I think you'll find that in New Guinea the name is Dah-lienhr." Thea walked briskly over to a tipped-up cardboard box that held a plate of green grapes and bit into one. "*Dah-lienhr*. From the Highlands, the hill country. They called you people the Night People because you were sooty and black, and even the whites of your eyes were dark gray. You wore ass grass. You put flowers in your frizzy hair. You hated work of any kind. You took away the wives of men, you took away husbands too. You drained their penises with a terrible thirst. You weren't picky! You made love to their wives in the long afternoons and then cunningly slipped herbs into their dark places, and made the women turn away from their husbands and long only for you. You were a troublemaker."

Donny stood up. "You must be some kind of a crazy person!"

"You were tossed out of that tribe by the time you were fifteen. You went down, on hard paths, to the capital. There, you were able to get jobs cleaning the big houses of *white* men and their wives. But you hated to work. You can see that in yourself even now, can't you? You continued old ways, trimming trees, planting slips of that same herb in their kitchen gardens. The men were easy. Men generally are. The women took a little longer, but in the end they loved you longer and wanted you more. They had been divorced from pleasure, never knew what it *was* until they might — the wives — open their closets in the morning, after their husbands were gone, looking for a clean street dress. You'd be kneeling there, a black shadow, waiting for them. You were small then. Black as anthracite. *You were an animal!*"

Thea paused to take another grape. She held it in her mouth, broke the skin. The juices brought tears to her eyes. Her green irises were shielded with sky blue contact lenses.

"But one man and his wife followed you from your Highlands tribe to the capital. Their stated purpose was to find you and put a curse on you that would last for several lifetimes. (And it will, as far as I can see.) But the wife only longed to see you again, and the husband knew it. When they finally found you they came to the back door of the place where you worked. I think the man there was in shipping, although his business had gone to hell, and the woman had become good for nothing, because of you. Your Highlanders had painted their faces bright red, and caked their mouths and eyes with dirt made into a frightful frown."

Donny took the trash can he had been sitting on, began to roll it, along its bottom edge, down the driveway, to be lined up with the other trash cans he put out every week. (He'd been throwing away more and more things.) He kept his eyes down, focused on the gutter.

"That was some scene in the kitchen." Thea's eyes streamed clean tears. She held up her right hand as far above her head as it would go. "The silly white wife fainted. She thought she was going to be killed. The wife from the Highlands immediately called out, 'Dah-lienhr! I see you! I lust for you!' The husband was disgusted with you both. He ran away into the yard and uprooted every plant that you used for your enchantments. He made a great green mop of them and brought them into the kitchen. 'May all your longings be visited back on you,' I think he said. 'May your thirst for pleasure continue to be terrible but may your lust never be slaked. May you be left longing! May your many children leave you lonely and scorned! May you be empty and sorrowful, and may that continue for three long lifetimes! May all your wives leave you, and may you remain ignorant of why this all happened.' By this time the Highland husband had taken a kitchen knife and stabbed you just where you're holding your arms now. Your soul was rising, not quite sure what had happened. You stayed around for a few seconds too long, because the husband went on with it — his feelings were hurt. 'Here!' he said, stuffing the herbs into your mouth and around your genitals, 'this is lasting three lives!' By that time the silly white wife had sat up, crawled off to find a pistol and shot the intruder dead, so it was his dying wish, and you bought into that."

Donny waited. "But why . . . ?"

"Don't ask me again," Thea said. "He built ignorance into these three lives. So there's not much use in your trying to understand. But wait until I get my tape equipment, we'll see if I can get this story back again. You can listen until you get it."

With that she drew down the double doors on the garage, plastered them shut from the inside with inch-thick lines of sky blue plaster.

Ten days later, on the side door, Thea put up a sign that said OPEN.

Thea never tried to do anything. She threaded her way through these overgrown houses at the far eastern edge of the San Fernando Valley built for families that had never, under any circumstances, been meant to stay together. She built up her world from scratch. She threw out everything she'd ever owned with cotton in it, or wool; she would divorce herself from everything with an animal base. Except one day in a shopping mall she espied a huge black velvet painting with a crouching tiger. Tig*ress*.

She bought it. Hung it up. Her favorite, her *essential* color, was blue. She bought a single bed and a blue bedspread, with flounces. Bought the remnants of a sky blue rug. Had it delivered. Got the boy to lay it for her by mentioning that the lion was the king of the jungle because he had sex up to forty times a day, and took naps in between, and had mastered the art of not-striving, just as he, this delivery kid, could lay a piece of rug in ten minutes while it would take an ordinary person at least four hours.

He left swaggering down the cement path by the side of the house, tossing his long mane of honey brown hair behind him. She could see sliding out of his hips and head and shoulders, the words *forty, forty, forty*! She went back into her wide white room with the sky below and white clouds all around and the tiger at once friendly and unfriendly, a perfect paradigm of the universe.

She stocked up on tape cassettes: she would record everything she saw, keeping one copy for herself, giving one to the subject. She would monitor herself.

She was thirty years old. She'd been telling fortunes off and on since she was five; in Brighton, on the beach, in a stall, with a mother sitting behind the curtain (who pinched her whenever she got near an unpleasant truth about wages or illness or adultery).

From the very beginning, of course, they thought she did it with tricks. They thought, when she held their hands, she was feeling them for calluses. When she looked at their noses and saw that horizontal line, she must figure out they were allergic, or chronically sick, but the truth was, she'd felt their cold, their bronchitis, coming along the beach, marching along before them, before she ever *saw* them.

She grew up that way, in England, and went to school, not thinking about it, yawning her way through beach weekends, making money for her whining mum, not *thinking* about it, because when you thought about it, it got dimmer. Like trying to focus on a star at night: to see it best you looked away from it. And she grew up, like everyone else on this earth, learning from her mother what she didn't want to be. No bangles. No pretending. No afternoons in the pub dulling any of it with beer. No lying on your back under some bloke, with your feet drawing aimless patterns in the air, pretending *that* was the be-all and end-all. She'd hear or see her mother doing just that, even though her mother knew that she was in the kitchen eating a fried pie and must have *known* that she, Thea, could see through the thin walls to the boredom, the thinness of the experience, even when her mother yipped the loudest. But did her mother even *know* what she knew? When you looked at that question it faded like a star.

When Thea was fourteen she began to go dancing on the Pleasure Pier instead of putting in the time telling fortunes on the strand; she'd had it with sand sifting in through the curtains and fog dripping in through the woolen underclothes she wore under her taffeta dresses; *had* it with saying to a man who had been an alligator in a past life, "You will be getting a better position very soon," or "I see a journey in store for you," when all she really saw was *him,* swimming across a muddy river, then pulling himself up onto a yellow, muddy bank, and (teeth out there in a great big smile) dropping off into a reptile snooze.

She noticed, in her last year at school, that when her chattering girlfriends called some churlish boy or other a pig or an ape or a snake, most often they were *right,* although she couldn't tell them. And she began, very reluctantly and sadly, to see why her mother might drink and keep gentleman friends to put some of this other stuff firmly to sleep. Because, really, it was getting out of hand.

In 1975, when she was fifteen, she got hold of some acid almost by mistake, right there on her home pier, where she'd grown up and earned money for the family. She saw she'd been going about it all wrong — that lives came in *layers*. Her customers wanted to know what was happening now, and tomorrow, and the next day, but she saw back (if back *was* back), as if a hundred slips of colored gel had been put between her and the Bright Light of the universe, to dull the light and make it prettier too.

The next day, a Sunday, after she knew about gels, she thought she'd try it out, in her curtained stall.

"Do you have any Italian relatives?" she said to a small sad man who stood before her in an undershirt, having paid his money for his fortune. "I see a white house made of stucco and some hills and some goats. Does the number seventeen mean anything to you? Weren't you one of seventeen children? Didn't you spend long times not doing anything — except sometimes something dirty, but nobody saw — !"

A vicious, vicious pinch from her mother, who still whiled away long afternoons and nights behind her daughter's curtain. Thea yipped, and said, "Maybe I'm mistaken. Don't you have a girlfriend now, and you're thinking of buying her some gifts, earrings, aren't they?" But it was too late, he grabbed his money, and blushing purple as bad wine, cantered off down the strand, and she could *see* the goat trotting in front of him, and him trotting after, his dick caught in that delicious grip, and no one around on these low rocky hills to stop him, and he could do this all *day* if he wanted to and drink himself to sleep if he wanted to on thick red delicious wine and sleep out on fragrant grass with all his sweet goats frolicking around him, and they loved it as much as he did, they liked *him* so much and time was so different to them anyway . . .

Her mother stood in front of her now, her hair blowing in the sea wind, a few pink curlers stuck in like seashells, and Thea almost saw a mermaid, carefree. Was that why her mother had to live by the sea, and made sure someone else did all the work?

Her mother smacked her, hard.

Since Thea was blond and beautiful and young and angry she asked the universe to send her away. The universe always says yes, so within the hour, a pink young couple on holiday came round for their fortunes. Instead of saying that they might have been together before, a thousand-thousand years ago, as two pink pebbles, or maybe sea urchins in a tide pool kissing each other with each salty ripple, Thea got a grip: "You're very much in love," she told them, clipped, British and professional against their wide good-natured Australian accents. "And you're on holiday. You are never so happy as when you spend time in each other's arms."

The husband blushed. His wife bashed him in the arm. "Too *right*!" she shouted.

"You have three adorable children, Charles, Grant and . . . Lisa?"

"*Alicia*, not Lisa," the husband said. Then, to his wife, "Did you put her up to this?"

"Charles, Grant and Alicia. They're a handful. You don't need a holiday, you need to take your holiday home."

They stood staring dumbly like a couple of pink rocks.

"An au pair girl, don't you see? To give you time for each other. *Me!*"

By the end of two weeks, when the Ashleys completed their English vacation, Thea had raked some fortune-telling money off the top, gotten her passport and (on the strength of heavy blond flirtation) her Australian visitor's visa. Five o'clock on a rainy afternoon she said goodbye to her uncomprehending mum, looked her last at tired gray faces, felt the grim Brighton magic that came from always burrowing in layers of velvet to keep out the damp. Goodbye greasy lights, sweet pier, old country.

After four months in a Sydney suburb where she did a terrible job looking after Charles, Grant and Alicia, Thea found herself free on a blistering summer day in late 1976, down at bustling Circular Quay on the lip of Sydney Harbor, the most beautiful bay in the world. At sixteen, she was as beautiful as she would ever be. She took the Manley ferry across sheltered water to the corresponding lip of land that sheltered the city and its harbor from the gorgeous, shark-infested open sea.

When she got off, she found herself in Manley Beach, Brighton's loutish younger brother. Codfish balls! Cotton candy! The smell of marijuana smoke thick as bush fire! The pictures in her mind blurred for a while. She lost the knack, looked at these brawny boys and pretty girls and couldn't see a thing, went swimming, diving into huge breakers on the far side of Manley, breakers that did what they were supposed to do, *break* whatever she had in her mind. She stayed away from drugs, drank beer to sleep, kept in shape by running on the beach, got it why her mum liked sex. Don't think about it. Don't think about it. She got along with these people as if she'd known them all her life. Au pair girl by day, party girl by night.

When she was seventeen, she left her job and married Randy, an electrician. She had two babies, Brad and Bob, and lived in little rooms, and pushed her tots on swings, took tea with Australian women who had trouble in their marriages. Maybe it was a bad move for her. She had been used to long evenings in pubs, and nights of sex with men who were, most of them, she noticed, just one dream-step up from dogs, the loyal German shepherds of the world, capable of love but not complexity. Life's plot hadn't thickened yet for them. These women were a mixed bag: putting in their time, learning patience.

As was she, with her children and the demands of the small crowded world she seemed to have chosen. Outside, somewhere, the waves and the ocean. Inside, miles from Sydney's bay, she lived in a row house with her husband and these two kids. A long hall down the middle of the house, bedrooms on either side, the living room at the very end, then a garden, then the outside privy. A wood stove. Woolen soakers, drying. Boiling beef. Everything from the physical body. Everything crabbed and small. If she had chosen to feel, she would have felt her own light dying. But the whole point in a life like this was *not* to feel.

That went on, for twelve years. And if she were to say — although she never spoke about it — that she had *forgotten* what she had been, the very word "forgotten" would have implied a wakefulness that was far beyond her. In the summers, when she took the littlies to the beach, she never went in now, only sat on a towel and yelled, "Be careful, Brad; be careful, Bob!" One summer they traveled by van to the center of the country, toward Alice Springs. They would make the further drive to the Rock, Ayers Rock, "a big stone pimple," one of the park wives had called it, knitting woolen soakers for her baby girl, "but the men like to climb it, it keeps them out of the pubs for a morning."

"I've never been so hot" went Thea's postcards from that trip, to her mother in England, her women friends in Sydney. "I've never seen such awful country." (And she didn't care if the postal officials in these awful towns saw her cards and tore them up, so preoccupied was she with being sure that there were enough lemon squashes in the van each morning for the boys and enough beers for her husband and for her. Two thirds of the way out in the outback, the *desert,* the camshaft went right through the motor, or that was how her husband explained it to her, but she wasn't listening. There was a wait for a new motor in the town of Rumbarala. They rented a car and wandered in the desert. Their three-week vacation stretched to four. Her husband phoned his shop and they were understanding. Which one of *them* had not had car trouble? Which one of *them* had not, at one time or other, driven the wife and littlies out to see the Rock?

In the rental car they wandered, during unbearable days, on the ribbon road. They passed truck-trains and dead kangaroos. Brad and Bob developed summer colds. Her husband had stopped talking altogether. Thea sat in the rental car, an Emu lager in her hand, warming faster than she could drink it, looking dully at sand. (And yet, she would not have said she was having either a "bad" time or a "good" time.)

When the van ran again they headed out for Alice Springs. "I'm not going home," her husband said, "until I've seen the Rock." In Alice, she bought toy goannas for Brad and Bob, goannas that came in wooden cubelets and moved on strings. She turned away from vast, sad aboriginal families that shambled down the scorching sidewalks of the one or two paved streets. Thea walked, on the second morning, past a tourist shop "of a better cut," as her mother once might have said. The kids stopped to peer in the window. Brad wanted a spear "the abos had made." Her husband wouldn't hear of it, of course. But looking through the windows Thea saw that the walls of the shop were covered with aboriginal paintings made of thousands of dots, huge pictures made of dots, and she flared with sudden anger.

"We work so hard," she said bitterly to her husband there on the sidewalk, with her two children getting over colds, and herself, her *body,* sweating from every pore, her once delicate feet wide now and splayed in the thongs she always wore, her light green sundress, shaped like a tent, baggy and damp with her sweat, the straps of her white cotton bra showing conspicuous and separate from the two-inch straps of her dress, her shoulders pink from the sun and pulpy with sweat; her *hair,* once her best feature, dark with dust and sweat, falling into her eyes. "We work so hard for our money and we drive all the way out here, and they try to take it away from us with things like *that,* Randy!"

He patted her on her shoulder. The sun came down on her with a mighty migraine and pain so intense she doubted she could get back to the car.

"Going to faint, then? Stay here, I'll be back with the van." But she couldn't stay here. She walked behind him, in the terrible sun, shielding her eyes from the white light that poured on Alice Springs, dizzy from blinding lights that arced through her brain.

She made the ride from Alice to the Rock with her hands pressed firmly across both eyes. The children were quiet. They hated to see their mother sick. They dreaded her bad moods.

That evening, her husband took Bob and Brad out behind their motel to watch the sun set on the Rock. Thea sat inside their musty room, fiddling with the channels on the temperamental TV. Terrible despair swept over her. She was awake when they came in, but pretended sleep, turning on the single cot she had picked to sleep in, her palms over her eyes.

"Nerves," her husband explained to the children, as he had so often in the past months. The three went out again, to some cheap cafe. When they came back, he undressed the boys. They stayed awake to watch TV because they were on holiday. Randy put them one on either side of him, the three of them an island of resolute contentment, banked in musty beige chenille — she a dot, a wire of misery, that lay outside their force field.

The next morning he took her outside and gave her a talking-to. "We've had some bad times and no mistake," he told her.

She looked at his face. He still looked fine, reptilian fine: but his eyes had sunk, from hard work and drink and denied hope, far in under the bony ridges of his skull. His lips were thin from pressing them shut to keep from complaining. He'd been a good husband to her. Never raised a hand to her. His face carried the tiny blotches of burst blood vessels from drinking. His eyes never met hers as he talked but moved, microscopically, to each side of the ridge of her nose. She realized that when he said "bad times" he only meant the broken motor, their unexpected stay in Rumbarala.

"But we're here, now, don't you see? We're on holiday. The boys are looking forward to what they'll say about it when they get back to school. This is a landmark we're going to, see? So try. Won't you try this morning? My own father wanted to climb the Rock, but he never did. I'm doing this for him. Climbing the Rock." He struggled to say what it was he wanted to say. "Have some breakfast. Come along with us to the base. That's the place where they climb. I'll be taking Bob and Brad. You don't have to climb. But you must come along. Take snapshots. It means a lot to them. It will mean a lot to you. I promise."

She dressed the boys and felt them shrink from her impatient fingers. She ate toast with them at the coffeeshop, drank three cups of strong tea. The four of them got on the early bus for the short drive to the base of the Rock. They put her by a window; she should have a chance to see what they'd seen last night. The windows were open, the air was fresh and dry, so harsh that it scrubbed her lungs, her sinuses. Sweat dried all over her, she cooked, she dried out. Slowly her foul mood abated.

Still, she kept her eyes mostly on the earth, the soft shoulders of red earth, the parched plants on blood red dirt. It rained, they grew, they died, it rained, they grew. That sort of thing. Her headache lifted, leaving her empty and spacey.

At the base she wondered, scornfully, at the folly of white men (and white women). Riding to the Rock it had looked cozy, like a giant breadboard pulled out of the earth. Up close it was nothing but *rock*. Some lunatic had spent a lot of time jackhammering holes in a purely vertical line, then jammed metal rods into those man-made cavities, and then strung those rods together with a looping, metal chain. The trick was to grab hold of that looping chain with your left hand and stride out and up, climbing to the very top of the Rock. You stood for a while, at the top, in a close clump like black ants around a jam jar. Then you took the chain, still with your left hand, and made your way back down, holding the chain from the other side. *Somebody* had thought that meant "conquering" or "climbing" or "doing" the Rock. But the chain looked so silly! The looping black chain up across the great sleeping stone shelf was so puny! The idea of climbing it at all was *stupid*!

But buses full of tourists had already unloaded, jog-trotted across the dusty flats to where the Rock (with impervious impudence) jerked up out of the ground. They hit the ground running and hit the Rock running. Men mostly, but children too — and women, though they didn't look happy about it. Thea heard words like *sunstroke, stroke, heart attack,* but again, that seemed to be the idea.

She wanted to lean back against the bus and take a look. Now that she had looked at it, it seemed like she might never get enough. Her husband and the boys had already trotted out and up. They hauled themself up along the silly two-way line, turning sometimes to wave. She saw that although a great many of the tourists began the trip, there were far fewer up along the top third of the chain — saw too that if you wanted to rest (or even look out across the middle of this country), you ducked under the thick, loose chain and sat on what would be the left side going down. Quite a few people did this.

Watching from the shady side of the bus, she saw them begin, cautiously, to inch their way down. She ran her eye along the long flat top of this . . . *thing*; no one was out there. Nobody strayed very far from this man-made chain. God, it was hot, and getting hotter! Seven-thirty in the morning in this godforsaken sweatbox and nowhere to go after this!

And unaccountably, she began to feel better. Much better. Her wet sundress took the rough, sandy breeze and fluttered out about her. She crossed the red dust, scrambled up the slippery rock thirty or forty feet until the chain began. She put out her left arm and tugged herself up, to where — one in a chain of determined humans who had no clue about this rock — she began to climb. She saw this rock could very easily be a loaf of bread with a shiny brown crust. She began to hear it mumble and murmur beneath her. She held on tight to the chain. She broke out in another sweat. She was terrified of heights. Hadn't she ever known that about herself? She stopped while the man in front of her stalled the line, ducked under the chain to squat, puffing. His face was vermilion, dripping. "The old ticker," he said to her. She reached for a higher hold on the links of the strong chain. A sudden breeze dried her out again. She felt crusted in salt, shining in the sun from salt; she was lightheaded.

She climbed farther, farther, up and up. Fewer and fewer people now: she was part of the air, an ant on a bread loaf. She ducked under the chain and crawled out about ten feet to a shallow indentation where she could sit and look out at the middle of the country.

Which went so far, *so far,* so far that she could see the gentle curving of the earth and know the world was round. Could feel the rock, which went so far, so deep into the earth, that its bottom lip rested in molten lava, melted rock. She heard its conversations. She saw beyond what she could see, and saw all the kingdoms of the earth, all of them. She heard a voice, some memory from Sunday school days: *Throw your-self down! He will give his angels charge of you! They will bear you up!*" The voice was shouting, blabbing away, and she looked around for where it came from. She saw the laboring climbers to one side but their eyes were blank. She became aware of a bloke, a *guy*, crouching five or ten feet farther away from her, ruddy and redheaded, so much the colors of the rock that she hadn't seen him, hadn't felt him. Now she knew — with what tear-making relief — that the voice had been shout-ing at him.

"It's great up here," he said to her. "Magnificent. But don't you think, well, it just occurred to me, that people are afraid of falling because they really want to jump? Or, come to think of it, fly? Just fly on out?"

"Don't you *hear*?" she wanted to say. "Aren't you *listen-ing*? Open up your fucking *ears*! Get yourself a fucking *hear-ing aid*!" Instead she asked politely, "Aren't you from Amer-ica? Do you have your wife and children here?"

"From Los Angeles. By the beach. On a business trip. My wife stayed home this time. We have two young children. But I've got to make it to the top."

He sat in an indentation of rock, and with his coloring, blended right in. He was well built, athletically handsome, in his middle forties. His forthright face covered discipline, fo-cus, consuming ambition; she could read that part of him like a newspaper. He was a good man, she could see that too. His freckles were so thick they turned his cheeks that pleasing peachy color. His mop of red curly hair already showed streaks of platinum. His eyes, a deep, deep brown, melted with well-being. I am making this climb, they said. I am mak-ing it to the top. I am enjoying this chance encounter with a stranger. His hands, folded comfortably across his knees, were strong and well kept.

"Business brings me here," he repeated. "I'm here on business. At first we thought we'd make it a family vacation." It was as if she heard three stations on a badly put-together radio. She strained to hear him as the wind stole the pleasantries from his mouth and across the outback over to Perth and across the Indian Ocean to nowhere, where tomorrow they would disperse. She heard her own wires, for so long tuned out, pick up: some whole other wife, slamming down a menu in a restaurant with pink walls twelve thousand miles from here. The wife said, "You put strangers before me! It isn't working out, Jerry! If you can't start paying attention, I'm leaving, and I'm not kidding, I'm not blowing smoke on this!" She wept as she bit down on some piece of bread with dill in it. He was fair-minded, he saw her point, but he had trouble paying attention.

Thea saw his lips moving, had to *read* what he said, because over all this came a lot of shouting, meant for him, she was sure of it. "Throw yourself *down*! Because you're bound to go *up,* whatever you do!"

Thea was astonished that he couldn't hear it, along with the wind whistling, and the weeping children just behind her whose bullying dads had decided they had to climb the Rock because it would build their characters, and the three-hundred-pound Australian females who billowed up this shaley slope, great whales in their earlier lives, serene creatures of the deep whose hearts appeared to pound, but they were swimming in the air now, up against the sky. All that came from their brains and hearts were sweet whistles (the noises whales make) as they coaxed their children up along the chain, so that they might get to the top, look around the circumference of their country, take some breaths of fiery air, either obey that booming voice advising climbers to throw themselves off the Rock or, disregarding it, slide back down on their buns, take the tourist bus back to their motels.

"Well," the man said, and got to his feet, holding himself

steady against the gusting, really very dangerous ovenlike winds. "I won't get to the top by sitting here, will I?" He smiled and his soul yawned out of his mouth, glistening. He was *terrific,* she saw; he knew the difference between right and wrong and he was coming down solidly on the side of right, but there was unhappiness coming down too. She wanted to say something to him, remind him to pay attention to the fucking *voices* if he couldn't see his way clear to doing anything else, but her old easy way of prescient advice was gone. She was out of practice, and she saw herself as he saw her, a tired wife in a wrinkled sundress, freshly laundered bra strap showing. He held out his hand, though, and she took it. "It was good talking like this," he said, his whole face and body and soul showing nothing but strength, health, well-being and a commitment to the right — a vague, very vague precept, now that she thought about it.

He was impervious to those voices, peevish now, which had degenerated into an insistent whine: "Throw yourself down, why don't you? Why can't you throw yourself *down*?" He took her hand to steady himself as he stepped past her across the treacherous rock to the black chain. "See you later," he said sweetly, and was gone, climbing up.

But his hand had brought back her electric headache, a migraine that knocked her silly, and she, goofy with the pain and lights, got up on her hands and knees to crawl over to where he'd sat. "Poor thing," she heard a matron say. She locked her hands around her knees, letting the pain recede, feeling the arcs, admitting that yes, after a twelve-year respite, she had it back. She closed her eyes, watching the swooping yellow-lighted arcs springing out of the left side of her vision only to sink down on the right, out of her line of sight.

She looked out at the great sweet curve of the earth, the red pulsing blood of the earth so close to the surface here, the plants like ruffles on earth's pretty dress, the voices that stopped chattering, now that they had her undivided attention and hummed now, in perfect harmony. The wind waltzed her, holding her in embracing arms. Demons crawled under her knees and stung her like fleas. The years dropped away. She went through the files of every dancing insect human who courageously toiled up this precipitous cliff, blindly to do something, anything that might bind them back into embrace with this beautiful, sailing earth.

"I've got it back," she said out loud. "God damn it!"

She stood up, held out her arms, thought one last time about flinging herself out into the dancing air, then skipped down the left-hand side of the chain. She searched the holding area for her family waiting for her by the bus. As they trailed back to the motel she said, "I'm in the mood for some champers, Randy!"

After the kids were down for an afternoon nap he went out and brought back two bottles. She gave him a series of fucks he'd remember for the rest of his life. And so must she. After tonight she'd be swearing off for a while. She'd give this stuff, oh, five years. See where it took her. Meanwhile, there was the champagne, and the body of her husband, so much cleaner and stronger and pleasanter than his mind. And here she was in this room, on a continent that sat like a calm matron taking a sitz bath in the Pacific, and she had it back; she had it back.

After they went home she took the ferry over to Manley, that scruffy beach town where she'd begun her Australian stay. "Tell me what's next!" she demanded of the universe. She liked the look of California, every city named after a saint. She wanted to go to the beach. Well, she *had* to. California. Los Angeles. The Angels. He will give his angels charge of you? But wasn't that voice a bad one? But what if there weren't any bad ones, just differences of opinion in the invisible world? The peachy, decent American who'd had to get to the top lived there. They had a desert there, just like Jerusalem. They had all that movie money.

Once she made up her mind it fell into place within a week. She found poor Randy with his pecker stuck inside the telephone girl at the place where he worked. Brad and Bob didn't pick up their rooms once too often, and when she taxed them on it, they told her that boys didn't do that work; *sheilas* did that work. They said she wasn't a real Australian and she mustn't come to school anymore to pick them up because she "looked funny." Thea called up Randy's mum and asked if the littlies might visit her for a while. She said, "Certainly, love. But don't think you'll ever change my son. He's been a scamp and a drunk since before he was born."

One morning Thea took half their money out of the bank, made a reservation with Qantas, drove her sons over to her mother-in-law's. "I'll be gone for a while," she said, but they were gone and out of the car, their embarrassment for her all over their stocky shoulders. She dated it from the day at the Rock — people turned to look at her now in the street. No wonder poor Randy wanted to stuff a regular girl instead of the one she had become. She drove to the airport with a plastic purse under her arm.

When she got off the plane at LAX, she took one deep sniff of the metallic air, knew she was home. She began hearing voices again: See Me! See *Me*! After a few days of driving around in a rented car she realized that See *Me*! was another of those misunderstandings. She was hearing *Simi*, some place inland where Indians used to live. On a hot day in January, she drove up and down the shabby neighborhood of huge wooden houses. The voices she heard were talking about chia seeds, and clouds, and honor. Small talk from the past, smooth and warm. She checked into a motel in the area, drove to a bar called the White Night, danced up a storm with burly boys who reminded her of her husband (only they were nicer), tossed back a few beers, sweated most of them out dancing and then, the next morning, drove straight to the house where she wanted to live. She knocked on the door and a haggard man answered. Was she a friend of his wife? Because, if so, forget it.

But when she told him, no, she didn't know his wife, he asked Thea into his filthy kitchen and told her a long, boring story. His wife was a cheater, and had ditched him out, leaving him with four ungrateful kids. He'd worked for General Motors and the railroad, but they'd laid him off. The country didn't care about honest work anymore. Thea listened skeptically. She edged across the room. "What's over here?" she asked, knocking on a California plywood wall, the house so ill constructed that the whole place trembled.

"Just the garage! She took the Olds and left me with the Winnebago."

"Can I live in there?" She clicked into his mortgage payment. "Eighty-nine dollars a month, and I can make myself a private entrance?"

The man folded his hands across his sweatshirt. "How'd you know that? Are you sure you aren't from her?"

"Just a guess. Can I paint? Do what I want? And don't you want to start throwing some things out?"

Donny told his neighbors, everyone who would listen, that he had once been something like a sex god in the South Seas. He lightened the vision from New Guinea — where people weren't the most attractive in the world — and brought it up to Tahiti. He bought a batik hanging from Cost Plus to put up behind his couch, found some paper umbrellas to stick in his drinks, changed his hard liquor from Seagram's to cut-rate rum. He even — at another of those almost countless garage sales that dotted the neighborhood every time someone got married, somebody got divorced — found himself a grass skirt. He swept up his kitchen, and changed his sheets. Word spread quickly among the divorcées down at the White Night bar that Donny was no longer averse to going down on ladies. He considered it his destiny, he said. They had all known each other so long out here in this valley that people were slow to believe it. They all knew each other from high school. Why should Donny, every girl's very last choice for as far back as anyone in Simi could remember, want to change now?

But it was true, and the manager of the White Night had the wit to put a couple of Hawaiian numbers on the juke, and lay in a semiprivate stock of those little paper umbrellas. Because happiness is catching, Donny asked his kids over for Easter dinner, making them candied yams with pineapple, and a big roast pork with poi on the table. Thea felt the waves of animal contentment leaking through the plasterboard like liquid butterscotch, which made her happy. Because she knew the best work came out of happiness. Suffering had nothing to do with anything.

Thea never used a bank, never worried about money. Never told a soul they used to be Napoleon or Florence Nightingale. If she did see some of that she picked another life. She found herself using the phrase "parallel universe." When people asked her about that, she couldn't answer them intelligently. Day by day she checked herself for unhappiness; couldn't find any. Checked for happiness, the ecstasy she might have supposed that she'd feel, seeing all this extra material. Couldn't find that either. She wrote long chatty letters to her sons and husband. They answered her as best they could.

She lived a quiet, circular life, walking in the morning, doing a little shopping, taking in movies with Donny, giving herself a holiday on Friday nights, dancing until her body, for a few sweet hours, occupied that place where her mind stayed so much of the time. She didn't know a damn thing about herself and didn't want to. She followed her skills, that was all.

But some of her clients were salespersons and she doubled their sales, or they doubled their sales and gave her the credit for it. And even out here, thirty miles across a long, low, dirty valley from where they made movies, there were youngsters who aspired to the fame and the glory that came from that occupation. Thea might snappishly query a gum-chewing slut, "Why do you put all that *junk* on your face? For your last five *lives* you lived in Wales and had skin you could practically see through, so why not respect your past?"

And the next day, the young girl, topped off to the brim with a history of herself, might lightly dance into a cold reading with no makeup, and be so radiant with unshed, unassimilated *past* that the producer might see, and give her the part. Thea knew that news of her spread off in every direction across the valley. She was good with love, loss and investments.

She saw them coming up the walk about three o'clock in the afternoon one day in May: sturdy, determined mom, her face creased, her hair skinned back, blue Brooks Brothers shirt, straight skirt. Behind her, looking frail and haughty, a blond girl in her teens, her left arm in a new-wave fiberglass cast. Thea spoke right up. "I see what the matter is. You were an Eskimo. You hooked up with the wrong bunch, and went to the wrong side of the Pacific. You should *always* go west or south. Come on in. *You,*" she said to the mother. "You can stay out back."

If the mother looked, she might see what Donny saw. It could go both ways. A meadow or a junkyard. Both very nice.

"If you'd just *notice,*" Thea said to the young girl, as she popped a grape, took hold of the frail right hand, and felt her own tears begin, "that you don't have to *experience* everything firsthand, you can rely on hearsay for some things, you'd be a lot better off. Now, when you were born to this Eskimo family, they bound you up to a flat board and *hung* you from the top of the igloo. That's what this cast is all about. *You* began to cry, because you were feeling sick. The more you cried, the more they swung you back and forth. You were disappointed! I know the feeling! They were going on at you in this strange language. Parents are *always* like that. But you could have avoided all of it, just the way you could have avoided that accident."

"So," the girl said with weary contempt, "she already told you?"

"Get this straight! That boy just slipped out of his body. He probably doesn't even know he's dead. Kind of a happy-go-lucky type, wasn't he?"

Thea's hands began to burn. She snapped them out of reach. "Excuse me," she said, getting up from her chair and reaching for three aspirins. "Now. You were a travel agent between lives. You worked with souls who were discouraged. You noticed that some of them from Earth got themselves in particular trouble. You knew the virtue of travel, of seeing something new. Switching their minds off the same old scene. Anything for excitement. But you take it to *extremes*."

Tentatively, she took hold of the right hand — bones, skin, flesh — again. She heard the accustomed jabber of voices, static, junk like a bad radio. She shook her head a couple of times, violently. Light arced behind her eyes. "You were always a grudge-holder, and a pain in the butt. You had attitude to burn," she said to the pale girl, "but everyone loved you so much they overlooked it."

The girl, her fine blond hair falling over her eyes, began to grin.

"You've got a surprise coming. Something interesting and very unexpected is coming up. You're going on a trip, all right."

Part 2

Travel, in the younger sort, is a part of education; in the elder, a part of experience. He that traveleth into a country before he hath some entrance into the language, goeth to school, and not to travel.

Francis Bacon

Whitney and Tracie

Downtown Los Angeles
June 21

WHITNEY DROVE, her left arm pale without its cast. Tracie deciphered directions that had come to the Temporary Success office printed out on a bad dot matrix. "*I* don't know," Tracie said, a little crabbily, "whether it's 1616 Wilshire, or 1111, or 6666 or *any* of those things." It was their eighth job assignment in as many days. A good summer job.

"What did D.B. say?"

"Miss Neimenthal? She's not a dumb bitch. I wouldn't call her *dumb*. She didn't say anything. She handed me the paper for tonight, is all. She said ten dollars an hour but that we didn't have to fraternize. She said they had regular hookers for that. She says Anita's coming as a liaison from the office, and she's coming too. Ten dollars an hour, a minimum of five hours and we get a chance at the hors d'oeuvres."

"Gimme that. And turn on the light."

Whitney pulled over to the curb in the darkening traffic. She drove the Volvo. Her mom said that with this big thing, if they *did* have a couple of drinks, or they got caught in a drive-by shooting, they'd have the highest percentage of safety. Encompassed by gray plush, strapped in like a monkey in a scientific experiment, Whitney reached for the paper Tracie held in her fingers. On principle, Tracie held it out of Whitney's reach. "I can read it. I can *read* it!"

In the yellow light of the overhead bulb, Tracie's fingernails glowed red as ten tropical insects. Whitney's own nails chased hers around the front seat of the car. They'd spent the afternoon over on Centinela, where six dollars for your hands and seven for your feet could buy twenty perfect toe- and fingernails — Vietnamese girls and women working on you, sometimes four at a time, the air heavy with hair spray, nail polish and incense. In the far corner at the back, a plaster Buddha reclined, all but hidden by a stack of sacrificed fresh grapefruit. Today, Tracie had brought a fresh peach, and with the cashier's permission, placed it on the altar as she'd gone to the back shelf to pick her polish. May we live long, and find cute husbands, but not *yet*!

The Asian women had watched suspiciously, but given them both four coats of polish. And then back to Whitney's mom's house to shower and change and get bullied into taking the Volvo. At the last minute old Wynn pressed a credit card into Whitney's hand. "We don't *need* it, Mom! We're earning our own money now!" But they left, protected on every level, by the Buddha and those Asian ladies, and plastic money, and gray Swedish steel. They wore black dresses with short skirts and V-necks, and black stockings with seams, and their mothers' pearls. Tracie's dress had fringe. The job Temporary Success had dealt them tonight was sitting at a table at a convention of Southern California realtors and writing up name tags.

Anita had tested them both for clear penmanship this morning. Tracie passed with flying colors, because of a private course in calligraphy she'd taken when she had mono during the tenth grade. Whitney's handwriting was clear and uncomplicated, inherited from her mom. Anita said they had the job for tonight but to do something about their nails. Well, they'd done something!

"It's the *Bonaventure*! And this number with the zeroes has to be for an auditorium or something."

But the Bonaventure was hard to get into, unless you used valet parking, and Whitney hated to use valet parking. "Like, those guys should get a *job*," she muttered, making a right turn and a right turn again, as they edged around the great turquoise mirrored building.

"Whitney, we can *deduct* it! Remember what Jerry says. 'Live your whole life . . .'"

"As if it were deductible?"

A silence.

"Wouldn't you like to just park the car," Tracie offered, "and go down *Broadway*? Buy a taco? Go to the Million Dollar? Listen to some salsa?"

"Nah. You only want to do that because of your *fringe*!"

"After they get their name tags do we get to dance with these guys? Is there going to be dancing?"

"Bar *mitzvah* dancing?"

"No. *Salsa*! I'm going to find a guy from Paraguay. That's why I've got this fringe. He's made his fortune from heroin but he's *reformed* now. And he's left his children behind in Asunción. They can't get visas. That's OK with him because he wants to start a whole new life, a clean life, in the City of the Angels. Juan Rodriguez. About fifty, but trim as a lifeguard. Five thousand dollar suits. His heart belongs to the samba. The rumba. He wants to start a *new life with Tracie*. He takes his new fun-loving wife to . . . where do you think, Whit?"

"Amsterdam. Or northern Sweden. He gets a cold and dies in the first snowstorm. You *always* wear black after that, because you're in mourning. Then you marry the prime minister. I'm going to use valet parking. But there goes our money."

"That's OK, Wheetney. *Muy bien,* you know? Because money's no problem for us. Because Juan's going to give me enough money for a whole other house, and you can come to stay. We'll always keep a room for you. You'll *always* be welcome at Casa Rodriguez!"

They slid out of the car, tossing their hair in the same gestures, striding out under the porte cochere, their fake Chanel pumps (bought for thirty-eight dollars a pair over at the Designer Warehouse in Woodland Hills) clicking in unison. Halfway across the lobby, Whitney peered over indoor box hedges to look into restaurants to see what people were eating, while Tracie looked for a directory, or at least the escalator up to the mezzanine — isn't that where they always threw bashes like this? On the mezzanine? Each took identical lipsticks out of purses that were, to all intents and purposes, identical, and colored in their youthful lips. But it was only Tracie who boldly ogled single men gliding down, as they sailed up the escalator. Only Tracie's hair that had been permed into a burning, frizzed blond halo. Whitney kept her eyes steadfastly focused on the escalator stairs. That way, her straight blond hair covered her face.

Up on the mezzanine it was easy to see where the party was. The reception didn't begin until six-thirty and it was only quarter of, but already one whole side of the mezz was packed with jowly guys in three-piece Hart Schaffner and Marx suits, many of them with dates — the kind of girls who gave Tracie the screaming *pip,* as she often said, because if she didn't get a Ph.D., or marry Steve McQueen, dead as he was, or get into International Smuggling or join the Peace Corps, she was going to end up like one of those women, she just knew it. That is to say, one of those poor dogs in their middle twenties who wore flesh-colored panty hose and white silk blouses that weren't even silk and thick gold chains that weren't even gold, and hangdog hopeful looks on their faces, and if they were lucky they were going to end up this night breathing heavy in some guy's apartment and have to spend tomorrow squinting into a computer in some dog-office somewhere, getting wrist-lock, waiting for a phone call so that — if they were *lucky* — they'd get to spend tomorrow night the same way. Office puppies.

Miss Neimenthal, D.B., was already there, with her *look* on her face, pacing up and down. She wore a name tag that said only TEMPORARY SUCCESS. Anita, hard-working Anita, had pulled up three folding chairs behind two long hotel tables, covered in fake pink linen. There were three sets of invitation lists, one each for Anita, Whitney, Tracie; three boxes of name tags; three pens, one at each place, each with a thick calligraphy nub.

"We were afraid you weren't coming," D.B. said. Her blue jersey dress plunged far down into ancient cleavage. "We were afraid you'd get lost."

"Hey, can I have my *name tags*?" A woozy guy, with a shy girl behind him, bent over Anita. "We've been waiting a long time." Anita, dark-haired and patient, sighed. "The party starts at six-thirty, sir. We'll be taking your names at six. We don't start work until six. You understand."

Whitney and Tracie took their chairs behind the table: Anita with letters A to L, Whitney M to T, Tracie U to Z.

"I don't have any *names*," Tracie complained. "Upshaw, Wharton, what kind of names are those?"

"American names," Anita said. "Thank your stars. They're mostly American tonight. From the Valley. Realtors and buyers. Investors. Lots of doctors. Lots of dentists. They've been over here already, wanting me to put their names with Doctor on them. I told them not until six o'clock."

"No Latin dandies." Tracie sighed. "No Juan at all."

Whitney giggled. "How do you think of those things?"

Anita turned her attention to her list of names, unscrewed a pen, spread out her name tags. "I'm open now," she said to the man closest to her. "Let's get a head start. Give me your name and I'll give you a tag. I'm A to L . . . Oh, *wait*!" She carefully printed out ANITA on a tag and pressed it to her blouse. Following her lead, Whitney wrote her name and stuck it on. Tracie carefully lettered SEÑORITA TRACIECITA BIENVENIDA M.

"M?"

"*Si, mija.* For the Virgin *Mary* who will bring me Juan Rodriguez tonight. A nice Juan, *ocala*!"

Whitney giggled.

D.B. said quietly, but with a terrible fierceness, "This is one of our most important accounts, girls. Look sharp."

For the next two hours, they looked sharp. People felt so strongly about their own names. Anita was right: the doctors wanted DOCTOR and some of the people who were no more a Doctor than Whitney was wanted DOCTOR. Some of these realtors (and there wasn't a Brooks Brothers suit in the bunch) wanted MR. written in front. Some of them wanted their nicknames put in quotes. Some of them had such silly names.

Sandwiched here between Hard-Working Anita (whom she never in the world had the least worry of growing up to be like) and Crazy Tracie, Whitney felt suddenly light as air. She was alive, she was better, she was working, she was free. Anita worked neatly, her head down, as if lettering name tags was the most important task in creation. Tracie, because she had so few customers, implored the men she wrote for to latinize their names for the tags. She took hold of their hands, read their palms to find out what kind of printing they liked. Whitney relaxed into being pretty and blond and nice and happy.

To every man who came with a wife, Whitney insisted on giving that wife her own first name. To every husband she volunteered, "You're a lucky man," leaving him to ponder his luck — had he sold something and not remembered it? To every office puppy she added what she could in the way of decoration and fancy lettering. And to one schmuckface who said about his puppy date, "Oh, she doesn't need a name," she said to the date, ignoring the cheap creep, "Give me every name you've got!" And added for good measure, underneath: RADIANT BEING.

"Señor *Schmuck*," Tracie called out after him, "Señor *Slumski*!"

After the first hour someone asked Tracie to dance. She disappeared. The crush was inside now, the bad live band began. Someone brought Whitney and Anita a couple of margaritas. D.B. noticed and took them away, but not before each had swallowed a couple of long, refreshing gulps.

Whitney tried to hear some of the conversation around her. What she heard, as pairs of men came out of the hot noisy ballroom, was real estate information about points and interest and square footage. It sounded like football to her, so excruciatingly boring. She wished that Tracie would come back. Or that someone would ask *her* to dance.

She wanted to say something to Anita, but she didn't know her that well. Anita worked so hard. Maybe Anita thought she was a lameshit. Señorita Schmuckette. But Whitney *knew* something amazing was going on around them, if she could only get to it. She would speak to Anita. She would say something.

Anita spoke first, not moving her lips. "Eleven o'clock. Take a look. Stay cool."

Obediently, Whitney looked out in the eleven o'clock direction. Coming up the escalator, popping up one at a time like twenty-five sore thumbs, the hookers came. That's what they had to be.

Anita ducked her head. D.B. stood vigilantly. We may be

unloved at Temporary Success, her demeanor announced, but *we* are not selling sex here! The girls came up to the table for their tags.

"Tiffany," said one.

"Holly."

"Goldina, D-I-N-A."

"Francine."

Conscientiously, Whitney and Anita leaned into their work. The girls, when they left, had perfect tags.

"The world," Anita said sadly, "is too strange." Then someone came up and asked her to dance.

"Go ahead," Whitney said. "I'll take care of it."

It was only eight-thirty. An executive came out and told D.B. that by special request they were extending the party. Could the girls stay?

"Yes," D.B. said, "if they get paid! And if it goes past midnight, I'll have to insist you put them up at the hotel!"

"That can be arranged," the executive said. "I think a lot of us will be staying."

And, *finally*, some guy came up to Whitney. "Can you, uh, dance?"

Why not? Why not dance?

He took her to the bar first. She ordered a margarita and offhandedly, almost like falling into the meditation that they'd taught her after the hospital, took up the dance, never even looking at the guy's face, noticing only that Tracie was dancing eight or ten feet away. The music blared and she moved to it, watching her own arms, keeping track of her own lavishly polished fingernails.

The man couldn't dance his way out of a Baggie. "I'm from Utah," he shouted. "Where are you from?"

"Right here!" she called, through the sweat and shuffle. "What part of Utah?"

"Little town."

So tonight must be important to him.

"Where?"

"Over by St. George."

She looked at him and saw him in a snare of self-delusion. Out in the big city. Away from Mormons. Dancing with a blonde.

"What real estate do you sell?"

"Senior *citizen*! Affordable *condos*!" He panted as he danced. Out of shape.

"I just graduated."

He hadn't asked.

"I want to go to UCLA. Stay. With my family."

He hadn't asked.

"I was in an accident. I had a cast on my arm until last week."

His face showed disappointment, disapproval. She was messing with his fantasy.

She managed to dance over to where Tracie was getting down with some puffy buzzard. "*Tracie*! This guy's from St. George!" Tracie, what a friend, took St. George and left her with Puffy Buzzard, who could only tell her that he had a wife at home, that he was looking at property on the California-Nevada border, and that if he had only two words to say to her those words would be *Buy Desert*. She made a note to tell that to Jerry. Buy Desert.

The music changed to a samba. Most men backed out and fled to the bar. Office puppies shrank to the sides of the room. They'd worked too hard, typed too fast, to ever learn how to samba. But the California dudes of this firm they were temping for stayed out on the floor; they loosened their ties and got down. This is what it's *about*, was their one-two-three message: if you buy in, if you own part of our downtown building, even if you rent an inside office, you'll learn how to samba!

Now Whitney saw why Tiffany, Holly and the rest had been summoned: dancing was their work, as surely as what they'd be doing later. Out on the floor in four-inch, spike-heel, fuck-me sandals: *one two three*! (Or was it a two-four rhythm?) The band enjoyed itself in salsa land. And Whitney rejoiced, because of Tracie's five-day-a-week schedule of modern dance, tap, ballet and, thank God, *Latin rhythm*. Tracie ruled this mezzanine ballroom and more than held her own with Tiffany and Goldina. Tracie lived to dance, and had taught Whitney (usually against her will) to samba, rumba, all those old-timey dances, plus the latest salsa steps . . . Whitney felt tight ligaments and muscles clack and loosen along her upper arm and collarbone and under her shoulder blades and over into her spine, but the pain felt good. She remembered: "Miss! Miss! Miss! What day is it? Who's the president? What's your name?" Oh, she wished she were dancing with the doctor who'd sewed her lip! She smiled at Puffy Buzzard with all her might. Where had *he* been that he could move his puffy trunk and head on such fast little feet? And looking into his squinchy face, she saw that he too was lost in the music.

Oh, wow. Oh, jeez. Oh, shit. Oh, thanks. Thank you, God.

A dozen couples out on the floor, and Tiffany was best but then she got paid for it. And how many people Whitney's age had ever met a hooker? Had ever written their names on a tag? But Tracie was best, her bright yellow hair flying out from her skull, her back as straight as a ruler, her bright red lips and perfect teeth so bright. But maybe Whitney, yes, yes, Whitney, her own self, was best, because she was as cool as a cloud, and moved like a cloud, because her cast was off and she was free. She wasn't hanging down from an igloo now, although the swinging part was OK. She swung, like that thing they had in the observatory, that moved because the earth was moving. How she loved this puffy guy for never giving a sign of giving out! And the St. George guy she'd given to Tracie was holding his own, but a crowd had begun to gather around Tiffany and her partner. When Tracie stopped to join the clapping crowd around them, Whitney felt that she could stop too. It was a good thing because her back was killing her and her whole left arm was numb, and if she didn't know better she'd think she was having some kind of total heart attack, so she moved with Puffy Buzzard, kind of a nice guy actually, over to watch the last couple on the floor, where they were combining lindy moves and country moves and salsa moves. Tiffany was hypnotized by the music and her partner stood his ground like a good bullfighter, his own feet barely moving, as he shoved her between his own legs and over his head and around his stationary body and over his head again, and the crowd, as Whitney had heard the expression, *went wild*. She thought with bewilderment and amusement, *this* is the world!

Then she saw two things. Off to the side, the far far side of the ballroom, she saw D.B. vivid and ramrod in her clinging blue jersey and chunky gold earrings, talking to the very head of this company, this would-be consortium. She heard, as if she were the Bionic Woman herself, that they must be talking about money. Then she took in, she *saw*, a blue-blur — Blue Blur Anita.

"*Go, Anita!*" Whitney screamed, and Tracie, across the circle, took up her voice. "*Go, Anita!*" The answering shriek. And Holly and Tiffany, who fueled good times for a living, shouted, "*Go, Anita!*"

It went on like that until the band took a break and Whitney's Buzzard took her over to the bar. Whitney went for a margarita, ordered another one. "You're not drivin', are yuh, honey?" Even though her shoulder was hurting like a bastard by now, danced more, and more, until she felt she had to, just had to, get a breath. She walked back outside to where the table and the last of the name tags and the folding chairs still were, fanning herself with a company prospectus. Tracie was already sitting down, with a fresh coat of lipstick and as much cool composure as she could muster.

"Miss Neimenthal has asked us to stay here until the end of the party, to say goodbye to the guests who are going home."

In her peripheral vision Whitney could see D.B., clearly on the warpath. Whitney sat, stilled her breathing. Wow! Her shoulder! She took a couple of aspirin from her purse and put them under her tongue. They worked the best of all the pain stuff. And she'd never have a heart attack. On the other hand, after all these, if she ever pricked her finger she'd bleed to death.

"I'm so disappointed in Anita," D.B. said. "I'm appalled."

Whitney kept quiet but Tracie couldn't, naturally.

"Why is that?"

"She's mulatto."

That explained it then! That's how she learned to dance like that. But she couldn't be! That couldn't be right.

D.B. moved off and Whitney whispered to Tracie, "That can't be right, can it? Wouldn't we have known?"

"There's no *way* she's mulatto. She's got those thin little lips. She's got that mousy hair. She's . . . she's *not* mulatto!"

Whitney's head whirled. "*Sir!*" she called boldly to a rumpled guy who'd come out for air, "would it be too much to ask if you could get us a couple of margaritas?"

It wasn't too much to ask.

The girls took identical healthy swigs, then hid the drinks down at their feet.

"What . . . what . . ." Whitney's head swam. All this noise, all this color, the mixing of tequila, aspirin, exertion, began to get to her. Just for a minute, she wanted to cry. Tracie, wonderful friend, watched her with immediate concern.

"Miss Neimenthal," Tracie called out, "what do you think? Could it be possible for us to stay here at the hotel tonight? Just the two of us," she added hastily. "No fooling around or acting silly or having guys up. I'm . . . worried about Whitney. No biggie, Whit! But there's no use getting tired."

"Of course, of course! I've already arranged for it. And Anita too, although, don't worry, I won't inflict her on you. She's mulatto!"

D.B. walked across the open area to talk to Mr. Head Realtor. The girls stayed put, ducking their heads below the level of the draped tablecloths to take hasty swigs from their drinks. "I know it's down here someplace," Tracie announced to no one in particular. "It's terrible when you lose a contact lens like this . . ."

"Tracie, you don't have to act like I'm the Perennial Hopeless Cripple."

"Yeah, but don't you want to know what goes on after we leave? Don't you want to see D.B. and Mr. Head Realtor leave together *in a limo in the morning*? You don't want to drive home now, do you?"

In unison, without thinking about it, they shook their heads *no* to an invitation to dance from two sweaty dudes, and went on talking.

"So what do you think about Anita? And why would D.B. get into such a spaz attack about it *now*? Wouldn't she have known all along? And if you call your mom, does that mean I don't have to call my mom? No, *my* mom is going to be asleep, so why don't you call your mom . . ."

Twin visions trailed along through their conversations. Tracie's mom, maybe sitting up with the baby watching TV, but what if they'd finally both gone to sleep? Tracie's stepdad asleep in the den, his mouth open, a nice guy. Whitney's mom in the big bed with Jerry because he was home, now, for a few days. And they'd either be asleep or doing it. So you couldn't call *them*. They decided to call Tracie's mom. Tracie went to do that and returned carrying two more margaritas.

A big, cute guy trailed after her. "Say! You girls are drinking margaritas! You like tequila? You like it more than — say — Harvey Wallbangers? Long Island iced tea?"

Tracie's eyes signaled *what a dork* to Whitney, but she answered civilly. "Harvey Wallbangers are for drunken college boys. Long Island iced teas are tasteless and deceitful, a way to get college girls into bed. Margaritas are a healthful drink. The lemon and salt are medicinal. They balance your electrolytes to minimize a hangover. Tequila is a natural cactus beverage that goes back to the Aztecs. And damiana — which I saw the bartender use instead of Cointreau — is an herbal cure-all found only in Baja California. It's good for everything. We respect margaritas. We deplore Perrier and all it stands for. *Darn!* There goes that pesky contact lens *again*!"

Tracie dropped to the floor and Whitney met her there. They rolled their eyes, pounded each other's shoulders, stifled their laughter, let it out in soundless gasps, let it out again. They took great swigs of icy froth, wiped away salt from their smiling lips, sighed with the silliness of it all and climbed back onto their folding chairs. This time, when the tequila man and a friend returned and asked if they'd like to dance, they both nodded *yes,* together, without thinking, and spent three dances out on the floor, and this party was getting to be after midnight. Tiffany and Holly or whoever she was had disappeared. They were earning their living now. All around in corners, old guys were selling buildings to each other. Whitney felt fine again, energized, fine; her pain gone, and really pretty sober. "Maybe it *is* true, what you said about margaritas." Tracie's knees threatened to buckle from laughing.

The guys escorted them properly back to the table outside the ballroom, disappeared and reappeared, bringing another four margaritas. "What would you say your favorite brand of tequila *is*?" one of them asked the girls. Tracie answered,

"José Cuervo, in America. In Mexico, we prefer Siete Leguas. That's the name of Pancho Villa's horse."

Whitney put her head down on the table to get her breath. *Why* was this so funny? *No one* else thought it was funny. No one else was even noticing. Even these guys were talking like they were at a funeral home. They excused themselves, walked away, then turned and stood watching them, talking to each other.

Tracie said, "If I have to get down to look for my contact lenses one more time, I don't think I'll ever be able to get up." In silent agreement they left this round on top of the table. What the hell! They weren't fooling anybody. And they *couldn't* be working! Because everyone in the living universe had a name tag by now.

"It wouldn't kill me to go lie down," Tracie said. "Would it kill you, Whit? They don't need us anymore."

"This is so weird here, you know? Like they're spending all this money. This is the world."

"Are you drunk, kid? Could that be happening to you?"

But it wasn't Whitney who was drunk; not she, not Tracie, who would end this night in disgrace. H.W.A., Hard-Working Anita, was the one, and even now, at 12:42 in the morning, D.B. and Mr. Head Realtor had taken things into their own hands. They were coming out of the ballroom now, and they were holding Anita up between them. Her hair fell down across her face, her feet made a brave attempt to walk, but every three steps or so her high heels wonked over to the side. She was far gone. People, not even realtors, but regular tourists passing through — Japanese businessmen, white Protestant couples, occasional kids, playing hooky from their folks' hotel rooms, stopped to take a gander at Anita, a disgrace to her profession, whatever her profession was.

The elevator clicked open, the strange three disappeared.

"Jeez," Tracie said. "Hard-Working Anita!"

Chastened, they took their empty glasses back to the bar at the end of the mezz, straightened the tablecloth, stacked up the unused name tags, put their pens in a neat row, folded their hands in front of them, shaking their heads *no* to various Drunken Bums who asked them to dance.

The elevator opened. Tiffany and Holly appeared, perfectly groomed and serene. They gave their name tags back, said good night, disappeared down the escalator.

"What do you think they make? They spent the same time we did, and they sure didn't get as tired."

They weren't laughing now, worrying about Anita. But then the elevator opened again, and the doors were quick and smooth enough that Tracie and Whit saw, for one glorious instant, D.B. and Mr. Head Realtor locked in each other's arms. Tracie's hand clutched on to Whitney's leg hard, hard.

The two adults, preoccupied and busy, crossed the mezzanine.

"We put her to bed," D.B. announced. "We didn't even take off her clothes. We left the light on so if — *when* — she wakes up, she won't be so disoriented. I *told* Jeff, this never happens in our organization. But I *told* him, I noticed it right away. She was *absolutely* blotto."

"No problem," Mr. Head Realtor said. "I told Debra she can be proud of her organization. You girls have done her proud. You've made quite an impression on some of our associates. You wouldn't be interested in taking a trip to Maui in a week or so? Two days' work? Everything on the up and up, of course!"

D.B. surveyed them critically. "You didn't know it, Tracie, but for a while you were talking to the North American Vice President of International Latin Imports. Mr. José Cuervo *himself* in this neck of the woods. He told Jeff that never, in his entire career with the company, has he heard such a spirited but wholesome defense of the product! The Cuervo people just happen to be participating in an annual liquor convention in Hawaii. Tracie, they want you to be Miss José Cuervo, and *you,* Whitney, you can be whoever you want. Ten dollars an hour, a total of about forty hours, all meals, all expenses, an opportunity to work on your tan."

"What do you think, Whit?"

"Airfare. Did I mention airfare? You'll be going business class. Our treat."

"We'll have to talk it over with our parents. But may we go upstairs now, Miss Neimenthal? We need to get to sleep."

"Of course! And *thank you* both. For everything. Here's your key."

They walked off, arm in arm, walking in step, heading toward the elevator. Pushed the button. Waited, not looking at each other. They stepped inside, faced front, waved good night to maternal D.B., paternal Head Realtor. Then, when the door had safely closed, Tracie hurled herself against the wall and moaned. Whitney lay down on the floor and closed her eyes. The doors opened at the next floor and a couple stepped in.

"Going up?"

Yes, they were going up. Once inside room 1121 they rolled around on the king-size bed and laughed. They rang — just before two in the morning — for one last round. Tracie laughed so hard that once, on her way to the bathroom, her knees really did buckle — she lost it entirely. Whitney, propped up on extra pillows with ice from the refrigerator under her shoulder blade and along her left arm, swam through wave after wave of perfect happiness. Around three or so, as they finally began to drift off, the television still on, the wreckage of a major party around them, aspirin at the ready and a long letter to Room Service ordering french toast and sausage and canadian bacon and belgian waffles and fresh orange juice and coffee hung neatly on the doorknob outside,

Tracie turned to say good night across the vast expanse of silly bed.

"Whit? *Mulatto!*"

"Blotto. Just *blotto,* OK?"

Their eyes closed, in unison.

Whitney and Tracie

Maui
June 26

BECAUSE THE PLANE was overbooked, they got bumped up to first class. A stewardess came by with a tray of free champagne. And they weren't even off the ground yet!

A few other travelers, who had just taken in the fact that they would be crossing the vast Pacific in a dangerous DC-10, turned their heads to train disapproving stares on these two giddy teenagers. "Are they old enough to drink?" one woman asked her husband.

Her husband was staring as well. These girls! How long had it been since he'd traveled with girls who wore shorts? Those *legs*. He could, if he closed his eyes for a few delicious seconds, feel either pair of those legs locked around his neck . . .

He opened his eyes. The two girls were still bursting with laughter. His wife wore a tailored white silk blouse and loose yellow silk slacks. Her waist was bound by a belt with bright stones. He knew about the two sets of scars behind her ears from her two full face-lifts. And yes, her thighs were strong, from tennis. But when he tried to remember when she'd last laughed like those girls, he couldn't. When he tried to remember when last he'd been around girls who laughed so heedlessly at nothing, he couldn't.

"Don't worry about it," he said briskly to his wife. On impulse, he kissed the fine skin stretched across her cheekbone. She turned from him, in habit and exasperation.

"Oh," Tracie groaned, "I can't stand it! Can you *believe this*?" Two days before, they had received their tickets and reservations at the old Sheraton Maui on Kaanapali Beach; instructions to bring bathing suits, party dresses, and to "go easy on the makeup," because José Cuervo's whole thrust was to appeal to "an upscale, wholesome market." Tucked into their press kits (along with pictures of the Mexican town of Tequila and photocopies of cactus fields) were designer sketches of how they should look during working hours: Hawaiian outfits with wide sashes saying *Miss José Cuervo! Miss Gusano!*

"You have lived a long and varied life," Tracie remarked. "You have lived so long that you have become Miss Gusano."

"Miss Worm, right?"

"Yes. It's a grave responsibility, let me tell you."

The plane coughed underneath them. The stewardess came by with a second swipe of champagne.

The plane taxied toward the runway. "I don't want to go," Tracie said, her face suddenly sallow with fear. "I think I should have passed on this assignment."

The plane took off. It's like the incline, Whitney thought, like driving up the California Incline, up from the beach along the cliffs, going home. It's not so bad. If I look out the window, I see the ocean slipping away, just like on the Incline. It's not so bad, I could almost like it. I could almost love it. When the plane banked sharply left, she thought, *So?* It's just like turning left or right on Ocean Avenue, no biggee! The plane, after a few shudders and rumbles, hacking coughs, finally decided to go ahead and fly. The men got up to go to the bathroom.

"I forgot to say," Tracie whispered weakly, "that I usually try to pack an extra airplane. Just in *case,* you know?" She put her palm on Whitney's arm, removed it and pointed to the wet palm print she had left. "Look at that. That's *pathetic.*"

"Look at that lady," Whitney whispered, to get her mind off it. "Would you say she's had a few *lifts*?"

Up here the sky was electric blue and the sun shone like a million-watt bulb. The ocean looked like bright ink and little boats sailed right under them. They were still close enough to the airport that the white sails must be traffic from the marina. *Traffic from the marina!*

Full of happiness, Whitney chose a mushroom omelet, with sausage on the side. Tracie asked for french toast. "It's nice, isn't it? Up here in first class?"

Five hours later, they stepped from the plane and felt, for the first time, the trade winds, the flowery, soft air, dampening their hair. Two men waited for them at the foot of the salt-warped stairs.

"Welcome to Maui," one of them said, "the island of romance. Remember us?" He was chubby, and thin blond hair fell on his round, tan face. He wore a short-sleeved khaki jacket with fake epaulets. "I'm Hal," he said. "This is my buddy, Steve. I'm José Cuervo, he's Gusano. I keep telling him he hasn't got a chance. How can you sell something with a worm out here? José Cuervo, *that's* the only one!"

Steve wore a clean white baggy shirt and overly stylish baggy black cotton pants. Standing next to Tracie, he came out about three inches short. The island spirit seemed not to have caught up with him. He shook their hands and, walking with them to the luggage hangar, explained what was what. "This thing goes for three days. We're coming in late for the first day. I'll be frank with you kids, nobody out here wants to buy tequila. It's rum with them all the way, because of the sugarcane. And when you put a margarita up against a daiquiri, they don't see the advantage. They don't want any *salt*."

"Well," Tracie said, "Here's the deal on those rum drinks. Two daiquiris and you're blotto . . ."

Whitney burst into giggles. Tracie shot her a severe look. "With margaritas, you can dance all night."

"Good point," Steve said. "The trouble is, though, with all this drug business and all this lead-a-clean-life-for-Jesus stuff, I hope I'm not stepping on any toes, but people don't want to drink anymore at all. We should be in the mineral water business, the Orange Crush business."

"*You* in the Orange Crush business? Excuse *me*!" Hal kept his hands jammed in his pockets, and let Steve handle the luggage.

"We had some time to kill, so we ducked in here and found you something to wear."

Here, by the cab stand, next to a souvenir store that sold Hula Girl floor lamps, was an expensive last-chance tourist trap that sold Hawaiian shirts and garish sarongs.

"I don't *think* so!" Tracie blurted, but Hal was already pushing them inside, where a saleswoman in a muumuu waited.

"Here they are, honey," Hal said. "Do your best."

"You lucky girls! Neither one of you can be more than a size six. Am I right?"

Something about the way Whitney clutched her arm sent Tracie around the bend. "Why *not*? Have you got a grass *skirt*? *We'll* go for it. Why *not*? Do we have to wear a top? I certainly hope not!"

The woman quickly chose them matching outfits with matching patterns. Skimpy halter tops and wraparound skirts that scooped up on the left side to show plenty of thigh. Whitney's came in vivid persimmon stamped with large white gardenias; Tracie's was a knockout in morning glory blue. They thrust their narrow feet into white sandals. Hal excused himself and came back with an armful of leis which he carefully put over the girls' heads. White carnations mostly, and on top several circles of pink and lavender baby orchids.

Tracie and Whitney went back into the dressing room to take a look. "*Spectacular,*" Tracie said. "And if I'm not mistaken, we've been getting paid ten dollars an hour since the plane took off this morning?"

Before they went to the hotel, Hal and Steve decided they all needed lunch. "Don't worry," Steve said. "We're not hitting on you girls. You're minors. We could go to jail for that, or at least have to change our temp agency. We've all got lunch coming to us. We can't sell tequila with low blood sugar."

They drove in a rented convertible to the Sunrise Cafe, a pretty place on the beach, on the leeward side of the island. Islanders greeted them politely and showed them to a table by the water's edge. It was shady here, under a blanket of palms. Whitney couldn't get over the feel of the air on her skin, the sweetness of the feel of the air. The ocean's waves didn't crash here. They rolled and rolled and rolled, then slapped on the sand like a series of love pats. Each wave, as it crested, was perfectly clear.

"Hal and I have known each other for years," Steve volunteered, after they'd ordered. "We served together in the army reserve, up in Newfoundland. We're new to liquor, but we've sold all sorts of things. We started out in New England. We were in fish for a while . . ." He looked over at Hal, who smiled.

"Cod," Hal said mildly. "We turned over plenty of cod."

"But cod tastes like cotton balls, and that's on a *good* day. On a bad day it tastes like cat food."

"Ends up cat food, a lot of the time."

"We went into furniture. Nobody ever buys furniture. Americans only buy mattresses every seven years. We both got divorces — we thought, life is *short*! We're salesmen, we're old friends . . ."

Their orders came. Barbecue jumbo shrimp for the men, shrimp salad for the girls, four foaming margaritas. The time was going on to three, but Steve said not to worry. "We decided to sell something that people would want forever, and that they'd have to keep on buying. We really couldn't get behind food. We'd had that cod experience. We thought — booze."

Hal spoke up. "Not the brown stuff."

"No. We thought, Go for the vodka. Tequila. Even gin. Things you can see through. We've done pretty well."

"We have a very clean route," Hal said. "San Francisco, Denver, L.A., Hawaii, and once a year a tour of the factories in Mexico. We're supposed to widen our markets. Bora Bora. Because honeymooners need margaritas. Singapore. They tell us we're supposed to get those guys to make their slings with tequila. Will that be the day or *what*? Melbourne, Sydney . . ."

"My stepfather works out there," Whitney said. It was the first time she'd opened her mouth in a while and her throat felt grainy and unused. "He works in developing hotels. Industrial complexes. Resorts. Things like that. He's a financier?"

Steve and Hal exchanged glances. This was good news! Then Hal put his arm across the back of her chair. "I guess we'll have to wine and dine you, then, Whitney. Steve and I are going to turn into ravening beasts. It's our duty to the company. You don't mind, do you?"

Whitney turned her wicker chair directly to the ocean.

"This is a strange world," she said. "What would you ever guess would be the odds on the four of us being together in a place like this? The odds would be long, like a . . . long shot?"

No one took the trouble to answer. The only sounds were the winds in palm fronds, the smack of orderly waves climbing up along the smooth beach. Whitney looked at Tracie who, in the last minutes, had begun to fool with her hair, absently making a few braids, so that they crept like little snakes through the mountain of her light blond frizz. Two hours ago, she and Trace had been in a plane. Two hours from now, they'd be, like, in a hotel. Somewhere. Here was just this gorgeous moment. Six months ago everybody had been telling her that she was "lucky to be alive." She hadn't believed it.

"Robin," Tracie said. She too had turned her chair to the sea. Her head tilted all the way back to catch the sun. "He'd like this."

"Sure would." But she didn't feel sad.

"'Kay, girls. We've got to get going. Think tequila."

They drove with the top down. They saw that the island came in layers: the sea, the sand, banana palm, coconut palm jungle; then dark green sinister patches that Hal said he thought were coffee plantations. Then up, up into steep peaks as bright as ice cream, and those peaks topped off by gray and white clouds.

Steve pulled into the parking lot of the Sheraton Maui. "Why they picked this place for a liquor convention beats me entirely. You need a regular clientele that fits the market. Everybody at this hotel outside of the convention is pushing eighty. You feed them tequila, it might work like Drano on their poor old bodies."

Tracie kept quiet. Whitney knew she had something on her mind. When the girls walked into the liquor convention, it was true, the action seemed to center over at the Bacardi booth, where they'd hired hula girls and invested in some flashing pink lights. But Tracie, after shaking hands with the pale, disheartened tequila salesmen in gabardine suits who'd worked the morning shift, went rummaging behind the table to see how they were making up their margaritas.

"What are you guys using for mix? Damiana instead of Cointreau? Radical. Steve! Want to sell some *drinks* here? Want to take some orders?"

They stared.

Tracie jabbered as she cut up limes, fresh and green, on a white china plate. "Go find waiters, borrow a couple of white jackets. Find if this place has a doctor. Get a stethoscope. Whitney! Find a felt pen. We're going to have some fun here!" With a pen she scribbled on the back of a sign: *Tequila, para la vida! Damiana, for immortality!* Then, while the men gaped, she stepped out from behind the table into the crowded aisle.

"*Don't* go over there," she ordered every passerby within hearing. "That stuff'll *kill* you! Don't you know rum is bad for your liver? I want to tell you something. Do you know that Aztecs routinely lived to be over a hundred years old? Don't you want to know why? The margarita is the culmination of over forty thousand years of experimentation. Lime to prevent scurvy. Salt for warm weather. Tequila as disinfectant. Drano for your intestines. But the secret ingredient here is the *damiana*! Because, you want to know why? Damiana is an herb that grows *only* in Baja California. It has the same properties as gotu-kola, borage tops, yellow dock root. It cures impotence — not that you'd have to worry — it does away with female trouble, it prevents cancer *and* the common cold. How do those Indians live down in Baja California, where there's nothing but stone and rock and hardly any fresh water at all? Tequila, distilled from the inside of the cactus, lime — *if* they can get it — and a tonic made from damiana, the true wonder drug of the Aztecs!"

By now Tracie was getting excited. "*Ice* is a modern invention. There's no value to it. Egg white is awful. They just put that in to keep the bubbles stiff, but it gets in the way of the total purpose of the margarita, which is to straighten out your heartbeat, clean out your liver. I'm telling you the truth now. My mother at home in California goes to some fancy Beverly Hills doctor who charges her a hundred and sixty dollars an hour. You know what he gives her? Borage! Boldo root! *Damiana!* So *I* say, Save the hundred and sixty dollars. Spend six on two margaritas! Wake up in the morning glad to be alive! *Here!* Taste this!"

Tracie held up a new margarita, thickly rimmed with salt. "Take a lick! Then take a swallow. *Now.* Tell me you don't feel better! And over there behind the counter, see that Gusano? The worm at the bottom means a hundred years of life!"

At Golden Oaks, during a seminar on guided imagery, some guy had come in and told them about energy fields. *Never let an obstacle get between you and your projected goal!* Whitney joined her friend in the aisle, working differently, *being* instead of doing. Being a blonde, out for fun. She carried a bottle in one hand, salt, lime and a shot glass in the other. Every man there — she knew it, she willed it — was going to halt in front of her, look at her breasts and her long blond hair and her bottle of José Cuervo and ask, as though he was the only man on earth, and she the only woman, "What you got there?"

And she would take his hand and hold it for a minute, then show him how to hold the shot glass, hold the lime, and in the fleshy folds between thumb and forefinger pour some coarse grains of kosher salt, and pour that first heartening shot into him. *Wow!* Then it was time to taste the new batch of margaritas. Hal and Steve, without being told, had shrugged into white waiters' jackets. Steve wore a stethoscope. Tequila for life! The men had the sense to confine their advice to a simple injunction to go easy on the salt in cold climates, and to be sure not to drive after three of these, because too much of any tonic was bound to make you feel dizzy. Mostly they stayed busy writing up orders.

Some elderly tourists sneaked in to explore the convention. Tracie and Whitney grabbed them, gave them one shot each, then sent them back out to the bar, where, incredibly, orders came in for extra fifths of José Cuervo, a couple of bottles of Gusano. Around seven, some of the other booths began to close for the night. The men from Jack Daniel's came by, submitted to Tracie's harangue, and refreshed themselves with a frothy margarita. The Seagram's men slunk off without a word. Hal and Steve ran out of invoice pads and had to borrow some from Gilbey's gin. By seven-thirty the hula girls, dead on their feet, had come over for a free sample. "You know where that damn dance gets you?" one of them asked Tracie. "Right here." She poked at where the joint of her leg joined her hip, her hand disappearing into fresh dry grass.

Whitney didn't say much. It wasn't her way. That's why, she thought, some people got the wrong idea that she was aloof. She tried to express this to one of the hula girls, whose skin glowed with eight hours' exertion. "You were beautiful," Whitney said. "I've been watching you all afternoon. I'd do anything to be able to do what you do. I'm too shy, I guess."

"No, man, it's *easy*! I've been giving hula lessons my whole *life,* it's easier than standing still!" Soon the girls were teaching Whitney and Tracie some of the rudimentary steps, but Whitney had trouble with the arm movements. "I was in a car accident a few months back," she said, and a Hawaiian girl answered, "Then you got to do it with your knees and your head."

Steve finished writing up the orders. "Three hundred and seventy cases since four this afternoon. And we're back-ordered on damiana for a hundred years. We've got to buy up some Cointreau and decant it into the damiana bottles for to-morrow. No yard sales this year, Hal. Thank Christ!"

Hal nodded, watching the girls and seven or eight sales-men dancing in the aisle. Last year, no, the year before that, had been so bad for him that he'd spent the summer in New England in his dead mother's old family house. His wife re-turned aluminum cans for pay. On weekends she took a selec-tion of whatever she found around the house and set it out on the lawn to sell for food money. They'd been up against it. He went along with her, because what else was he supposed to do? There wouldn't be any other money coming in until he went on the road in the fall, and they couldn't go on welfare because they knew everyone in town.

One afternoon in August he woke up from a nap in the backyard, heavy and sweaty and insect bitten. He heard, down the driveway, hushed voices. "Can you believe?" a woman's voice said. "She *gave* them to us?"

He roused himself and shambled out to the front lawn, where his wife, pale and tired, was folding away two bills into her coin purse. On a blanket, spread out on the lawn, kitchen and dining items made a forlorn display.

"Did you just sell something?" Mosquitoes buzzed around his head. His son's pale body hung in the loop of an old rubber tire from the elm in the front yard.

"Salt and pepper shakers. They gave me five dollars apiece."

"*The silver ones?*"

"Were they silver?"

He remembered the antique salt and pepper shakers and the castor set and the silver candlesticks and all the other silver that used to sit on the dining room sideboard, that he hadn't noticed in years and years. He went back inside, looked at the sideboard, completely bare now, tried to remember the marks on all that stuff, things that had gone back to before the Revolutionary War. He came back outside where his wife stood, staring at the blanket.

He must have been so unpleasant that he lost his wife that day. (And gave her the house, since he didn't want it and didn't have anything else to give her.) He wrote his son once a month or so, and the kid generally wrote back, but he'd lost his son too, over those salt and pepper shakers. Which he would still have now, along with his family, if he'd had these girls on a Hawaiian island, two, three years ago.

So he stood and watched, and didn't join in the dancing, although every time Whitney moved quietly by him with a shot of tequila, he downed it. The girls were right. There was something about the lime. Something about the salt. Since the breakup — which he could never say broke his heart, although thinking about it depressed him — he tried to keep his world within the confines of what his eyes could see. The less you thought, so to say, the less you thought.

He followed the quiet blonde with his eyes because she was so restful, so easy on the eyes. He thought he saw flashes of alternating ease and melancholy that she gave off like a faulty electric light. Hadn't he heard her say she'd been in a car crash? So . . . maybe she saw what he did. That all it took was one brush with the cosmic drum brush, one blast of the cosmic drum cymbals, what did they call those things? The cosmic *high hat*!

"Time to close up. No more customers. And we've sold out. Totally."

The last thing they all needed was another drink. But Steve and Hal pointed out to the girls that what they had bought to wear under their flowered skirts and might even have dismissed as so mundane a thing as underwear were actually the bottoms of bikinis. After they closed the booth, the four of them, bone-tired but elated, headed for the smallest of the resort's four pools. Here in an artificial grotto hidden from the ocean and hotel rooms alike, a partly submerged bar with a bored bartender waited for their business. Under tiki lamps, the bar stools were placed so that if you were tall, the water might come up to your chest, and if you were short, the water lapped your chin.

Now they could peel off their long skirts, half wade, half swim over to the bar and sit up at it, under water, the tepid wavelets washing away sweat, hard work, plane fear. The Hawaiian behind the bar gave them each a gardenia for their hair and a new orchid lei. Why, there were plenty of flowers around here! You could never use them up!

Steve and Hal excused themselves and returned by the time the girls had taken sips of their first drinks — something with fruit juice and pineapple and paper umbrellas.

Here they were again, Steve and Hal, old guys in their late thirties, who, it was pretty well established, were going to be coming on to these young girls. Their appearance in bathing suits was going to be crucial. "Are we going to be embarrassed by this?" Tracie muttered. "Are we going to *die* from this up-coming moment?"

The old guys handled it pretty well. Steve, who, Whitney decided, looked a little like Dean Stockwell, had a nice brown hairy chest, and baggy black and white trunks that came almost to his knees. *I'm harmless!* his whole body said. *Don't worry about me! You've got nothing to worry about!* Hal, taller, chunky, had that light, buttery tan. His shorts were innocuous khaki, almost part of him. Pool lights caught his sandy hair. And the lines in his face.

They had three rounds of drinks at this quiet bar, but there was no question of the men trying to get them drunk. They spent two whole hours, from eight until almost ten, very quietly sipping, talking, leaning into the water. Steve was making Tracie laugh, and Whitney thought there was no better sound in the whole world than her friend's reckless, insistent laughter. She had Tracie to her left, Hal to her right. He turned on his stool, facing her. Whitney could see, from where she sat, blankets of greenery behind Hal's head. He told her a little about losing his wife, his child, his house. About how his wife had been as good as she could be under the circumstances, until she just couldn't do it anymore. That he tried not to think about his son, because it made him feel bad. "There were things I could have done, I guess, but I couldn't think of them then, when they might have made some difference. So I try not to think about them now."

Whitney put her head down on the bar. "I know. I know exactly. Because when I was in that car crash six months ago, it was very bad. A boy I knew made a right turn and a truck slammed into him. He got slammed. But I didn't know that because I went unconscious. When I woke up I looked over, and I knew he was dead. His head was tilted back against the seat, and the steering wheel had gone into his chest, but I didn't see that then. His mouth was closed and his eyes were closed but blood was coming out of his eyes like he was crying blood, and I . . . drifted down. I drifted down for a minute as far as I could go. I thought, Please God, take these last five minutes back. Let us be turning out onto Santa Monica, laughing and talking. Let Robin be alive. Please let him be alive! But he wasn't alive. And you couldn't get those five minutes back, no matter what. So I came back up. I'd lost a bunch of teeth. They were still in my mouth so I moved my right arm, my left arm was broken, and fished around and found my teeth and balled them up in my cheek, because they always say you can put them back in, and I didn't want to be stuck with false teeth for the rest of my life. And I concentrated on remembering my stepfather's last name, and our telephone number, and my social security number, and the name of our insurance company, and even who the president was, but I couldn't remember. Because I knew those were the questions they ask you when they come with the ambulance. I even had the sense to reach over with my right hand and turn the ignition key off so we wouldn't have a fire. I didn't look at Robin anymore. When I got out of the hospital, he'd already been buried for two weeks."

Hal took Whitney's shoulders and turned her around so that she saw, past Tracie and Steve, to the other side of the grotto.

"Take a look," he said.

At first she set her shoulders impatiently. He hadn't been listening to her — well, who ever did? What was she supposed to be looking at, the *view*? What was the big deal, some *plants*? But as she gazed, the landscape began to move and breathe for her. She saw vines curling and clinging to trees; she saw leaves, breathing good stuff back into the air. She saw hanging flowers and blossoms, and from the way she perceived them, she knew that they effortlessly existed simply as a way to ornament the universe. She reached with her injured arm to touch her lei, and got the message from all around her neck: *still an orchid, still being an orchid.* She tensed to turn to the liquor salesman to say *wow*! But his fingertips on her shoulders told her to stay the way she was. *What more was there to see?* Then she saw natives who had been there all the time. Half-naked brown-skinned men and women moved soberly in a clearing that seemed far away, but not so far that she couldn't see the men clustered together, painting their cheeks with fine lines of white paint, and tying up their loincloths. She flicked her eyes to the girls, so beautiful! Their long hair fell over their shoulders and across their haltered breasts, their legs moved under full grass skirts. Their bare feet gleamed like dark coral in the dust. Seriously and carefully they plucked flowers from the vines around them and put them in each other's hair.

Once again, Whitney barely began to move her shoulders,

to turn to her companion. Once again, her companion kept her steady, turned away from him. "Wait," he whispered, and with that whisper, his breath in her ear, she became aware of all the sounds that went with all the sights. It was fierce! Not just the steady thump of waves on the beach, but the whine of mosquitoes, the hum of some kind of gnats that she saw now, floating around them, since someone had turned on the pool's underwater lights and tinted the water and the air just above the water an iridescent turquoise. She heard the skid of Tracie's straw as it poked around through crushed ice for a last taste. She heard the light slap of water against the sides of the pool. To her right, out of sight in the dark trees, she became aware of human murmuring. There must be a bunch of other people over there! And they were getting louder, hitting a yearning, greedy note. The brown-skinned kids heard it too. They sped up their gestures, flicked out their skirts. A few boys jogged in place. One of them handed around a bottle of baby oil which some of them took and some of them didn't, spreading it on their chests, their muscular arms.

It was almost too dark to see! But one of the boys turned on what looked like a faucet by the side of a rickety building that Whitney just then saw — if you went on looking like this, what else could you see, like, *if you went on like this*? A boy struck a match under the faucet, which squirted out a yellow flame. He turned the flame down. The girls retreated to one side of the clearing, keeping their skirts out of the way. The boys, one by one, picked up poles which had been propped up against the side of the wooden building. As each boy passed the end of his pole under the faucet of flame, the pole, which had a cup of something at its end, caught fire. Brilliant yellow fire lit up the clearing. There was a ramshackle balcony along the upper story of the building. Across the top of the balcony, laundry hung every which way on hand-strung lines. Some of the most vivid flowers weren't real at all, but part of the patterns that huge dark women were wearing as muumuus. A hand-lettered sign flapped in the soft leeward wind: EM-PLOYEES ONLY.

The girls fluffed their hair, and sorted themselves out in pairs. One snatched off a wristwatch at the last minute and handed it to a big woman in a muumuu. Two men picked up drums. Then, off to the right, lurid red and blue lights lit up the manicured tropical forest that surrounded an outdoor restaurant. Under these lights, Whitney saw, as through a scrim, the sad faces of several hundred Americans, all very old. Their faces stretched with longing. A record, very scratchy, came on over the speaker, the Hawaiian war chant.

The boys shook out their arms for looseness as it came their turn to run. Carrying their torches they trotted, chanting, out into the center of the restaurant, bowed to the customers, then ranged themselves around the sides. One man pulled out a conch shell, and blew. The music changed, to "Sweet Leilani." *Sweet leilani, heavenly flower!* The girls waited in the clearing until their cues came. Then, in pairs, they lifted their arms in hula position and undulated out onto the restaurant floor. The applause increased. In the clearing, lit now by the single gas jet, the older women watched, critical and proud, like mothers anywhere.

Hal's right index finger tapped her shoulder. "OK," he said, in an almost normal voice. Whitney turned to see Tracie and Steve watching too, their elbows set back on the bar, pool water curling around them. Tracie was pretty drunk. "Not *every* day! You don't see that every day." Hal smiled off at the clearing. It seemed a shame to stop looking.

They decided it was time to order something to eat, and sitting out of the water now, up at a table, high and dry by the side of the pool, they ate great plates of spareribs and fresh pineapple. The girls finished everything on their plates, and most of what the men left. From where they were sitting they could catch most of the floor show, which got cornier and cornier. By the time it ended, all four of them were back in the water, doing laps. Whitney thought, With every stroke I shed the past. With every stroke I shed the past.

Hal was the first to quit, and a few minutes later she swam over to the side to be with him, while in the pool the competition got heavy, and Tracie shouted out, "*Another* one, you bastard? Not *another* one!" Their strokes got more erratic, but finally Tracie rested and Steve did two more laps, triumphant. When he swam over to them he ducked his head over to sleek his black hair back, then said, "We could go over to the ocean. See what *that* looks like."

No later than eleven-thirty, maybe midnight. Still eighty degrees. Why not? The bartender made them up double daiquiris in green coconuts. "That way you don't mess up the beach!" The four of them ambled down a set of stepping stones that took them past outbuildings of this old, pretty hotel. Just before they got to the beach, the men stopped at a deck where hundreds of palm mats were rolled and stacked for hotel customers, and picked up a few. Then the path ended. They picked their way through rocks and outcroppings onto a sheltered beach no bigger than a living room. The ocean thumped and foamed, and the sand was creamy as a carpet.

Whitney's eyes filled with tears and for a second or two she went back down that long black slide. Robin will never see this. He will never get to see this. Then she remembered the English lady out in Simi Valley. "He doesn't even know he's dead! Be honest!" If you're here, Robin, take a look.

The men unrolled the palm mats in overlapping patterns, while the girls held all their drinks. The four of them lay down in a row. And it wasn't as if Whitney's mind hadn't been working, ticking, all along. It was. It had been. This is all a come-on. This is what they do all the time. Take a look at how they put those *mats* down! Don't you think the two of them have done that a thousand times before? But the moon registered a kind of whimsical *So*? So *what*? And the waves thudded, so *what*? Tracie, quiet now, registered, under her lashes, so *what*? You've got to do it sometime, why not now? Because, for one reason or another, Whitney had never gotten around to doing it.

Still, she thought she might not do it, because wasn't this a silly way to do it? Shouldn't she wait for something, someone, more significant? But the moon, once she lay back on the warm mats and sand, loomed over her as big as a bicycle wheel. More significant than *this*? Get serious! *Robin*? Are you here or not? Hal, as quiet as she had been, leaned over to kiss her. She'd reserved judgment until then, she really had. Her bathing suit came off, she shut her eyes and let her body feel pleasure, pleasure instead of pain. What a zinger. What a buzz! Notice that, Robin? Hal tapped her at one point to get her to open her eyes, smiled down at her, opened the palm of his hand. What is that, a medal of some kind? A quarter, maybe? She saw it was a condom, neatly rolled. Shut her eyes again. And one way or another in the hours that followed got rid of her virginity, felt pleasure, more than she would have ever guessed, and a couple of times lost her self completely, as any sounds the four of them made were swallowed up by the thuds and wheezes of the waves. Once, her hand, carelessly flung out, caught Tracie's arm, carelessly flung out. They took each other's hands and held on tight, cheating the gods.

Whitney, Tracie
Maria, Anita, Ed

Los Angeles/ Ensenada/Tijuana July

WORD GOT OUT through the office that they'd had a great time in Maui. A letter came from the Cuervo people stating that sales had gone off the charts because of those two "efficient and vivacious young ladies." On the one-week anniversary of their first night on the beach, an arrangement of seventy-five orchids sitting on a log arrived at Temporary Success, addressed only to "The Goddesses." Everyone knew that wasn't Ed, tall, thin, and gray-faced, sitting all day hunched over his word processor, or Maria, a Spanish girl with blond hair, whose main job seemed to be filling in for ticket-takers in first-run movie houses all over Westwood. It certainly wasn't H.W.A., Hard-Working Anita, and, no, not D.B. either.

Whitney and Tracie, Tracie and Whitney. Goddesses! And no one seemed ready to let them forget it. Maria wiggled her hips whenever she saw them; Ed yelled, "Down the hatch, Miss Joe-say Cuervo!" every time he saw either one of them. But the person it got to the most was Hard-Working Anita.

There didn't seem to be much the girls could do about it. They detached blossoms from the log and gave one to everybody, sticking one on Maria's chest and one behind Ed's ear, and made up a cluster for H.W.A. and even gave some to D.B. Carefully and soberly, they broke off perfect orchids, pinned them on each other, not saying anything, but Whitney remembered that night; how she'd been a blossom and part of a blossom, and no doubt Tracie remembered something of the kind because she shook her head and smiled, and standing by the reception desk, after they'd given three to the receptionist, they looked down at the log still full of orchids, bursting with orchids, and Tracie said, "*Amazing.*"

All of which really depressed Anita, even though she was too good-hearted to say anything much. Whenever, in the next weeks, an out-of-town gig came up, she went on it, when any fool could have told her it wasn't going to be any fun. She drove to Chico for a hardware store opening. She flew to San Francisco for another real estate party and came home with nothing but a bad hangover. She went on the MGM Fancy-Flight to New York, as a temp sec for some producer, but she took dictation the whole time they were in the air, while everyone else played bàckgammon.

Anita came back from that trip thin-lipped and sad, and talked about having fun. "There's no point in waiting around for fun to happen to you — you could have one long wait! We owe it to ourselves to have fun, because none of us is getting any younger. Look at what happened to *you*, Whitney, it could have been you in that accident instead of that poor boy, so I want some suggestions, what can we all do together that's fun? Before we lose the summer, and you girls have to start in college, and we're all a year older again?"

Was it such a bad idea Anita was having? It was probably a good idea. Ed said he'd always wanted to go Cajun dancing down at the Masonic Hall on the second Friday of every month over in Inglewood. Five of them went in July, Ed and the four girls. They stood in the drafty hall, ate gumbo off paper plates, took the dancing lesson at seven-thirty before the eight o'clock dance began. Whitney knew right away she wasn't going to be able to do it because there were so many arm pulls and swings and she still couldn't do much with her left arm. Tracie gave her a hard look as they stood in the crowd — full of dweebs and dorks and sad people; single parents with their kids and plenty of Cajuns and lots of geezers in walkers and plenty of mixed couples, black and white, Asian and Mexican. "Don't hang around," Tracie told her. "Go next door. We'll catch you later." Then Tracie turned her back on her, found a Japanese bachelor with excellent posture and commanded him, "Dance with me! I'll never figure this stuff out otherwise."

Ed did very well, having his pick of single women of every age and race, and Maria, with her quiet blond looks, danced a lot. But Hard-Working Anita got stuck with a burly redneck who knew the steps but was dead set on dancing for two hours and then going home with her and fucking her brains out and maybe stabbing her to death in the bargain. So at nine o'clock Ed and Tracie and Maria told Anita it was time to go home, and grabbed her away. They found Whitney next door where she stood in the doorway of a Hare Krishna temple, dreaming the time away, watching the gold Buddha and the flowers inside, and clusters of Hare Krishna families outside, as they flocked about on the steps and on the lawn, and some Hare Krishna kids ran around playing tag.

Together the five of them straggled past lines of stucco

bungalows back to their cars. They talked about where to go next, because it was only nine-thirty on a Friday evening and they had the whole city to choose from. But Ed wasn't drinking and it was silly to go to a bar and there wasn't any point in going to a movie because a movie wasn't fun, and no one was really hungry because of that pretty bad gumbo. Maria and Ed seemed content to let it go because they had low expectations anyway. Just by pure accident, Whitney seemed to have drawn the good time, hanging out watching the Hare Krishna people. "I didn't know they had apartments and laundromats and all that stuff." She was talking to Tracie, who was still pretty winded from dancing. Both of them bumped their hands along fences and peered, as they walked, at families shut up tight against burglaries, safe inside, having dinner, watching TV. "Some of those women, they were real dark, and had their saris on, and caste marks and long hair and the whole shot, so I thought, *of course* they were Indian, but they were *Mexican,* with their caste marks and all."

"We could go to East L.A. and listen to Mexican music," Maria suggested. "That would be cool."

But they couldn't figure out how to get to East L.A.

"Third and Evergreen," Maria said. "I'm pretty sure there's a place on Third and Evergreen." But when they got to the cars and found Ed's *Thomas Guide,* and walked back to Winchell's Donuts to get some coffee and plan the excursion, it turned out that Third and Evergreen didn't even intersect. "Besides," Ed said sadly, "we don't want to get our heads blown off. Too many gangs. We wouldn't know what we were doing over there." Coffee in Styrofoam cups. Doughnuts. A greasy table. Tired people all around them. Whitney crouched, withdrawn and sulky, pondering a future where she'd never be able to dance with her arms. Or do gymnastics. Or swim seriously. Or have fun ever again. Even Tracie looked bugged. How many Friday nights, Saturday nights *were* there in a person's life?

Not that many. Not enough to waste one like this. Or end up like Anita.

But Anita was the one who had the idea. "Look!" she said excitedly. "I have got it. I have *got* it! How long does it take to get to East L.A., even if we *could* go without getting our heads blown off? At least an hour. But what if we . . . Look! What if next Friday we head south on the San Diego Freeway, two hours to San Diego, another hour to get across the border and through Tijuana, take the toll road south, that's just another hour. And we'd be in *Ensenada*! We don't have any big jobs next weekend. We could close down maybe three-thirty next Friday and by this exact time next week, we'd be *in another country*, you know what I mean? Right by the ocean. Dancing. Listening to music. The whole thing. Come back Sunday afternoon, get to work on Monday. I think this is it. This really *is* it!"

Ed had never been across the border. Tracie remembered going once, with her real dad, long ago. Whitney had some memories, from her real dad too. When Anita sighed, "*Just to go somewhere else,*" they all said yeah. "Yeah. Let's do it."

Which is why, ten-thirty the following Friday night, the five of them checked into a Holiday Inn on the American side of the border, because Ed's carburetor was acting up and he refused to cross until a mechanic had a look at it. The drive to the border from L.A. had taken seven hours, not two, because of an oil spill across four lanes just north of Leucadia. And they'd gotten off the freeway at San Clemente for coffee and pie and Ed couldn't figure out how to get on again. And a few other things like that.

They rented *The Terminator* on video and holed up in one of two double rooms they'd rented. Ed said he'd sleep in the car. It was his responsibility for the delay, and besides he was watching his money so they could all eat at El Rey Sol, the fancy French restaurant down in Ensenada where you could

162

get a two-hundred-dollar meal for only one hundred dollars, or so they'd heard. Anita went out and came back with two twelve-packs of canned margaritas and four bags of Fritos. They watched *The Terminator* twice.

Whitney and Tracie finally decided they had to sleep and went next door, but at one in the morning Maria woke them up, with her pillow under her arm. "Anita and Ed," she said. "They're *doing* it in there. I'm sleeping in here, OK? Don't worry, I'll take the floor."

They flung her their bedspreads. Then Tracie groaned, got up to get them all glasses of water and three aspirin apiece. "I don't know what they put in that canned stuff, but it can't be good for you."

"*La bonne vie,*" Maria said, up on the floor on one elbow, her face green in the light from the bathroom. "The good life. But think of Anita."

"Don't make me *laugh,*" Tracie pleaded. She turned out the light. "Where are we? What is this place?"

Whitney sipped at the airy, not very cold, tap water. Her head pounded. Her teeth ached in her head. Her shoulder hadn't been right since she'd taken that dumb Cajun dancing lesson. "San Ysidro. *North* of the border."

The wall behind them began to vibrate.

"Jesus," Tracie said. "Listen to that."

Whitney gulped some water. She didn't have the heart to laugh. Neither did anybody else.

The following day, on the other side of the border, which crossed two of the steep, dangerous chasms between traffic-packed Tijuana and the raw beachside buildings of Playas de Tijuana, Ed's car got a flat. It had to be close to noon, the temperature way up there over a hundred. This road floated in the air like a suspension bridge in a bad movie. At its end, clusters of houses made of cardboard and tin clung to arid cliffs for dear life. Goats scampered up and down the raw dirt.

The stalled car caused a traffic jam. There was no real shoulder; only slippery dirt and *air*. They were stuck right at the edge of the road. In the two lanes heading west, out to the Pacific, cars hurtled past — callow American college boys shouting, catcalling, not one of them stopping to help. The Mexicans seemed bound by a different imperative: stop one of those pickup trucks running on stinking diesel fuel and you might never get started again.

"It's not even a bridge, Whit," Tracie yelled. "Get out and look! I think they built it up with dirt from the very bottom. It's like the fucking pyramids." But, in the back seat, Whitney couldn't move. She'd listened to Anita say that at least Ed should have crossed over the gorge before stopping. She'd heard Ed answer shortly that he wasn't ruining a tire just for her convenience — a new tire cost a whole day's work, or didn't she remember?

Anita's eyes teared up at that. She'd gotten out of the car, looking silly in high heels and panty hose, and wobbled until she came, in two steps, to the edge. "Oh!" Whitney heard her frail voice, snapped from her mouth in dust and fumes. And it came back to her, the truck barreling down from behind, the thoughtless smash, the destroyed, torn metal, Robin's closed eyes, weeping blood. Ed, unable all morning to meet anybody's eyes, opened the trunk of the car. Whitney felt the car lurch, then lurch again toward traffic, as Ed hauled out the spare. Then his sweaty face peered in.

"Get out. Get out of the *car*! I'm not going to jack the two of you up too!"

"Come on, Whitney. He wants us out of here. We'll walk along the side of the road, and get off this thing, and wait for him over at the mountain. It's only a little walk."

Whitney didn't know Maria very well, knew only that she was blond, hailed from Dallas, and before that, Spain. In her wallet, where others carried their prom pictures or pictures of their fiancés or even snapshots of their dogs, she carried, somewhat secretively, a holy card of the Sacred Heart.

"Come on come on come *on*!" Ed said. "Get out of the fucking car so I can change the fucking *tire*!"

Maria's smooth cool hand closed over Whitney's forearm. "We're going to get out of the car. Then we're going to get Tracie away from the edge because she's acting cuckoo. And we'll get Anita because Ed's being so *mean*. Then we'll just walk on over and see what they're doing in the barrio. You know what? I used to have a boyfriend who took me down here all the time. We'd go to the bullfights, and you know what?" She cracked the door toward the open air of the gorge and got out. "Don't worry, there's ground here, because you know what? If there wasn't ground, I wouldn't be standing here. And you don't want to get out on the traffic side, it's too dangerous."

Dangerous! No shit! First you were here, driving and smiling. Then you weren't here and your face was jam, and *you weren't here.* And it might even be true that your soul hung around, thinking it was still a part of things, but it was never going to get a chance because your body had dashed down upon a rock and gone. The car began to move on Whitney's side, up, up, up.

"See? He's already jacking up the car. You have to move real soft now so as not to hurt him. Come on. We've got to go."

Anita was already walking out ahead of the car. Trucks swerved close to her. Men in flatbeds gave her gestures, fucking gestures, leaning out into midair. But what was the point of ever fucking because in an instant, rubber brakes! The car swerves. The boy's beautiful face pours blood. "We could have gone off so easy," Whitney whispered. "There's no guard rail here."

"My boyfriend used to take me to those fights, you know? And sometimes they'd be in downtown TJ, and we'd stay at Caesar's or the motel where the bullfighters stay. But every other Sunday they put them on at the new bullring out by the Playas. And it's a fairly new ring, you know? But the sea breeze comes up every afternoon and no matter how much water you pour on that cape, the cape is going to flap. But you know what I heard? Even the bullfighters like the new ring, the one by the ocean, the one with the breeze. We're going to hold hands now." She took Whitney's slippery hand, held open the door, and pulled her out of the car.

"Whitney's feeling pretty bad," Maria called to Tracie who squatted on her haunches now, picking up pebbles and throwing them down into the gorge. "I think she must have a hangover. That was *awful* stuff we drank last night."

Outside, cars and trucks flew by, creating gusts of hot wind strong enough to take three women and blow them straight into the middle of the air. Or the cars might run them down, for sport. Cars did that.

Tracie stood up, pressing with her palms at the small of her back, looking regretfully at free space. "OK."

The three girls walked single file, Maria in front of Whitney, Tracie behind her, the quarter of a mile to the mountain and houses and little crowd of Mexicans who waited by the shelf of brown, parched land. Such was the force of Whitney's terror that all of them had the shakes by the time they got to the others who waited, watching with some interest as the foolhardy gringo changed a tire out there where he could get killed. Anita stood with her arms folded, furious. "He thinks he's such hot stuff. Well *he* isn't such hot stuff . . ."

"What's the matter?" A chunky wife addressed Maria in Spanish as if she knew — well, she *did* know — that the pretty blonde spoke the language.

"*Ella tiene miedo. Su novio sufrió muerte en un carro.*"

"*Que lástima!*"

Maria pulled off her jacket and a wide belt. "Please, take these. It would make us happy."

"*Gracias!*"

The woman disappeared into a house which seemed alive, so desperately did it cling to the raw cliff, and returned almost immediately with a cup of steaming tea. "*Tómela. Es contra el miedo.*"

Whitney accepted it, began to sip. A few children watched, then turned away, throwing stones into the air. Whitney finally whispered, "What is this?"

"For a hangover," Maria explained.

"*Si, si. Por una cruda!*"

Whitney put the palm of her hand across her forehead. A few tears streaked her cheeks. Maria and the stout wife eyed each other and shook their heads. Up the slope, men speculated. Poor girls. Not loved, not protected, not respected, not honored. But then, when Anita began to walk back out, against the traffic, to harangue Wretched Ed — Anita, too dumb even to take off those high heels of hers — everyone laughed. Sad men tending goats or mending tires on their almost perpendicular slopes stopped their sad thoughts to laugh. Mexican women and children dressed in filthy clothes that didn't fit covered their mouths. Tracie snorted. Maria, though it was bad manners, giggled. And Whitney's mind, registering the image of that wobbly, self-important female, tottering out on a precarious pier of dirt to assert her ownership of Wretched Ed, finally let that image wipe out the picture of the beautiful boy, his eyes pouring blood. Because what if Anita *did* fly straight out into the air like a kicked football? That would be pretty *good,* wouldn't it? Finally she smiled. The Mexican mom took her tin cup away.

When they hurtled past the Playas and the bullring, its flags flying against the greedy sea, Ed absolutely refused to stop to get the tire fixed. "We're late enough already, we've missed the whole weekend."

They drove the toll road too fast. Up front, Anita objected.

The three girls in back held hands and closed their eyes as Ed took curves at foolhardy speeds. They stopped at the Halfway House, full of drunken Americans. Ed wanted to drink, but Anita said only if he let *her* drive, so he poured down eight or nine beers, not talking, in a piss-poor mood. The three young women went out on the balcony to look at waves.

Little Indian girls came up to sell them Chiclets. Maria emptied her wallet, took off her shoes and removed barrettes from her hair to give to the girls. Tracie took off her bracelets. Whitney gave them a sport watch. The little girls quietly held out their hands for what they would get, then asked for some money. When Maria handed all their Chiclets back to them, they pattered away in the hot sun. "You can't worry," Maria said, "about the way the world is. All you can do is change what you see."

They couldn't figure out how to get back on the toll road so Anita drove the last fifty miles down Baja to Ensenada on the *libre* road, past farms in the dead desert, and skinny cows and frisky goats. When Ed complained that he was going to puke, Anita irritably instructed him to roll down the window and *do* it. When Ed said that would wreck the passenger side of his car she cuttingly suggested that he might have thought of that, back when he was putting down foreign beers like they were Diet Pepsis.

"Not many big O's last night, I bet," Maria whispered.

"No O's at all, would be my guess," Tracie responded sagely.

But Whitney, between them, could only look at the road as she perceived it, coming up between Ed's and Anita's heads; the kind of landscape you see on a pinball machine, once you put in your quarter. "*Slow down!*" she wanted to scream. "*Downshift!* Just because there isn't a line down the road, doesn't mean there *shouldn't* be a line down the road!" Although this narrow two-lane thoroughfare was far less trav-eled than the toll road, when a truck came in the opposite direction, it came straight down the middle: get out of the way or die.

No pretense here, Whitney thought. Nobody even pretended the world wasn't dangerous. When a *curva peligrosa* came up, and Anita took it at fifty miles an hour, Ed rolled down the window and puked. The smell of vomit filled the car. Whitney watched him from the corner of her eye. His neck was thin and gray, a streak of sweat trickled down into the collar of his not very fresh shirt. He needed a haircut. He sat back, gasping, wiping his open mouth with the back of his hand and closed his eyes. How could Anita have done it last night? Let his poor little dick wander around in her, let his gangly body fall asleep all over her as he drunkenly said *oh baby, oh baby,* before he totally passed out? (Because all of them had heard him.) And what if he had a disease? Except he couldn't have a disease, because no one else in his or her right mind would ever sleep with him.

Again the window rolled down. Again Ed puked. From the back seat, Tracie asked, "Are we having fun yet?" Maria muttered in Spanish. Whitney sat upright, her eyes wide.

"What's that?" she asked, as they whizzed by what looked like a metal sculpture, painted pink.

"In Mexico, when you die, they put up a shrine. You pray for them when you go by."

It was too much for Whitney. She closed her eyes, felt the tears go down her cheeks again. "Don't worry," Maria said. "God takes care of everybody. They just remember it down here."

"Nobody." Then she stopped. "Nobody put up a shrine for Robin."

Tracie grabbed her leg with strong fingers. "Get serious. Who would the shrine be to? Couldn't have a shrine anyway. *What,* right there by the Santa Monica Cafe? Get a grip, will-ya?"

Whitney wept. "I miss him, Trace. He's gone." The others

ignored her. Even the blue sky was in a bad mood, it didn't care, and the ground could care less.

Which isn't to say that when they passed the Miracle Ranch Orphanage and the fish cannery on the outskirts of Ensenada and finally drove down the dusty main drag around three on Saturday afternoon, they didn't end up having a pretty good time. Maria read some posters in Spanish and hauled them out to a *charreada* — a Mexican rodeo where they drank more beer and turned out to be almost the only Americans there and got a bad sunburn.

Poor Old Anita (P.O.A.? No, that was too mean, too cruel), insisted that they go to Hussong's, the *in* college bar. Maria said her father had known Victor Hussong, the younger brother, down in Mazatlán, who'd been shot by an upset husband and they'd written a *corrido* about it. But in this bar, this Hussong's in Ensenada, only a hundred miles south of the border, adultery was not the story. College boys throwing up was the story. Anita got up to go to the girls' room. "Don't do it," Maria cried, but it was already too late. Anita came out, a bucket fell down out of the sky, cowbells rang, college louts hooted. Time to leave.

By six o'clock they'd driven down the beach where Maria, who never said anything much at the office, found a dance hall and collected a stack of money, to pay musicians for sad songs — "La Cama de Piedra" (The Bed of Stone). It was her turn to cry then, about her rich father who had deserted her family, and thought he could buy her affection. "And he *can*," Maria sobbed, "he *can*. Now, *conosce ustedes 'La Llorona,'* The Weeping Woman?"

Ed buried his skinny head in Anita's neck. "Oh, baby, you know how I feel about you! Otherwise, I . . ."

They checked into La Mission Something or Other that had a pool and plenty of tile. They walked the length of the town, looking at leather goods, followed by musicians who strummed along to Maria. At the hotel, loaded with cheap souvenirs (an alligator whip that Anita insisted was the perfect gift for Miss Neimenthal back home), they cleaned up for dinner at El Rey Sol. This time, it was the three girls in one room, Anita and Ed in the other.

They met, around eight, in the tiled patio of the hotel, and walked down the main street of Ensenada to El Rey Sol. "This isn't like a Spanish city or a Mexican city," Maria said. "This isn't like a city at all."

The food was more astonishing than they could have wished for, with appetizers and a fancy salad, and a sorbet course. Pretty soon, the magic of French champagne began to kick in. They were American, they all worked at the same office, they were having a good time. They tore apart big lobsters and Ed ordered up a steak. Ended with profiteroles and cognac. The musicians had followed them in, and alternated with a trio across the room that was playing for a table of Mexican businessmen. When Maria ran out of money, the businessmen sent over the message that they'd stake her indefinitely as long as "true daughter of Mexico" agreed to sit with them.

"Should I?"

Of course, of course.

Ed escorted her over, returned with the men's business cards.

But without Maria, there was nothing to do but go back to the hotel. Back in their room Whitney and Tracie turned off the lights and got in twin beds, which smelled of mildew. The wall behind them vibrated, stopped. They thought they heard Anita, crying. The only English-language television channel they could get had a Martin Sheen movie about a professor of English married to a neurotic wife who couldn't accept his other child born out of wedlock.

"Hard to be a wife," Tracie remarked from the darkness.

"You *know* it."

"But what else have you got?"

They slept after that but woke up, taking turns being sick. Was it the lobster? Too much liquor? That sorbet? When Maria came in, she was sick too.

The next morning, shaky and dim, the three girls walked down a tiled hall to the breakfast room of the hotel. Quietly and cautiously they ordered coffee and *pan dulce*. From their window they caught a dispiriting view of the harbor, cement and unpainted metal and unattractive ships in dry dock.

"The Love Boat," their waiter told them, "is in town. You can go and see it, *mas tarde*."

"Tracie, you know what?" Whitney's eyes filled with tears again. "I'm afraid to go back over those bridges."

"Don't tell anyone. There's nothing you can do about it. We'll be home soon."

Whitney managed a smile. "Are we having fun yet?"

Tracie said, "Look at the bright side. We're having more fun than Anita."

Maria looked out the window. "Life is a bed of stone, sometimes. I don't know why."

Jerry

Singapore/Jakarta/
Komodo/Irian Jaya
August 18–21

THEY TOOK NEW GUINEA away from him. A dozen and a half brown-skinned executives, who scrabbled and gibbered and held their sides tittering, took his dream from him in a snap. They sat in a newly air-conditioned board room in Singapore's renovated Raffles Hotel and simpered and covered their teeth with their hands while they snatched his dream away. Two or three Australians who'd come up from the North Coast weren't paying attention at first; when it dawned on them what Jerry had planned, they too burst out in great guffaws. They thought he was nuts.

Jerry, trapped with a prospectus and close to a hundred million in ready money, had to take their weaselly derision. It was, after all his planning, all his dreaming, a matter of those saltwater crocs. When he pointed out that Port Douglas on Australia's Gold Coast still had a croc or two, as well as the biggest goddamn Sheraton in the world, they only snickered. Jerry remembered an unlikely parallel: the Hollywood producer who had wanted to annex Belize, and make that hellhole into paradise. And what a fool he'd seemed.

Jerry turned the pages of the prospectus, letting the money, the architecture, the planning, speak; too proud to break down and cry. Loring gazed calmly down at the facts and figures that Bartch, Bridges, Freed put in front of them all — the World Bank financing they'd jimmied into place. This project would be a bonanza for some fourth-rate country somewhere and everyone at the table knew it — if they could just get past their horror stories of limbs getting crunched off in six inches of ocean water, and the Rascals who shot arrows at you as you walked down the main street of Port Moresby, and Russel's vipers that slept under your pillows, and more crocs who slid in kitchen doors and down bungalow halls and yawned with great grins at people playing bridge and "took the dummy away, ha ha!"

Loring must have known all along the idea wouldn't fly. Jerry saw it in his face. And now the talk went to shrunken heads! But these small, dirty, ill-educated little specimens — *they* were the ones with shrunken heads! Jerry got hot about it, once he saw how clearly BBF had been set up. When the Malaysians made a counterproposal of Penang and the mud flat, just north of "that charming city," he vetoed it rudely.

After an hour, the Indonesians made their offer: a ninety-nine-year lease on the eastern end of Komodo. Jerry shrugged in despair. He'd seen the silly movie with Marlon Brando! Giant *lizards*? Was that the key to a twenty-first-century utopia? The deal almost fell apart right in that moment. His own frustration and temper almost killed it. But the Japanese received the offer neutrally. The Australians liked the idea.

Underdeveloped land, they pointed out. The climate was dry. Good for work.

But see, Jerry wanted to say, if we wanted to put all this time, money and investment into a *shithole,* we could have bought up Nevada and put it *there*! Loring tapped his fountain pen on his wrist — a light warning to his more impetuous partner. But Jerry was sick with disappointment. Because they didn't *get* it. He wanted, he looked for . . . something else. Something new. And that was where he nearly lost it again — when an oily Filipino began talking about how he'd made a study of how high you could keep the temperatures in your factories before women and children started fainting.

They must have seen the disgust on his face because they chilled out after that. They were only joking. Except that the Filipino billionaire who owned the factory wasn't joking.

The consortium had no trouble with the idea of Komodo. "Untouched," they kept saying. The Japs said OK. The Filipino thought he had another billion in his pocket.

The Australians said OK.

Loring said they'd have to go down and take a look before they could commit BBF assets. He reminded them all that BBF would be the major holder; that they'd been the ones to put the World Bank on notice. Some ferrety brown man answered back that everyone knew they needed a third world country with correct politics in order to put that extra financing in place. An Indonesian said that — with their permission — he'd immediately arrange a trip for them to his country, to Jakarta, then a hydrofoil to Komodo. "In our small world, a trip like this is nothing. You could be in our capital by tonight." He left the room to arrange for visas, by phone and by fax. Loring and Jerry were checked out of their hotel by underlings as the meeting petered out. A limo waited with their luggage outside the trimmed, lavish gardens of Raffles. A place that had been worth something, once.

Loring asked him, how about a Singapore sling before we go? In the old Kipling bar?

"It's *not* the old Kipling bar!" He had lost it. The South Pacific had been his, the cool blue pool of his mind. They took it away from him. Before he could recover his balance, by three o'clock on the same day he had gone in for a breakfast meeting in Singapore, he and Loring got dumped onto the Jakarta plane. The bastards had blindsided him.

Talk about a new direction. Jesus. They would land in Jakarta tonight and go on to Komodo tomorrow. Nothing, Loring told him in the limo, had lived longer on earth than the Komodo dragon, except maybe the cockroach. No, they weren't like they'd been in that movie. They weren't even the same reptile.

Jerry wasn't interested.

He didn't know zip about Indonesia. He knew that some decades back they'd massacred Chinese. He knew that in Bali women routinely forgot to wear the top half of their clothes and allowed their full and beautiful breasts to be photographed. It was a paradise there. Everyone knew that. But all those other islands along the archipelago?

Jerry realized, with chagrin, he didn't even know what religion they'd be dealing with. Bali was Hindu, everything west of that presumably belonged to the Nation of Islam. But Komodo was east of Java, all the way out there! Loring knew, had to know, but he had slipped quietly into his plane seat and closed his eyes. His face gleamed with sweat, his shirt showed damp patches. This wasn't the time to ask him anything. Jerry pressed his lips together. He couldn't allow himself to be disappointed. It was true, he would not in the next several years have his blue-black Highlanders in the smoking jungles of New Guinea; fierce men who painted themselves in dazzling yellow and blue, and wove old copies of *Look* magazine into their headdresses. What would he have done with such men anyway?

The plane took off, flew, landed. They were herded into buses and driven across bumpy tarmac to the lobby of the Jakarta airport where they read an enormous sign: BEWARE OF TOUTS! Touts began, mercilessly, to badger them.

"Allo, Papa! You wan' turtle? You wan' good sex, you wan' alligator? You wan' love spell? You wan' hotel? Good hotel? Stay home with my sister, spend the night?"

Jerry held fast to his luggage. "No," he said. "No. No. *No!*" But one old woman had dug in her heels as she played tug-of-war with these ungainly Americans. She wrested Loring's bag off his left arm and scurried away with it, running out of sight. There must be a thousand furious people in this stark, brightly lit room. The temperature must be over a hundred. The sound was something out of Jerry's experience, like a party, only not a party; a continual screech of human voices so overpowering that Jerry had to put his mouth directly to Loring's ear as he yelled, at the very top of his voice, "We've got to go after her! We can't let her get away with your things!"

They pushed toward a door that opened on to a dusty field, dotted with old cars. BEWARE OF TOUTS! Someone handed him a scrap of paper with that message scrawled upon it, then asked for a tip. Jerry threw the paper down, clutched at his bag. So soon, then, had they walked into disaster. He foresaw the next morning in anterooms of the local American consulate, making lists of Loring's possessions; would they ever get *out* of here?

"You want your bag? You want taxi? You want hotel?" A man Jerry's age, taller than his countrymen, bobbed and danced in their path as they pushed through the doors.

"No," Jerry said, tugging on Loring. "No. *No!*"

But when they passed into the dank heat of the parking area, Jerry spied Loring's garment bag, opened out and spread, conspicuous in silvery magnificence, across the hood of an ancient, filthy, private car. The old woman stood guard beside it. And even in the stress of the moment Jerry noticed that this woman, like all other Indonesian females he had seen, either on the plane or here on this damp, teeming ground, dressed more modestly than nuns, with high-necked jackets and sleeves that covered their wrists, skirts that covered their ankles.

"My mother bring bag. You want hotel? You want home for night? I give you good price."

"We have reservations for the Intercontinental. Can you take us to the Intercontinental? How many piasters? How many rupiah?"

The old woman snatched Jerry's suitcase — and his laptop IBM — and slung them into the open trunk of the jalopy. Loring's bag slithered in on top of them. The din, even outdoors, was deafening. Jerry saw the people around him obscured by *dust* — ground dust, coal dust, smoke. *Beware of touts!* But it was too late. Dazed, he slid into the back seat. The old woman slammed the door behind him. The swarthy driver handed Loring in, slammed *his* door and went around the car to take the wheel.

"Is this a bemo?" Loring asked, beside him. His voice sounded frail and old. "Is this what they call a bemo?" Even Jerry knew it wasn't a bemo. Bemos were jeeps or pickup trucks, but he thought he knew why his companion spoke — to keep up his courage, here in the murky twilight, to remind himself he was still alive. With some anxiety Jerry reminded himself that this must be an adventure. More accurately, it was no more than a lowly cab ride, a *nothing,* something an adventurer wouldn't even remember to record. Loring spoke again — querulous old man — "Is this the way to the Borobudur Intercontinental?"

A city where electricity was still an iffy proposition. A city where the roads were dirt, and only dirt; where every set of wheels sent up waves of choking dust, where roadside stands were lit by torches and smoldering fires in trash cans. They flared erratically on this stooped and tired people (or was *he* the only one who was tired?). And what smells! The rot smell of dead greens, dead cats, sewage that had been around for years. By rights, by everything Jerry knew of sanitation, all these people should be dead, drowned in germs; dead men, dead women.

"This can't be the way to the Intercontinental."

It was true, now that the road had taken a turn or two, that the burry glow of downtown Jakarta seemed distanced. They were going farther and farther away into dense dark. The ghostly apparitions by the side of the road were paying less attention. Would it still be an adventure, Jerry wondered despairingly, if they ended up dead in a ditch, their bodies part of the smell of decay, their luggage up for sale in one of these torchlit lean-tos?

"I take you to Marco Polo, in Teuku Cik Road. Nice swimming pool. Nightclub. Good breakfast. Potable water. Good spot."

The driver turned into a black alley, made another turn, and pulled in under the crumbling porte cochere of the Marco Polo. A mean little man relieved them of their passports and hoisted them in an elevator that smelled of urine to a room on the eighth floor. The room was stifling, lit by bright blue light, the windows sealed tight shut.

The man accepted his tip. "Nightclub in basement," he said.

There were two skinny twin beds in this room and one low dresser. The telephone's disconnected wire trailed uselessly along the dirty floor. Trash in the wastebasket. When Jerry stepped into the bathroom and turned on another buzzing fluorescent light, he saw immediately: clean towels, thin and stiff, hung up on rods; dirty towels, left in the corner from the last customers; a few pubic hairs in the basin; and an army of the biggest roaches he'd ever seen, scurrying for cover. Well, he thought, no worse than what you might find in New York. He walked ten steps back across the main room to wrestle open the painted-shut windows. Looking out and down in the friendly darkness he thought he could see the swimming pool of which the cabbie had spoken. And remembered that they hadn't been killed, or even robbed. *Alive!* Jerry, holding to the window's molding, felt himself free-floating with happiness. What if all fear were like this? Utterly baseless, with no grounding in reality?

"Let's go down to the club," he said to Loring, who sat numbly on the edge of his bed. "I could use a beer."

They took the elevator down to the B floor. The doors opened to darkness. Jerry fought down another brief wave of panic. How could he be such a coward? If the point of travel was self-knowledge, couldn't he be done with the fear part?

Another dour man stood before them now and, like a ghost, led them to a table in the corner. Now, music, Johnny Mathis, came over loudspeakers. Mostly men here, wearing Sukarno hats, ignoring them. They were the only Caucasians, the only ones who knew who Johnny Mathis was — if, indeed, Loring had that information. They were seated. Without asking, the man set down two icy beers.

"Dutch," Loring said, his voice, in the dark, readjusting itself to what was normal for him. "The beer is Dutch. They got here before we ever thought of it. Set up good breweries. Got those Dutch wives. Know what a Dutch wife is? A piece of wood you stick in bed with you. Drains off your sweat."

"I know," Jerry said. "I heard about it."

Jerry drank. Had Loring guessed the depth of his fear? It didn't matter. After Komodo, they'd be taking the same plane back to Jakarta but then separating: Loring on Garuda Airlines to Singapore and a United flight to L.A. Jerry would go home another way. He'd be flying from Jakarta east to Jayapura, the capital of Irian Jaya, that other half, darker half, of the island of New Guinea! He had to see it, he knew he was right. He would gather information on his own.

Another, more sour part of his mind queried: What was the advantage in possibly being *eaten*? Why did that seem more attractive, more appropriate, than being slung in a ditch by a Jakarta cab driver and his ancient mother? Why elect to civilize a jungle rather than a desert? Why couldn't he simply be a team player on this?

Because sometimes a man really did have to do what he had to do. What if Napoleon had stayed on Corsica? What if Brigham Young had passed right by "the place," and the Mormons had set up in the wrong godforsaken spot, like . . . Las Vegas?

Those weaselly men wouldn't "let" him go to Papua New Guinea! They only "let" him go to Indonesia! That was the only visa in his passport now. But such was their blindness that, even looking at the map of the archipelago, they must have failed to see that far, far to *their* east, across the Banda Sea, Irian Jaya was the last (and the most recently "liberated") part of *Indonesia*. The other half of Irian Jaya was the fiercely beautiful place, the place, his Papua New Guinea. He would fly to Jayapura, on the Irian Jaya side, get his PNG visa there, then fly to Lae, on the other side, *his* side. He would fly from there to Port Moresby. He would befriend the Rascals. (Could they be worse than the cabbie they'd had tonight?) He would inspect and inventory the ocean-going crocodiles for himself. He would count the Russel's vipers (because didn't rattle-snakes come down from the chaparral in the Santa Monica Mountains, and didn't the American middle class make their peace with *them* all over again, every single smoggy summer?).

They had been playing the theme from *High Noon*. In this room there were three women, one dressed like a Hong Kong whore, the other two in modest Indonesian dress. The whorish girl danced by herself, plainly bored. Then another kind of music came on — not the wind-chime tones of the Indonesian gamelan but something else, music Jerry had never heard before. Everyone in the room got up and began to dance — everyone but Loring and Jerry. They danced, all of them, shifting their weight from foot to foot, facing sometimes one person, then another. They held out their arms in front of them, as if they held skeins of yarn. A waiter came up to the two American men. "Dance," he ordered them. "Dance!" They stood then, shifted their weight from side to side, held out their arms, supporting invisible skeins of yarn. They danced, danced until a little after the music had stopped. The others, seated back at their tables, looked at them curiously.

"Two more beers," Loring said. They drank a few more, not looking at each other. When, forty minutes later, the dance came on again, they got up; they danced, then headed for the elevator.

"Strange, too strange for me," Jerry sighed. "Got any haiku to cover this?" Loring didn't answer.

Through their open window they could see the moon, same old moon. Jerry swayed, beery, safe. This would be the first time that he and Loring had spent the night together in a single room. But he was glad to half see the chunky older man who shed his clothes, sat in his old-fashioned undershirt, loose boxer shorts, long socks held up by garters. Like having a dad in the room with him. When Loring lay back without saying good night and began an irregular asthmatic wheeze, that too was comforting.

Jerry slept in his shorts, only a sheet to his chest, and fell asleep, looking at the moon. He woke with dry mouth, hearing the sounds of Loring in the shower.

He got up, looked out the window. Yellow dust hung in the air. Down below there was indeed the swimming pool, yellow, with cloudy things floating in it. The planter outside his window held parched earth, and a few paper cups. Well, what was he bitching about? Wasn't this why he had come on down here, to be of some help with all of this?

"Coffee. Get your shower. World looks better after coffee."

Had he looked so dejected, then, that Loring had seen it in the slope of his naked back? Jerry saw, in the elevator, as Loring lit up a morning cigarette, that his fingers were puffy, his hands trembled. He looked sick and sad.

In the lobby they said that breakfast was served downstairs. They descended once again. Last night's rancid room was full of morning light, filtered through lattices and trellises. The tables had been set with paper place mats and napkins. Waiters (from last night?) loitered in corners. Unguided, Jerry and Loring made their way to a corner table. The coffee was strong and sweet.

"American breakfast, Indonesian breakfast?" The boy stared out the window, waiting.

"Indonesian breakfast," Loring said flatly. Jerry ordered toast. Loring's breakfast lay like a third world reproach, an underdone sunny-side-up egg lolling on a bed of pink rice, with pink and green shrimp chips flanking the borders. The waiter, solicitous, brought soggy salt in a shallow bowl. The egg white, cut, seeped like semen.

"Look at this. Fertile egg. We used to get them on the farm." But Jerry couldn't look.

By nine they were on the hydrofoil, having made contact with Mac and Gus who'd decided to come down, and some other Japanese. Some Australians were making the trip, and a few phlegmatic Dutch. The Aussies wore tropical white linen suits, and carried large linen handkerchiefs. "My aunt," an Australian said, "knows Sumatra like the back of her hand. She says, only *new* people step outside in the tropics without serviceable kerchiefs!" He had brought along a box of these to give away — a deductible business present? Jerry remembered his Australian trip a year ago, the clear air, some woman who spoke to him when he climbed Ayers Rock. What *he* wanted to know, was: How could people stay home? Let it all go by? Never even get a *look* at it? This beautiful world?

The hydrofoil sliced through monstrous blue swells, southern waters. Businessmen vomited matter-of-factly over the side, then reached for glasses of Perrier that Indonesian crewmen, dressed in sarongs under starched white waiter's jackets, handed them on silver trays. The captain, as they set out, gave them a stock speech: the sea was where Indonesian devil gods lived. But not even the native crew worried on a hydrofoil, because it streaked like a bird and fooled the gods.

Jerry heaved, and heaved again. Guzzled Perrier. They would reach Komodo by six. Land at the far end of the island.

He saw the Dutch guys, stroking their red chins and necks. For hundreds of years they'd been after these islands, dead-set in love with them. What was it these large dullards wanted from these stringy natives? To *mate,* maybe? To have attractive children, for a change? Across the deck, twenty feet away in this open hydrofoil, Loring Freed hung his head and discreetly got rid of his egg, his shrimp chips. Six hours more. Jerry coated his face, the back of his hands with sunblock. He waited for his next set of heaves, then gambled, opening a box of Dramamine and swallowing six tablets. He took a long slug of Perrier, allowed himself a last look at this sea, and, disciplined, composed himself for sleep.

He woke, wretchedly sick, boiling in his own sweat. The hydrofoil had slowed, chugged up through chunky sharp waves to a rickety pier. Around the inside borders of the boat, pink, damp Western bodies pulled up, sat up, stood up. The Indonesians hardly bothered to conceal their contempt as they scrambled up on bleached planks, extended sharp monkey paws to pull obese Dutchmen to sure footing.

And once again Jerry felt dread, the childish fear. Anything could happen. They could desert us, start up their motors, leave us to rot on this beach. He remembered — *only now*! — that a guy he'd gone to high school with, years ago, a Jehovah's Witness, had been left for weeks with his second wife and stepson, on a beach just *like* this, and had only been picked up on a fisherman's whim. It made the pages of *People* magazine (but not the cover), and his classmate had said their family prayed their way through hard times on the beach and in the jungle. But what if you didn't believe in God?

"Two by two! Take two hands. Come *on*, Papas!"

Like a school kid, Jerry hunted out Loring. And was comforted to see that he, at least, carried himself with some dignity. They walked the length of pier together. The hot sea breeze carried off some of their sweat.

"They say the Indonesians withhold information. What do you think that means? Couldn't they just *lie*, like everybody else?"

Behind them, in front of them, they heard Belgians, Dutchmen talking, each in his own language, each with a partner.

"Come on, Papas! We go by village."

It looked . . . exactly and perfectly . . . the way it was supposed to look: a world, a life, in primary colors, and yet filled, at this afternoon moment, with depth and shadow. Along the foaming, noisy ocean, the sand took the sun's light and seethed citrus yellow. The pier modulated into a narrow ribbon of sun-bleached planks embedded in the sand, which shimmered with heat and undefined life, crabs and flies and silver water bugs. As they toiled along this plank road across the hard beach, the sweet, deep, impossibly lovely green and brown of coconut palms made a lacy border against parched cliffs (and yet, in L.A., he drove past palms every day, and thought nothing about them, except that they made good homes for rats).

And here were women — bare-breasted, finally — in sarongs; tattooed, bored, waiting, incurious. Here were children, naked and scampering in the liquid heat. A few goats. A few chickens. Thinking of the eggs which they must lay, watery and filthy and warm to the touch, Jerry felt his stomach turn.

The crew spoke to one woman — while the white men kept their glances to the ground, studying tiny lizards and a few shards of glass and tin. As money changed hands, a woman fatter than the rest, pregnant, surely, made her way through a small flock of goats that seemed, suddenly, to shy away.

She bent over the body of a young goat, her big breasts flopping down on either side of the animal's skinny backbone. Her arm went under the goat's neck. By heaving her weight against the animal she knocked it off its feet. With her other hand she tied its front hooves, then those to the rear. Two members of the crew scooped up the goat, snared it, slung it down, hanging from a double bamboo pole. They shook the goat, getting the weight right, so that it hung, head down, neck stretched out, its dainty hooves crossed and tied above the pole. The goat sobbed like a baby, and the rest of the little herd vamoosed into the scrubby jungle.

"Not exactly your *petting* zoo," Jerry muttered. Again, men in pairs mumbled to each other in their various, out-of-it European languages.

The Indonesians set out, quick-step, up a narrow, steeply sloped path. The growth here was thin and unattractive. With each step they took up into the sky, the air grew both hotter and less oppressive. To live here! Under this blue sky so clear, *so clear,* that if you looked up, and took your time about it, you might see stars and planets, even before the sun went down. The hydrofoil crew, he saw, four of them, not counting the goat-bearers, had positioned themselves, two at the front, two to the back, of the huffing Westerners. They carried long wooden poles, and repeated querulously, "Keep to da pat!"

"What a way to make a living," Loring grunted. But the older man had kept fit, his sickness had fallen away, and the climb didn't seem to bother him, the way it did some of the others.

The colors here! The dusky shadows of rock, the red earth that must be some continuation of the Australian land mass! Jerry realized that astronauts cocooned in their rockets who uttered such banalities about the universe they ventured into, must be — not dumb, but only dumbstruck. For the natives, this must be the same old hike, but for those who had eyes to see, each step took them closer to the sky. Scalloped sea foam crept upon the land. This was it, it, it.

More walking, more complaints from the soft Europeans, but Jerry went on, feeling the way he had a year ago at the Rock. Just as that day had offered a final, breezy triumph (that is, *you got to the top,* the way man was meant to do), this walk ended, and they found themselves on a mesa that opened onto a crevice which, in turn, formed a crease in the earth's crust. Jerry remembered that in *The Jungle Book,* Mowgli had lured his enemy tiger into a place like this, and buffalo had trampled Shere Khan to death.

Along the side of the cliff a rickety fence, slapped together with lengths of splintery, bleached wood, kept the tourists back. Pushing against each other, but at the same time hanging back, they attempted to get a good look down into the gorge. Were there *dragons* down there?

"Stand back, Papas! Stand back. *Stanbak.*"

One man, who had carried a coiled length of rope, made a loop, jerked it tight along the goat's silken neck. Jerry saw how easy it would have been to position the knot against the furred throat, to kill the damn goat *then* and be done with it, but the knot went to the back of the goat's neck, and the goat (just a kid really, why hadn't they let themselves see it?) stopped its pitiful crying and began to shriek.

"Holy shit." It was his own voice.

187

"You like, Papa? Good meal, huh?"

Now the guides, the escorts, were pushing the white men up against the splintered fence, so they could look, *had* to look, into the arid crevasse. The native who held the goat dropped it out over the cliff, unreeling his rope as it screamed and struggled. The air itself seemed to scream. A smell was added to the screams and the wavy air, and a sound of rattling and scratching, as the goat's hooves skittered on shale and rocks. From every side of the gorge the huge lizards came, hideous and speedy, heading for the goat. One tore off a hind quarter, then sat back to grind his jaws through the hotly bleeding leg. The goat screamed. Another lizard ripped away the other hind leg, and steaming intestines spilled onto red-caked dirt. Another dragon nosed through the offal, snapping up pulsing organs. Still the goat screamed. Then, from opposite directions, two more lizards came rushing and split what was left of the goat between them.

The man with the rope pulled it back up, carefully winding it, loop after loop, over his bare brown shoulder. "You like, Papa? We come back tomorrow." Behind Jerry, sounds of vomiting came. He turned and saw two men, their hands braced above their knees. One was a Dutchman, the other, Loring.

"We go back now. Two by two. Keep to da pat." With all their unconcealed scorn, the Indonesians did their job, jog-trotting with their lances held so that the Europeans, the Americans, big pink fools, were safely fenced from any hostile wildlife. And the natives weren't completely immune to this, because while the lizards, the dragons, hadn't fazed them much, the setting of the sun appeared to worry them a lot. They hurried along, they were skittish. This world wasn't set up for them. Or for anyone. Easy to see. Once you looked at it.

The village waited for them. The group had been scheduled to spend the night. The women had prepared a meal of fish and rice. After consulting the others, a Dutchman held a long conversation with the hydrofoil captain, but came back, defeated. "We have to spend the night here," he said, not looking at any of them. "There's no changing plans. He won't go back at night. The currents are treacherous, and devils live in the ocean."

Loring had his flask, and Jerry divided out what was left of his Dramamine. They sat at plain wood tables in a long house lit by kerosene lamps, drinking, and wordlessly took to their beds. In the morning, as the sun rose, they took off again, back to Jakarta. That airport, with its homely bedlam, its sign, BEWARE OF TOUTS, seemed almost laughable now. Jerry stood in the crowd in front of Loring's Garuda flight to Singapore, shoulder to shoulder with his partner, holding on to his luggage, viciously striking out at diminutive passengers who tried with all their might to push in front of them. "We're not supposed to take it personally," Loring panted. "*Malaam* is the Malaysian word for 'line.' Except that it means to push and shove . . ."

"And act like an asshole." Jerry had trouble with his voice.

Then there was nothing to say. They waited, shoved, kicked, got to the counter, picked up Loring's boarding pass. The officials wouldn't let Jerry into the waiting room, and charged Loring twenty dollars American to go through the door. Behind them an Englishman raved. "This is it. The straw that broke the camel! Underhanded dealings . . ."

"Withholding information," Loring murmured, and then shook hands with Jerry. "We'll find another place. It's a big ocean. You've still got a good trip in front of you."

"We've both got trips."

"Be careful."

"I'll get to L.A. before you do."

"Watch your step, Jerry, is all I ask."

Two hours before the biplane took off for Irian Jaya, Jerry went outside, walked along the dusty roads by the airport. The words of peddlers ricocheted off him. He bought sarongs for Wynn and Whitney and Tina. He found toy fighting cocks for Josh. Then he sat at an outside cafe and drank a Bin Tang beer.

No crazy crowds waiting for his plane. Only seven passengers. Four white men. Two brown men who looked like aborigines. A man in a business suit whose blue-black skin was furrowed with elaborate tribal markings and tattoos. The ride was long and turbulent. If the plane crashed into an island mountain or into the sea, they'd never find him.

The landing at Irian Jaya was uneventful. The smell of the place, a smell of fog and rot and decay and pesticide and coal fire and wood fire and some kind of food, seemed ordinary by now, the way a place was supposed to smell, the way the earth *was,* before it got cleaned up.

Jerry's troubles met him in the airport waiting room, when a tattooed bureaucrat pronounced his faxed visa from Singapore to be a forgery. His idea of obtaining papers to travel to PNG had to be a form of treason, since the two halves of New Guinea were soon to be at war, and the whole world knew it. He would have to wait here in this room for the provincial governor to OK his passage back to Jakarta. Or he might be jailed, "put in a house." The other passengers left this small, barnlike room and — how else could Jerry think of it? — melted into the jungle. Because here *was* jungle, the place he had imagined, so long ago.

No food here, no drink. They took the money he offered and put it in their pockets. Was he guilty now of bribery, besides everything else? A man wearing khaki shorts and carrying a gun came in to sit beside Jerry, a man as blue black as the marked businessman on the plane. (Jerry knew, from reading, from dreaming, that he must come from the Highlands.) No bed tonight. No booze. No long house. No rice. No fish. The man behind the counter fiddled with a radio, brought in a station across the Arafura Sea from northern Australia — crass accents, pop music.

These benches were dirty. A few insects buzzed around a lamp. Compared to the airport in Jakarta, the gorge in Komodo, this seemed a reasonable place. Windows, several of them, to the north and south, opened out onto a veranda on the one side, and onto the runway — with its hand-set torch lights — on the other. Windows to the east and west opened onto darkness, nothing, the jungle. At one of these windows, Jerry spotted a movement. Something, someone, outside, looking in. Jerry glanced at his guard, then gestured with his own head: Could he get up? Look out? The guard indicated with his body: Sure. Go on. You're not going anywhere.

Somewhat stiffly, Jerry stood. Quietly and slowly he measured off his steps to the streaked window. Exhausted, worn out, warning him once again, his heart began to pound. A man, a blue-black man, stood outside the window, taking a good look at Jerry. The upper part of his body was muscular, hairless, beautiful. His forehead and the area between his eyes had been dabbed with white ointment, in the same way a surfer — Jerry himself — might have used Noxzema. His nose, too, was covered with white goo, stippled on. All this was nothing, though, to a wide, flat, white-painted metal mustache that threaded through his septum, widened his nostrils, curled out far beyond where his cheeks ended and came back to entirely obscure his lips. On his head he wore a modish, teal-blue Aussie outback leather hat, with a hatband of darker, shiny blue, and two holes to string rawhide so that the hat might be fastened under the chin. Jerry, staring, turned his face slightly to the right. His left eye was better, *saw* better at night. The man outside turned his head to the left. Jerry put up his hand to the glass. After a minute, the man did the same.

I'm here, Jerry said from his heart, his soul. *I am here. I've come so far. I've come out here to see you.*

Jerry looked away first, worried that the guard might come up behind him. When he looked back, the man had disappeared.

P a r t 3

Keep me away from port or
whiskey. Don't play
anything sentimental. It'll
make me cry.

Van Morrison

We have the sentence that
mankind craves from
stories — the Maker of all
things loves and wants me.

Reynolds Price on
the Book of John
Incarnation

Wynn, Kathy
Whitney, Tracie
Josh, Tina
Baby Jonathan

Friday evening, Pacific Palisades September 21

"IT ISN'T AS THOUGH he didn't know about it. Not like he didn't have notice from *five weeks ago,* when he came back from that damn trip. I told him we didn't have any family life anymore and he said he wanted family life, but it was my responsibility to put it together. I even asked him, did he want to go to the circus, no big drive, just the one right here at the beach, and he said sure. Actually, I put it another way. I said I was planning to take the kids to the circus, and he said, 'Without *me*?' And I said, 'Get *serious,* Jerry! You're a good guy, but the last time you saw your kids, or my kid either, was back in the seventies sometime, wasn't it?' He didn't think that was funny. He got all miffed."

Kathy nodded her head. She was knitting an afghan and

having some trouble with it. Wynn had moved the furniture around in the screen porch once again. The hospital bed was gone, had been for months, but still this seemed the right place in the house to be. The two women lounged on a couch, their bare feet up on a coffee table, partly talking, partly watching a late afternoon talk show on television, keeping an eye on the room above the garage where the older girls were. The little kids were up there with them, Wynn's Tina, who'd been jabbering her brains out about the circus, and Kathy's Jonathan, who was coming up on his first birthday — how old was he now, ten months? — and just beginning to walk. Josh was around here someplace, playing in the main house with some kind of roaring robot-helmet stuck on his head. On television, the talk show man was pestering sad women who had been taken in by con-men sweethearts, asking them all sorts of mean questions: "How could you let him sell your house and put you into a rental property without signing something? At the very least you had to sign something, so why didn't you notice then?"

"Is he home yet?" Whitney banged in through the screen door bringing a blast of September air with her. "Can Tina and Jonathan have a drink? Some kind of fruit juice?" She glanced at the two empty bottles of Dos Equis on the table. "That stuff is going to put weight on you if you don't watch out."

"Look who's talking," Kathy answered idly, "Miss José Cuervo, right?" Her face, tanned and lined, was divided by a nice white smile.

Whitney shook her head. She'd take more from Kathy than she ever would from her mom. "Twenty-two inches," she said, and put her hand across her flat midriff. "We've got the youthful metabolism. You two are going to pay for every calorie. Anyway, Tracie and I are going on the True Diet. Very soon."

Wynn watched as her friend dropped a stitch and wondered if she should say something about it. The stitch just slipped off without her noticing. Would it matter in the long run? She turned on a lamp. Twenty minutes after four. What was she getting uptight about? There was still plenty of time. Still, she couldn't help saying to her daughter, "*You* haven't forgotten, have you? That we're all going to the circus?"

"*No,* Mom. I haven't forgotten. I'm getting them the juice, OK? I'm taking the whole carton."

They watched as she disappeared into the kitchen, heard her poke around in the refrigerator and appear again with carton and a short stack of paper cups. Because of Whitney — *and* Josh — they weren't allowed to have plastics in the house anymore. Josh, in the first two weeks of his first grade, had learned two things: an overwhelming fear of aliens and an equal fear that the planet was about to extinguish itself from pollution, like a candle flame in a mine going inexorably out. Last Sunday morning at breakfast, Jerry tried to reassure his terrified son. "There *aren't* any aliens, no aliens, no life of any kind on any other planet that our scientists have been able to find. So that's just a supposition, a hypothesis. There *aren't* any aliens!"

But Josh's teacher had said there was bound to be life out there somewhere, that because we hadn't found it didn't mean it wasn't there; that because we couldn't recognize it didn't mean it wasn't there. "It doesn't have to be in our image," Miss Holt had told her class, and Josh had repeated that fearfully to his father.

"*Softheaded!*" That's all Jerry had been able to come up with, which left Josh more scared than before. Tuesday of this second week of school, Whitney finally got the idea to buy him some noisy junk to fight off these aliens if they should ever come around and that's what Josh was doing now, rehearsing for the upcoming War of the Worlds. When Wynn asked Miss Holt about it, she said that was a stage every first grader went through — fear of the external world, after having been sheltered at home. Wynn thought, *Sure,* after you scare the *socks* off them, what other stage have they *got?*

The pollution promised to be more of a trial, a real problem. Because of Miss Holt, and only half a month into the semester, they had seven metal containers in their garage now, for newspaper, green bottles, white bottles, plastic, aluminum cans, the other kind of cans and cardboard. They had to bring in a Polaroid picture of Josh standing by the stacks of trash. Wynn worried. Shouldn't the containers be *half* full? If they were stacked high, wouldn't it look like they were neglecting things? Letting it all run away with them? Josh didn't think so, and he wanted containers made of mesh, so that the trash could be measured. This Wednesday he'd learned from the odious Miss Holt that the Amazon rain forests were being chopped down, so that Brazil could raise cattle, so that America could eat beef. He came home crying. "Just *a stage,*" Miss Holt had said to Wynn when she dropped her son off at school. "The first grade is *always* like this. I've told everybody. Children experience fear when they find out about the larger world around them. Then they calm down and learn to do something about it."

But Wynn was helpless to comfort her son. Again, it was Whitney who told her distraught half brother that most cows lived in the United States, the ones who ended up in an American hamburger, but that if it would make him feel better, why couldn't they try a new way of eating — no meat three times a week, and no more plastic in the house? That way the world wouldn't go out like a candle. And she took him out to buy a tree, which they planted in the yard.

Yesterday after school Whitney and Josh had gone through the kitchen stripping the place of Saran Wrap and plastic, and taken all of it down to a homeless center in Venice, south of Santa Monica. But last night, just before Josh's bedtime, Jerry had raised his voice at Wynn, at the kids. "What's the point of teaching anybody that stuff? Nobody's even proved this kind of thing. We're not going to save the world by planting trees. That's not going to do any good. *Listen,* Josh! By the time there's a problem, if there *is* a problem, we'll have the technology to fix it. That's what America's about. That's what the *world's* about!" By the time the lights went out in Josh's room, his father had the kid crying again, and one way or the other he'd used the word *moon* in conversation, which had sent Tina into a howling fit because, if Jerry ever came around, he'd know that whenever anyone used the word *moon* in her presence, she cried and said "the *moon,* the *moon,*" until the whole family went half crazy from it. You couldn't ask Tina *why* she did it, because to ask her, you had to use the word *moon,* which would send her off again. Besides, she was three years old. What could she say to any of them? Wynn thought that maybe her little kids were right. Maybe they knew what her husband didn't. Maybe the ozone layer above them really *was* shredding and tearing like a lace curtain above the earth. The world would go out like a candle, but it would catch fire first, from the sun's awful heat. Maybe their only hope was the moon.

Whitney hadn't been home the last two weekends. She stayed in her dorm room at UCLA, still partying with Tracie, but she seemed to have calmed down a little from her late nights, her partying summer. Thank God, thank God, she was getting so much better. Wynn was glad she wasn't home for this new round of Sunday breakfasts. Because Whitney was taking the Air Pollution class at UCLA with four hundred people in it, and they all went out on the roof of the Medical Center every day to measure how far they could see, and even from there, safely over on the West Side of the city, just a few miles from the beach, they could hardly ever see the Santa

Monica Mountains and sometimes they couldn't even see up to the north part of the campus. That's what Whitney said. And Wynn knew that if Jerry talked about technology — or even if he mentioned that a few hundred acres of jungle were ultimately going to have to be razed for planned communities or whatever the hell he had in mind — Whitney would sigh. Of course she knew his deal had fallen through.

How self-sufficient Whitney seemed now: how composed, how ready to take her share of responsibility. She was *calm*, with a calm Wynn never had, never would have. Last week, when Josh had come home howling from school, Wynn had asked her older daughter, "Did you use to get scared like this? I don't remember anything like this with you."

Whitney answered, "Sure, yes, don't you remember? Mr. Russo in the fourth grade said we were all going to blow up in a nuclear war, either that or the big quake. Remember, I cried because our house didn't have a basement?"

Wynn didn't remember. Not one thing. That other life was so far gone now. She didn't talk about it, she didn't think about it. What was the point of thinking about any of it? Or thinking about the ozone layer, thinning, tearing little by little, as if earth's delicate lingerie had been put in the wrong wash cycle?

The talk show finished. The world news, nightmarish for so long, lied through its teeth. Here in the city, things went on pretty much as usual. Gang wars, poor boys killing other poor boys, over a piece of sidewalk. A vagrant was squashed by mistake in a trash compactor. Kathy noticed the lost stitch five rows back, grunted.

A roaring noise approached. Wynn turned to see Josh in the kitchen doorway, his head encased in an anti-alien helmet. He was talking; she could see his lips move. "Turn it off!" she yelled. "*Take it off!*"

"When's Dad coming? Aren't we going soon? Do you think he forgot?"

"He's on his way. Why don't you go look in the refrigerator? You should have something to eat before you go. We won't be going out to eat until afterward." But the original plan had been an early dinner, and then the circus. Except that now it was after six. Fifteen, seventeen minutes after six. She looked over at Kathy, who peered carefully at the square she was knitting. "Dropped a stitch," she muttered.

"I saw."

"Listen . . ."

"It doesn't matter. It doesn't *matter*!"

"That's what you used to say, I bet. That's what I used to say."

So the past was with them.

"You want another beer?"

Kathy counted stitches. "Sure."

Wynn got up. Went into the kitchen. Pulled out another couple of cold ones. It really *was* like the old days.

Would Jerry notice when he came home? Would he care? No, no, no, no, no, no. Because he never noticed anything. Like it even mattered. Like she gave a shit. But that didn't mean she was crazy about the immediate future, the next hours, next day, next week. The planet, going out like a candle. The loneliness of getting old. *No!* Just the chickenshit next fifteen minutes when she'd have to tell the kids that they'd be going alone to the circus and what a lot of fun *that* was going to be.

But as she returned to the porch, Whitney and Tracie were already there, their hair outrageously backlit by the late setting sun, Tracie holding Jonathan, Tina tagging along.

"Mom? Is it OK if Tracie and I take the kids to the Cirque? Let's do it *that* way, because you don't need to see it. We'll take the kids and we'll be back by eight o'clock, nine at the latest. We'll bring back a pizza." Her daughter's eyes were free and serene, so why did Wynn feel like her own heart was breaking? It wasn't as if Jerry was fooling around with some dumb slut, and it wasn't even a real *circus,* for God's sake, that she — or the "family" — would be missing, just some French-Canadians with a little show down on the beach. Everything was fine, everything was swell. Her children were in her house, and her older daughter, who'd gone through so many trials with her in the old days, and come through such a bad accident, was such a wonderful woman, such a wonderful girl. Wynn knew, she *knew,* that if she could just hold on for another ten years, Jerry would have a moderate heart attack the way people like him often did. Then he would finally focus his eyes. Then she could talk to him. Except in that same ten years, Whitney would be out in the world, and Josh would be driving a car, and Tina would be thirteen and, my God, she was *already* such a handful . . .

"Because we were thinking," Whitney said quickly, "there are only five tickets, right? And this is Carmela's day off. So you, Kathy, Jonathan, Tracie, me, Tina, Josh, that's too many. So the best way is for you two to stay home."

"I'll carry Jonathan," Tracie said. "He can sit on my lap. That way if Mr. Bridges can make it, he can meet us at the circus and he won't —"

"He won't be left out," Whitney said, and silently added, There won't be anybody there like you to get mad at him, and spook the kids.

"Mom!" It was Josh, ready to go. "We're going to be late!" His anxious face was pale, his eyes blinking and sad from the time he'd spent under his roaring helmet.

"OK," Wynn said. "Why not? It's a good idea." She bent, found her purse and fished out the tickets. "You're going to drive carefully, right?"

Kathy asked her own daughter, "You sure you want to take Jonathan? He won't even know what he's seeing."

"He can stand up. Whitney says the tickets are right in the second row. He'll be able to see. He'll like it. Why *not,* you know? Since we're taking both these other little rascals."

Then, inexplicably, out of the blue, Tracie leaned down and took hold of Tina's little hands. "Come on, Sweet Lumps! We're going to see the Man in the Moon!"

"Not the moon! *Not the moon!*"

Tracie backed off, bewildered. Baby Jonathan began to wail. Josh, totally strung out, shrieked, "Does this mean we can't *go*? Does this mean we can't *go*? Shut up! *Shut up!*"

Wynn pushed the ticket envelope into her daughter's hand. "OK. *OK!* Just go. Thanks for doing this. We'll keep Tina here."

"What'd I *do*?" Tracie asked, but by then she'd started laughing, and so had Whitney. Because there was Tina, spinning like a top, howling like a banshee, about the moon.

"Go on, you don't want to be late! We'll stay here. Tina, will you *can* it? Use your seat belts, remember. All of you be sure to use your belts."

They were gone. Wynn caught the sound of the Volvo in smooth reverse. Then there was relative quiet, except for Tina's shrieks, which gradually lessened.

"What's *up* with her?" Kathy pointed at the wacked-out little girl with one of her long plastic needles, then asked her directly, "What's up, ding-dong?" But Tina only sniffed and shook her head.

"It's a word that begins with an *m*. It has to do with something that comes out at night." Wynn's sigh raked the air. "Something — don't say the word! — silver. Don't ask me why. Could *I* ever know why? The word sends her off. Tina, please! Will you come and sit up on the couch with me?" Wynn patted a place on the couch, the middle cushion. Still sobbing, but more quietly now, Tina climbed up, put her head in her mother's lap, her left thumb in her mouth, and pushed her feet against Kathy, right foot, left foot, kneading like a cat.

"If you're going to do that, you have to take off your shoes."

But Tina had already turned her head away from the light

and toward the squashy comfort of the back of the couch, determined to sleep.

"What I used to do," Kathy said, half watching the news, half watching her needles, "was wear this pair of pink shorts. I wore them the whole damn *time,* waking and sleeping. Under dresses and under jeans and over bathing suits. My mother was at her wit's end."

"I used to carry a salt shaker." Wynn didn't mention that she still had that salt shaker out in the garage somewhere — dotted with crimson nail polish, holding three pieces of gravel, an inch or two of thin steel chain, and magazine cutouts of Charles Bronson and James Coburn in their extreme youth. The gravel came from the construction site where she'd first been kissed — a soft wet kiss from a boy named Bobby. She'd been smoking a joint — *at her age* — and the gravel was magic, she knew it. Bobby! Thirteen, and as tentative and soft and as dubious about the whole thing as she was. She'd been twelve. But by the time she was sixteen she believed in the magic of the salt shaker in another whole way. The gravel, with its memory of the first kiss. The pictures of Charles and James. The thin steel chain, to pull in handsome, magic men. The salt shaker could make it happen; bring glamour and jokes into her ordinary life.

Her father had been a construction worker and her mother a fairly violent alcoholic, so one night, in a fit of piety, and wanting to meet a new set of boys, she took herself down to a Unitarian church. In no time at all she bought a sleeping bag, camped out with a youth group under stars, where a bearded minister sang them songs of brotherly love as he tried to prolong the sixties. But Wynn got caught by real life; pregnant at eighteen by the bearded minister, a married mother at nineteen. She sank down to the dead, dank, rented bottom of the San Fernando Valley.

"The best years of our lives." Kathy smiled, did her knitting. On the same wavelength once again. They hadn't known each other then, but they shared the past. Quite a few Golden Oaks parents carried that dark, unacknowledged DNA. Memories of sitting in shorts in sweltering Valley summers as their babies, whining little girls, babbling little boys, squatted in dry grass, smoothing the scorched backyard stubble with their baby hands. Young moms, hating to wash those kids (because motherhood wasn't such an *in* thing then), waiting until the diaper smell finally got to them. Then they'd strip those little tots and squirt them off with a garden hose, making a game of it . . .

Years and years; first married, then divorced, a dim-lit past, made up mostly of cooking. Breakfast. Lunch. Dinner. How sick Wynn had gotten of her poor first husband's soft blond beard, his limitations as a minister and as a guitarist. He loved her the way he loved God, and that was no compliment. He sang to her. And sat on his butt and watched her work. She heard him sing about the Spanish Civil War or the Vietnam War, and, in her vengeful mind, divided their sparse community property, planning ahead for a hard freedom. Still, Wynn kept the salt shaker. Waiting for the hard edge of a cheekbone, the irrational delight, the wit, the fun, the glamour she knew was out there, even though she knew now, for sure, that she'd never find it.

"Tell me again, how you snagged Sol." (Because Kathy, in her youth, had been worse off than she was. Married to an unemployed speed freak.)

"Oh, Wynn, *you* know how. I went to a computer place. I knew all the guys I'd grown up with couldn't hold a job, so I figured there had to be an equal number of guys who were working too hard to have any fun. Like they had their noses in a computer? *You* know the story. I've told you enough times."

"Tell me again, what you said." The sun was about to go

down. The room floated in twilight. Tina was dead to the world. Across from them, in a small bright picture, television represented another world to them. Sports, now. Baseball. Hit the little round target with your long hard stick. And it never struck any single man funny. Stupid! They were so bonehead stupid!

"First I went to Valley College, full time, for a year. *You* know all this stuff! I took Art History and Music Appreciation and Great Books and Geography and French. Then I went to a computer place and hung out, taking lessons. I told everyone I met that I came from Cincinnati, and that I was a widow. My husband had died of lung cancer at a young age, and that had shaken my faith in God. I said my little girl was used to the finer things in life. I couldn't give them to her because my husband had been just starting out in his profession when he was stricken, and we'd spent all our money in a futile attempt to *keep him alive*."

"And Tracie never cracked? She never let on?"

"I told her all she ever had to say about anything was, 'Oh, poor Daddy.' She's a pretty cool customer."

"So?"

"So, *what*? What are you asking me?"

"Was it the right thing? Did you make the right move?"

"If you ask me, you expect too much. Your expectations get up too high. The way you still talk about poor old Al . . ."

"That *Guy* Al! That's what we call him around here."

Kathy acknowledged it with a shrug. "I'm a thousand times better off than I ever was before. Sol lets me do as I like. And he's too old to cheat on me, and I always know where to find him. And I get to go to the ballet as often as I like."

They nodded together. It was what Kathy had told her twenty times in the last five months.

"Yes," Wynn answered abstractedly. She picked up the phone. "I'm sorry. I've got to call Jerry." She dialed one number, shook her head. "Not in his car. Why doesn't that surprise me?" She dialed again. "This is Mrs. Bridges. Is my husband still there? I'm afraid I *have* to interrupt him. Please put me through."

Wynn waited, hand over the phone, her breath coming in uneven gasps. "Jerry? This is Wynn? And I was wondering where you were? Because tonight is the circus? And you were supposed to be home by five?" She listened to his answer, watching a commercial. "No, they left already. They said they'd meet you there. No, I told you many times. Many times. You can . . . you can meet them there. *You'd better do it,* Jerry!"

She slammed down the phone with a mighty bang. "I can't take much more of this."

"You'll take it, though." Kathy reached out to turn on the lamp closest to her. "Because you have to. Besides. Jerry's a nice guy. He's *twenty* times nicer than poor old Sol."

"That *Guy* Sol?" But tears welled up in Wynn's eyes as she laughed.

"You expect too much. You know it, too."

"But listen, Kathy. Remember when you were married to Whoever? You told me he was always on your case for not sweeping up enough, and he'd look for dust bunnies under the bed and when the cat brought in that dead possum —"

"*Part* of a dead possum. The last *half* of a possum!"

"And you put it under the bed right at the place where he always stuck his nose? Because you were playing *hard*ball? Well, I can remember, before Al and I got married, someone in the congregation got a drunk-driving ticket, and he got so mad at the cops that he gave a cop-shooting party."

"You told me. You made him cop targets and everybody brought BB guns and stood out in the backyard blasting away at those pictures of cops . . ."

"And remember I told you when Al said, 'It's not *right* to

shoot at these cop effigies! Violence of any kind, even pretend violence, is not right.' God, he was tiresome!"

"He took his guitar into the living room, right?"

"*Yes!* But when the neighbors complained and cops came —"

"The *real* cops!"

"Poor old Al gave the same goddamn sermon he gave every Sunday morning and every other living hour of the day and night! 'It's not *right,* officers, to come storming into someone's house with your guns drawn!' He said later they just looked at him, *stupefied,* while he went on and on, and outside, we were so *stoned! God.* Have I told you how stoned we were? Running back and forth the length of the backyard like we were in a three-legged race, taking down the cop pictures off the targets? I *never* laughed so hard. And Al waited as long as he could to give us a chance to get those pictures down, and then he pulled that mournful face — he was so proud of himself that day. He said, 'All right, officers, I want you to know I'm not part of this party, that's why I've absented myself into this living room so I can play the chords to 'The South Coast is a wild coast and lonely . . .'

> '*You can win at the games at Olon!*
> *But a lion still rules the barrancas!*
> *And a man there is always alone!*'

And when he finally took those two bruisers out to the backyard, there were eight of us, nine of us, but the targets were gone. And everyone was so nice to Al the rest of the afternoon. Which was all he ever wanted anyway. Poor guy." Once again, Wynn felt the tears well up. Her hands were tangled up with Tina, one under her neck, the other in her curls, so the tears couldn't be dashed away. She felt them draining, pouring, whatever. She sniffed, and looked at her friend. "Do you think we got gypped or not?"

Kathy shook her head, concentrating on her knitting. She'd already given her advice for the day.

But Wynn remembered: a past she could never get back into. A two-bedroom home out on Victory Boulevard, and every single dish and plate came from Pier One, and the rug she swept and vacuumed every day cost ninety-nine dollars, a deep blue fake Oriental that showed every single separate cracker crumb. She remembered a terrible, terrible chair made of iridescent fake gold velvet that got dirtier and dirtier but never, never lost its shine. She remembered how angry she was all the time she lived with that poor guy Al, and how he'd wept sloppy tears when she left him, and what hard work it had been from then on, until she'd met Jerry.

On a tennis court. Because her plan, after Al, although different in particulars from Kathy's, had been uncannily the same. She'd taken up tennis. Wynn's only subterfuge hadn't been hiding the fact of "that guy Al," or her first marriage, or those dark years afterward, but her fury about how things had turned out. Her knowledge that life was grimy. A knowledge that Jerry never had, never would have. Wynn had turned every bad thing she knew about the world into sexual tricks, so that for the first five years of their marriage he'd never known what hit him. She'd jumped his bones the way she'd swept Al's fake carpet. Fiercely! With persistence! Now Jerry was drifting off into deals and notions and car phones. But he'd never leave her for another woman. She knew that like she knew the front page of the *Times*.

So what was bugging her? A siren started down on the Coast Highway, a long yipping sound like a howling dog. Inland, somewhere in downtown Santa Monica, another siren answered.

"Did you hear something?" Kathy looked up at the windows which faced out onto the safe green backyard.

"Just the sirens. They're always doing that."

"A car went down the street. Didn't you hear it?"

"I guess I need something to do. I'm getting a little strung out."

"You're coming down off all that worry about Whitney. It's natural that you'd have a reaction."

It's not that, Wynn wanted to say, to shout. Our youth is gone, my dear, dear friend! We haven't lived the lives we should have! Somewhere between poverty and riches, we lost it. We're alone. Yes! We are. When we had some good things, we didn't recognize them. Even now, with another set of good things, I can't feel them. *You* can't feel them. Can this really be it, life? The Big Deal? This can't really be it, this dread, this dissatisfaction, this imperfection in the midst of so-called perfection, the suffering I saw in Whitney, the indifference at the heart of the world!

Again, Kathy answered her thoughts. "I told you before, you expect too much. You make yourself unhappy." She spoke impatiently. With a sharp gesture she put Tina's feet down on the couch, got up, went to the french doors, opened them. "Do you smell something? Does the sky look funny to you?"

"It's getting dark, is all. Listen to this, Kathy, and don't get on my case for complaining. Why do you think people don't get stoned anymore? Why is it, when we give a party, everybody says they only want a Perrier or a white wine but then we open the cupboard and all the scotch has disappeared, and nobody's even had a good time?"

"I don't know." Kathy disappeared down the hall. Wynn heard her opening the front door, could hear her, feel her, looking, first inland, then down the street toward the palisades, the grassy strand, the edge of the cliffs and the thin ribbon of sea you could just see from their front porch.

"Something's happened." Kathy was back, looking puzzled. "The hedge at the end of the street by the palisades? It's gone. There's smoke coming up . . ."

The phone rang. Wynn signaled with her body that she was holding Tina's head, and would Kathy mind getting it?

She sat, annoyed with Jerry, anticipating another excuse. And maybe what she'd said about numbness was true, because she watched with no more and no less than her usual dread, as catastrophe mashed her friend's face.

"What is it? What's wrong?"

Tina woke. "The *moon*," she cried. "The *moon*."

"It's nothing at all. I'm sure of it. But we'd better get in the car and go see."

Robin

Pacific Palisades

WHEN THEA TOLD WHITNEY there was no such thing as an accident? I was there for that, I was interested in that. When she said, "That boy just slipped out of his body. He doesn't even know he's dead. He may be still, you know, hanging around with a smile on his face waiting for something to happen," I had to pay attention. I took it badly, I admit, standing around, as I was, in radio-and-dreamland, blinking, trying to get used to new doses of light and time and thought.

I was there. I was there. I was there, smiling, as that English lady surmised, in the fingers of the doctor when he sewed up Whitney's lip. As I was in the breast of my little sister as she sat on the ramp in the school theater, and everyone was saying nice things, but I was in her blood and felt her saying to me,

It's your own damn fault, and she was right, I guess, I see, I guess.

I was playing dumb, at some level, sending out the message, who *me?* Playing dumb, playing sweet, at the corpuscle level; not just watching "Robin" tumble around on the screen but being Robin, being the screen, being my mom, being my dad, being that grief, and still feeling, Hey! Like, hey?

Like, *hey?* Where's the *party?* Because also I was by that time part of the buzz, the whole proton/neutron buzz, a piece of egg yolk being whipped into an omelet, but not yet, a speck of gasoline waiting for my second in the carburetor, but not yet, not yet.

I was a part of, and remembering, in absentminded ways, what I'd learned in school about the music of the spheres. I was a note in the music now, thinking that the reason they called some things archangels was because the whole thing is set up in arches, in circles maybe. I don't know. Intelligence was never my strong suit. I was lovable. I was funny. I could get anything I wanted by love. No! I *had* everything I wanted because of love. I was happy.

So the grief thing was strange. The suffering thing was strange. I didn't recognize it. I was like . . . reading a magazine, not paying attention, the rest of the world far far far far away. I was the blond hair on Whitney's head, I was especially present along the back of her neck. I was present in my old room. Or I lay back, resting and calm, between the sad hot bodies of my parents the way I did as a kid, and then I arched around, picking up material the way you pick through a magazine, just skimming, feeling alive and feeling at home, caught between my parents, whisking along on the back of Whitney's neck with exactly the same sense of bratty happiness I'd always had. So when that woman said, *He's probably hanging around with a smile on his face waiting for something to happen,* it cut through me, the way some teacher's acid remarks cut through a classroom daydream. *What* was the question?

I did what I always did, I smiled, and passed on the commotion. Because my whole being this time was to wear an invisible cap on my head with bells on it, to turn cartwheels that broke lovably in the middle to test the patience of others. To provide joy.

So when Thea said that, I shivered. Pulled myself together for a blink; tried to see what I was a part of. My mother, in a supermarket, put her face in her hands and cried. My sister put her head on her desk and cried. I was their tears. My father, in his office, picked up a letter opener in his right hand and stabbed the back of his left hand; I was the blood. The hair on the back of Whitney's neck stood up. I was in the air, on the back of her neck.

So after that, I "knew." But it's all the same. It's *all* the same. Just as *you* can know, and not-know, "know" and still be in the total dark about what your knowledge means, that's how I was, how I am, how I will be. I see my past, pasts, I guess. I see my caps with bells.

What I know now is only this: things go in golden arches. The man in this life who made that idea go with food was divinely inspired. Things go in arches and circles and they hum. They make a noise as they pass by. To think of a place is to be there. To think of a boy is to be him. To think of a girl is to be her.

My sister alone that first night after they all came home looked at my picture, smiling and sweet, dopey as hell, and got it absolutely right, before she, too, went into grief. "You lameshit!" she said, looking at my picture, and I was her and I was the picture, and I was by then a part of the hum, of the matter arching around the earth in spheres, so I didn't pay much attention.

Not that I ever did.

Waiting for something to happen was the other part of

what had happened to me, and so? I waited. Because I could see, at the very least, I was part of a crowd, a field of particles over the Pacific Coast Highway. The sufferers, the curious, all that. And I looked at all that, and looked at what was wrong, because my purpose on earth was a cap and bells and a cartwheel broken off in the middle, and the trying of other people's patience. The tears and blood and sorrow I felt were only part of the accident.

Because accidents must happen! What kind of a place would it *be* if a few accidents didn't come down? Even I could see that. I could see it both ways and every way. But that wasn't what I was here for. I could see suffering, hear it. I could arch away across the world and see places where suffering, seriousness, sadness, sorrow, were the order and the norm, but it wasn't mine. It wasn't the norm where I'd lived.

Where I was now was a place where the placid golden face of hand-carved Buddhas ruled, and glitter fell from them, and calm afternoons with flowers ruled, and only in certain lights did the wide blue eyes of Kali flash with pale rancor or lack of rancor, arching out, sending screams into the afternoon, for fun, to remind people — just to remind them. My cap and bells stood against those flashes of pale blue light. I said, I *always* said, "Don't listen to that pale blue scary stuff! Do a cartwheel like this! Let's go in the car and get some coffee!"

Looking for love, but not the sorrowful kind. When my mother would think of me, I'd arch back over to her darkened room, by her sad body, feel her loss but feel, jeez, Ma! Get off my back, willya? Sometimes she'd sit up. Go look out the window. Or, in between sobs, pick up a copy of *Vanity Fair,* not thinking of anything, and I'd think, *That's better*! Because I wasn't put on earth to be responsible for *this* kind of shit! But she was so far away from getting the picture that I slid away and off it; forget it, it isn't worth it. Pain is pain and it *always* hurts, whether you're a mom without a kid or a tomato getting sliced or a car changing into scrap metal. And that wasn't what I was hanging around for, waiting for something to happen.

Which is why I hung with Whitney. Her arm hurt like a bastard after the accident, and she was sorry about me but in the light way I appreciated. What had happened to her after the first months of pain was: she woke up every morning or in the middle of the night, and while she got mad or sad, her main swish was the *swish,* the breeze of happiness, and the close attention now that she paid to being alive. I was there when she patted the baby and the baby patted her. The baby was saying, "This isn't too *bad,* this *life,* with people / things / ideas / stuff like this in it. I made a good choice, far out, far *out!*" When I danced, lodged like a pulsing invisible heart, on the back of her neck underneath her hair, I felt her joy in the music, I *was* her joy in the music. And I saw, in instances, the kind of man I would have been, should have been, plenty of black, curly hair, an actor, good television parts, a kind wife and decent children and a good house, just enough fooling around to keep myself and everybody else in a good mood. Intelligence wouldn't have been my strong suit: I would have had joy and love.

Well, I *did* have joy and love, wasn't that it? When I arched to Hawaii, *at her express thought,* at her unexpressed words bright in her pleasure-blurred brain, *Oh, Robin, I'm thinking of you now,* I lodged in her neck, then on her breastbone, then in her hand, which reached out across the sand to Tracie's. I felt what I'd never felt either in my life or out of it, love without strings, love without winning, love without ache (although the man above her ached and ached; he yearned for stuff I knew wasn't important in the long run). But I was the beach and the sound and the fun. The sound! Close to humming, you know?

Whitney felt joy. She felt love. She felt happiness. She held it like a transparent piece of china. She turned over in it like a seal in the water. She put it on like a coat. She held it like she held that baby. Which is one of the reasons I stayed with her during that blink.

For the last few months there had been a French circus down on the beach, just north of Santa Monica pier in a neat little corner under the cliffs of the palisades. I'd seen it last year, when it came. My folks had taken me to that one-ring circus that didn't have animals and was just one long wonderful joke. For me, it was something to see. They were people just like me, cap and bells: you could leap in the air forever and pile forty-two people on one little bicycle, and people would love you for it. Now I saw that while they wore sequined jackets with messages like YOU TOO CAN BE A STAR, they were really *French,* you know? They spent a lot of time out on the sand rehearsing, working hard, and almost as much time arguing (in French) where they should eat. Tonight, between shows, a twenty-eight-year-old guy named Jean Pierre who worked with the lights said he was sick and tired of the food at the Belle Vue up on the cliff just across from the pier. He said he'd drive north between shows to a place above Malibu that sold fresh oysters right out of a barrel of salt water. They talked about it, and another French couple took a car and went south, over to the Boulangerie for baguettes, and a cake for somebody's birthday. Another guy went inland on Wilshire for a case of Dom Perignon from the discount liquor store across from the car wash.

At about the same time an Asian couple from Inglewood, driving an Olds, pulled away from their shabby home. They planned to spend the weekend in Santa Barbara at the Villa Rosa — a hundred and ninety dollars a night but it was worth it. The husband, Eric Ming, worked as a systems analyst. His wife stayed home and was going nuts with fear and worry. There were gang shootings all around the house but Eric knew that if they could just stay there for about four more years they could sell their place and buy a decent house at the beach. Amy Ming was Hawaiian Chinese. She wanted to go back to the islands, and cried with homesickness most of the time. Eric, without talking much about it, had embarked on a campaign of appeasement, so that Amy wouldn't bag it all, saying "I want to go back to Hawaii. I can't stand it in this cold and awful place." On some weekends like this, some treats might slowly, sweetly, straighten her mind, keep her here, on the mainland. They turned north onto the San Diego Freeway, west on the Santa Monica, then down through the McClure Tunnel out onto the Pacific Coast Highway — the ocean tinted midnight blue, with a little last hint of the day's pink, and about seventeen stars in the sky, the very brightest that Amy had ever seen. She welcomed the crisp, clear Pacific night and began to think that California, and her life, might be all right.

In a parking lot out on the beach, Whitney and Tracie wearily struggled to get the kids in the car. The circus had been great, the total best, but now that it was over, the starch had gone out of all of them at once. Jonathan, strapped to Tracie's chest in one of those canvas strap things, was snoring, literally snoring, and it gave the two girls and Josh the giggles. "If he does that when he's a year old what do you think he'll be like when he's twenty? Or *forty*?" He began snoring in the parking lot, and in the car, as they waited for the traffic to clear. It was almost impossible to turn north onto the highway. The traffic was fierce.

But they did. Just after Eric and Amy, just in front of Jean Pierre. They detoured inland, and came back down.

The traffic heading south was pretty normal for a fall Friday night. I saw a big beige American car with about eight Mexican illegals, just rousted from where they lived under a bridge up in Topanga Canyon. They'd had a close call with the INS; very close, too close. Their sadness at losing all their stuff under the bridge was drowned in relief at getting away, still being free! They would head south, go under that McClure Tunnel and zoom across town, all the way on over to the East Side! Tonight they'd listen to music; they'd party. Tomorrow, they'd party some more. Then Sunday mass, and another party. *Monday,* they'd worry. *Si porque tomo tequila, mañana tomo jerez!* They passed a bottle of tequila around in the car, none of them worrying, none of them drunk.

Far above them all, at the intersection of Seventh and Georgina, a divorcée in her thirties who'd come back home to live with her long-suffering parents, hung up the phone on her ex-husband. Tomorrow morning he was going to marry some bimbette, up in a chapel in Malibu Beach, but the divorcée wasn't going to stand for it. She'd been thinking for months about the best way to spoil their wedding, and she was up for it. She went outside, got in her mother's old Chrysler and strapped on the seat belt. Forgetting to smile or wave at her house, forgetting to hate or even say goodbye, she headed the Chrysler west, toward the Pacific Palisades. She floored the pedal, let out the clutch, pressed it again, hit second, settled for hard-grinding third. Like a plane, like a plane taking off. Sixth, fifth, fourth, third, second, the streets ticked off to the beach.

Even her intention was not strong enough to divert traffic traveling north and south on Ocean Avenue. She saw the faces of two old people as her mother's Chrysler pushed their Japanese compact *out of the way* and onto the grass strip. She saw a cyclist skid *out of the way* and give her the finger, watched his face arrange itself in astonishment as her mother's Chrysler crashed through the guard rail and took wings in a short but astonishing arc out over the Pacific Coast Highway.

It hovered in the air, losing momentum. Gravity took it. Thoughtless, the divorcée steered. The Chrysler pancaked directly onto Whitney's mother's Volvo, which skidded westward in front of the beige American car with the eight Mexicans, who swerved to the left to avoid it and caromed into the Oldsmobile of Eric and Amy Ming. Behind them all, to the south, Jean Pierre, the workman from the Cirque du Soleil, slammed on the brakes, but he'd slowed to watch; had seen the golden, graceful arc, the headlights swishing through endless air. Entranced in the spectacle, he forgot, for a twentieth of a second, to put on his brakes.

His car slammed into the wall of tangled metal. Eric Ming was alive and aware and in unsupportable pain, knowing his back was broken, his wife was dead. He had made — from his limited point of view — a terrible mistake. But the slam of Jean Pierre's car ended his agony. Within the showers of broken glass, and fire that started up from leaking gas tanks across seven lanes, and showers of sparks, and pinging, flying metal, *I began to hum, and to come alive, and to watch, and to wait for something to happen.*

A ragged sheet of flame came up, a curtain across seven lanes of highway. Pieces of box hedge the divorcée's car took out on its way down lodged in its grille now, like straws in a farmer's mouth. Then they caught fire. The noise of the cars still echoed, as their metal bodies clattered and clanged into new shapes. Other cars and trucks going north and south screeched to a stop. People began to pour out, but backed away as soon as they did. This whole thing was an explosion waiting to happen, so you saw curiosity warring with caution: people looking at all this bright and gaudy stuff, peeking at it through their fingers, willing to risk the burn to the backs of their hands for the chance of seeing this once-in-a-lifetime panorama.

Then the heroes began to run forward to attack the wreckage and pry out the victims, but some ran back, vomiting and crying. Some stayed, in the terrible heat and bad danger, using their own tire irons to see if they could force open doors and break out windshields, while others yelled at them to *Stand back! Be careful!* All over the West Side, fire trucks and cop cars began their trip to this "accident," since many men in the clogged traffic carried car phones and had immediately dialed 911 to report the amazing sound and light.

Altogether fifteen people would die — one of them a rescuer who inhaled burning gasoline. The car full of Mexicans went up all at once in a puff of ignited fuel. In essence, they died together, and together thought of their lost lives, their lost wives and children, and how long it would take for their families to find out; how their loved ones so far away would suffer more and more, but at least the glory, the *size* of this accident would guarantee that they might live in memory, maybe get to have a *corrido* written about them. They smiled as they thought about it; ascended, and left. They sailed instantly away to the East Side.

The blood of Eric and Amy Ming slid from the front door of their Olds, blackened and reddened the highway. As it slipped closer to the double-decked cars, the Volvo with the Chrysler on it, the heat from the car of burning illegals caused the Asian blood to sizzle and scorch. The smell of burning flesh and blood filled the air. A sound of screaming joined with sirens, an aria of sorrow and terror; and men joined, in tenor voices, *Oh God, Oh my God.*

But the God they were thinking of wasn't present. This one was a goddess with bright blue eyes and golden arms that arched across seven lanes of traffic. At first her eyes rolled back into her head so that all you could see was that fathomless, aimless, endless pale blue: I am Nothing! I am Chaos! There is Nothing behind my eyes! And I myself am nothing! So much for all your hopes and dreams! Then her eyes clicked back into focus and she surveyed the mess, the brightness, the carnage, the red and yellow lights, and just thinking of the *traffic jam* that was coming tonight to the West Side of this cosmopolitan metropolis, the inconvenience, the changed plans, the skewed points of view, the garden-variety night-mares, the *sig-alertness* of it all, she began to smile and to show her teeth, which happens no more than once every ten years in any spot on the earth's shell. Children as far south as San Diego began to screech. Women fainted, men had heart attacks and died. She didn't have to count the dead, she had a feel for that sort of thing, and her smile widened into a grin. One survivor. And the rest . . . will change. She opened her mouth and her teeth flew out into the popping flames and stinking smoke. Change, yeah! That's what I'm about! So don't go getting your plans in order, any of you within the sound of *my* mind! Or I'll send this whole coast over to Japan! Her eyes rolled back again to pale blue, she disappeared, if she ever disappears. The ambulances and fire trucks rolled up the center lane. The heroes worked with bitter determination. They had no sense of anyone living out of this.

Did I say that Jean Pierre was actually the first to sail away? He lingered at the margin, watching for a while until most of the flames went out, then, orienting himself in time and space, he clicked back to the circus, where they were get-ting ready for the nine o'clock show, fretting that the bleachers weren't filling because of the accident up the road. He took a place a few feet above where he always stood, a much better view, and waited for the show to begin. His friends, with a lot of French exasperation, gave up on the oysters and sent some-one else across the street to the Boulangerie again, to get some paté to go with their champagne.

The Mexicans were *so cool,* and so clear about what they wanted, that over on that East Side parking lot where Mari-achis wait for jobs on weekend nights, a young girl with a vi-olin, ordinarily very respectful and silent, glad to be able to play with the big boys, drew her bow across the strings of her instrument and played nine pure notes: "Ochos Muchachos de Topanga." It would not be her first song, but it would make her reputation, and in the first decade of the twenty-first century as she waited in lavish, beflowered dressing rooms to appear before audiences of thousands, in this city, she'd remember that she'd begun to write the *corrido* before she heard about the boys, and figure, flat-footedly, that's what it meant to be an artist.

> *"Ocho muchachos de Topanga*
> *Viveron una vida tranquila*
> *Debajo del puente en la barranca . . ."*

The Asian couple died as they lived, not speaking. Amy zoomed to bright stars; Eric clamped himself down into an intelligent computer. I began to realize my place at this time and hummed *louder*: the vibe of curiosity, pleasure, my own kind of intelligence, cap and bells. There remained, at the center of this set of fireworks, the two cars, and the set of souls I was supposed to be interested in. A truck, a crane, had come by now. They came to lift the Chrysler off the safe Volvo, oh, sadness! Families by this time had been notified, or found out (because out at the edge, this city of millions broke down into neighborhoods of hundreds). In this beach traffic there were people who knew these cars by make and license plates. Cars had made U-turns out of traffic and driven to pay phones (or used car phones) so that from different directions, families came. The divorcée's parents, unwilling to believe it, already believed it, since they had stopped where their street met the cliff and seen the hole in the hedge, and seen for themselves that the Chrysler was missing. They knew, they knew. Still that woman waited, dead as a doornail, but smiling her mean smile until they drove up, and only then allowed the car to be lifted with a great groan from the Volvo. Only then did she send a last message to her ex-husband: Have a nice wedding! Then she disappeared into a parallel universe. I felt better right away: there must be some reason for people like that, but I didn't want to know the *reason*, OK?

From the north, two women, with much more doubt and disbelief and hesitation, made their way down Santa Monica Canyon to the highway. "We've been told . . . We've gotten calls . . ." Wynn drove, trembling. Beside her Kathy sat, her hands covering her eyes. Behind them in the back seat, Tina shivered under a blanket, sucking her thumb. She had developed a fever and a sore throat, and that sickness would be connected in her memory forever with what was going to happen next.

And that . . . that was . . . not so hot. The two women stood, pressed back by cops made brutal by the nature of their work. The women took out their terror on the young men in the blue suits, who even hit them a few times to "calm them down." The little boy in the back of the Volvo was crushed. He was so tentative, so *not there,* I didn't even see him. His body was unrecognizable; so was the rest of him. Wow! It was pretty bad! His mother couldn't take it in, and now she began to moan a terrible sound. Whitney had totally bitten the big one, boy, she was deader than I was, and *then,* for a change, I got it. I turned up my hum, and turned it up again. Oh, hm, hm, hm, I'm feeling so alone, Whitney, Whitney, Babes! And flashed my dopiest sweetest smile into the furry air, and did half a cartwheel, flashed my cap and bells. Hm, Whitney! *Hey!*

Is this what it is? she asked, clear and polite; beautiful as always.

Hm, I told her, as we folded together into one. Hm. Better. Hm. Oh, yeah. Better.

But still, we both knew, we had to wait around for something to happen. I knew, for this blink, I was only there for comfort and for curiosity. Just take it for what it is, I said / telegraphed with all my might. Take it for cosmic Jello. A cartwheel, half finished.

Down on the ground they didn't see it that way. Even I had a hard time as I saw the three men on the Volvo's passenger side working with what they call the jaws of life. They pried Tracie out of death's throat, they held her down when she thought she was already safe, in darkness. They screamed through the window at her until she opened her eyes. They held smelling salts under her nose until she shook her head irritably, then they told her not to move, she might hurt her neck. They asked her who the president was. They told her to put her hands at her sides, to keep them there. She knew what that meant and disobeyed them.

Her eyes were brown, brown eyes, and like a trapped dog's, a coyote's trapped in a trap, where she or he is looking at chewing off a leg. She or he will do *anything* to avoid the immediate future. But there is no way that future will or can be avoided. The door of the car came off. "Don't move, don't move!" they yelled at her, as if they owned her suffering and her affliction, but she put out an arm to push them away and the apparition she presented was such that none of them could bring themselves to touch her, to push her back. She got to her feet unsteadily and stood in the bright glare of every kind of light. Now it was Whitney's mother who hid her face in her hands. And Tracie's mother, alone, who stepped forward, flinching, to her daughter, who could move no more, and ashamed, turned her face away from her mother's as they clasped the last crushed baby, still strapped to Tracie's breasts, between their two broken hearts.

Don't look, I advised Whitney, as strongly as I could. Pay no attention to that at all. Just hum. Along with me.

■
===
■

Jerry

─────────

**Westwood
September 30 –
October 7**

THESE FUNERALS USUALLY were easy to set up but this one
was hard. Kathy's husband was Jewish, when he thought
about it. He felt that baby Jonathan was Jewish. He knew it
didn't conform to Jewish law, but he knew it was true. He
blamed his stepdaughter and her girlfriend for the death of his
son, and threatened lawsuits, not against the divorcée in the
Chrysler, who was, anyway, dead, but against the Bridges
family. Wynn, crazy with grief, knew only one thing. She
would not allow a Christian service: she blamed Whitney's
"real" father for everything, and sobbed that she would not
allow a sermon to be said over her daughter's body.

It was unbearable to think of having separate funerals. Un-
thinkable to have a "light memorial."

People behaved badly. Josh's first grade teacher called to offer her condolences and Wynn grabbed the phone. "You made his last two weeks *hell*!" she screamed. "Couldn't you have let him alone?" Miss Holt had a hard time of it, because her first graders, scared to begin with, were afraid to get in cars to come to school. When they got there, they wept easily. Pressed to give answers about the afterlife, she could only hedge, caught between vigilant Christians and Jews, and even a Muslim or two.

People blamed Whitney. Wasn't that her second accident in under a year? Was there cocaine in her system? Hadn't she been driving recklessly? Yes, they *knew* about the divorcée's Chrysler, but kids drove so badly now.

The wedding of the divorcée's ex-husband got postponed, then canceled. He sent flowers to all the dead. The *Times* ran an interview of him in the View section. A man from the INS, an unpopular man with heavy jowls and crimpy hair, blamed the whole thing on the illegals, who he said had been driving without lights. He asked for a clampdown.

Jerry stayed home. Carmela took care of Tina, who was so sick for a couple of days that it looked as if it might be a clean sweep in the Bridges house — no children left at all. Wynn was lost to the world. She stayed in their bed. He camped out with Tina and Carmela. He brought home Patty from the office to answer the phone, which never stopped ringing. He had to go down to the morgue and identify Josh. He had to OK an autopsy on Whitney and let them do all kinds of tests.

He couldn't think of what came next. When reporters called from the *Times* and the *Outlook* to ask for pictures, he turned them down. When they asked when the service would be, he told Patty to say they didn't know. When they asked what charities should be remembered, he told Patty to say they didn't know that either. No, nothing to do with drugs. No, not AIDS. Not even the tree people. He didn't know.

He'd heard of people who behaved well in a crisis. But he could only admit — he had just found out — he wasn't one of them. When people called from the office to ask if there was anything they could do, he had Patty say no, there wasn't. When Al Geffin, Whitney's father, called and insisted on speaking to his ex-wife, Jerry told Patty to say she wasn't home.

After two days he steeled himself and called Kathy's husband. Because Tina's fever had gone down. And Wynn wasn't talking. Something had to be done.

They arranged to meet at Sol's country club. The man who rose stiffly off a bench in the waiting area was old enough to be Jerry's father. He wore a white shirt and yellow slacks with a sansa belt, and white patent leather shoes. His tan face was splotched with crying, his small eyes reddened by tears.

"She won't go for a synagogue. So you do it. Do what you like."

Jerry realized, as golfers rushed past them into the building, that they weren't going to have lunch. They weren't even going to sit down together.

"We'll have a coffin. But there's nothing to put into a coffin."

Jerry fought his terrible paralysis. "We'll do the service together then? Is that all right with you?"

The old guy was crying. But at the end of ten minutes the two men had decided on the funeral home at the corner of Wilshire and Westwood, the crowded place behind the bank on the corner, hidden by skyscrapers now; the place where Marilyn Monroe had her crypt. "I'll ask the guy at their school," Jerry replied. "Because the kids went there —"

"Not *my* kid," the old man cried. "He never went anywhere at all."

"But is that all right, as an arrangement? Can I have my girl go ahead and make the arrangement?"

"Sure," the old man said bitterly. "You go ahead and do that." He went to the heavy doors to the main part of the club, opened them, disappeared. The receptionist gave Jerry an icy stare.

The principal of the school didn't want to do it this time. "Can't you get someone else?" he asked. "I don't think I can handle much more of this."

"Look," Jerry said. They sat together in the principal's cluttered office. And through smudged glass windows they could both see typists and student-help together in the outer office, whispering about them. "You have to do it. Because I don't know anybody else to ask."

A thousand phone calls went out. Cars parked at the many-storied lots at the Wilshire and Westwood corner. Some passersby thought there might be a sneak preview at the nearby Amco theater. The chapel filled an hour ahead of time, and the management hustled through the courtyard with folding chairs.

Almost the whole last graduating senior class of Golden Oaks was there. Some kids who had already gone off to eastern colleges came back for this night. All the parents from Josh's first grade class were there, the mothers crying, the fathers fearful. Everybody from Bartch, Bridges, Freed was there, even though Jerry had sent out a memo saying it wasn't necessary for them to come. A dozen couples from the San Fernando Valley were there, having read about it in the paper, turning up for old times' sake, either for Kathy or for Wynn.

Couples from Sol and Kathy's country club showed up in somber groups, overdressed, clattering with metal accessories. Some people whose hearts weren't involved in the grisly proceedings whispered to each other, pointing out the gulfs between Jew and Gentile, old and young, rich and poor. And many young men showed up, the boy from 31 Flavors on San Vicente, a postman who worked the Palisades, the man who had given Whitney her driving lessons — all the boys and men who had ever been in love with Whitney. And all the faculty from Golden Oaks, the upper, the middle and the lower schools. And everybody from Temporary Success — Miss Neimenthal, Maria, Ed, Anita.

The chapel was banked with flowers. They ranged across the three tiered coffins: Whitney's at the top of this Protestant, nonsectarian sanctuary, then Josh's, then — heartbreaking — the baby-size box for Jonathan. White, all white, the coffins and the flowers around them. On one side the Bridges family sat, hidden by a fabric veil. On the other side — barely visible — Kathy, Sol, Tracie, and a family that Jerry didn't know. There was no music. After the chapel and the courtyard and most of the parking lot had filled to capacity, the principal got up to speak. He gripped a blond wood pulpit. The three coffins stood between him and the assembly.

But his voice faltered. His voice broke. The congregation whispered and coughed.

"Our casualties are too great. Our young men. Our young women. Our children. Josh couldn't finish his first year of school. Baby Jonathan couldn't even walk. Can that be right? Can it? Can it?"

The voice of the boys' vice principal broke in. Those standing outside the comparatively small building heard him over the loudspeaker, cutting through the twilight. A few blocks away the rush hour traffic at Wilshire and Westwood, the busiest intersection in the city, made a soothing noise.

"We'll do the service the way we always do. To keep this short, to get this over with, Tracie will speak for her friend Whitney. We told her she didn't have to, considering her other loss, but she said she wanted to."

Tracie's voice, bright and hard as steel, grated through the speakers to the parents standing in the courtyard, over the weeping parents crammed into the brightly lit chapel.

"Whitney was always the beautiful blonde. She didn't care about going to college. She wanted to get married and be a wife and mother and go on picnics and take care of her kids when they got sick, and have fun. Sometimes she thought she'd never find a husband or if she did find him, he'd be a spaz. Whitney hated poetry. She hated math. She liked to drink margaritas and dance. She used to get so *mad* at her stepfather for not wanting her around. She loved her mom but she got impatient with her. When her mom had Josh, first she was jealous, but she got so she loved him. And she loved my brother Jonathan. She was the best, the best you get as a friend.

"OK! Her favorite singer was Elvis Costello. Her favorite food was pesto and watermelon. When we were thirteen we gave each other socks where each toe was separate. Her favorite color was white. She laughed so hard you could see the fillings in her teeth. She hated poetry, did I say that? She was good on a computer. With Whitney gone, I've lost my best friend.

"And . . . there was a night, when we were working as temps, because you should know, that's all we *really* have waiting out there for us, when our boss said someone was mulatto, but we misunderstood. What she really said was *blotto*! Whitney *laughed*! And I want to say to my own mom and to Sol that there was never a better, more beautiful baby than Jonathan. And his favorite book was *Pat the Bunny* and we think his favorite song was 'Little Red Caboose.' I want to say to my mother I'm sorry. If I could change what happened, I would give my life."

The crowd in the patio, uncomfortable on folding chairs, listened to the sounds of weeping, of fragmented phrases of encouragement, of someone's voice inside the chapel: "We love you, Tracie! We'll always love you!" But outside people shifted their feet and shook their heads. A few went off to search out the crypt where Marilyn Monroe lay cold and dignified in her own distant death.

Then came the sounds of the Pachelbel Canon played pretty well by some students of Golden Oaks. A moon swept up over Westwood. A few blocks away, couples parked their cars and rushed to the movies at the Bruin, the Mann, the Crest. And even here, some men and women surreptitiously checked their watches, because if they left now they could take in a show, and have dinner later.

It was dark inside the chapel. A series of slides mutely celebrated lives gone now: Whitney during her life at Golden Oaks, mugging for the camera. Dressed for the snow. Striking out at baseball. Crying in some class. Touching her tongue with her nose. And now, some of Jonathan, the baby. Then, for three minutes of blistering agony, slides of six-year-old Josh, alone, in T-shirts too big for him. Standing with his half sister, frowning into the sun. Dressed in a snowsuit. His main color, the slides told it, was red. His main two expressions were grinning and crying. His least favorite activity was combing his hair. And every picture he was in was backlit, until a man's voice cried out.

"Turn on the lights!"

The lights came on. The vice principal, Mr. Whitelaw, said, as though anguished shouts were nothing to him, "We cannot let these deaths become meaning*less*. Whitney will have a scholarship in her name and those wishing to contribute should do so. The boys would have grown to be athletes, and we urge you to contribute to an athletic scholarship for minority boys. And for all of you who need the sustenance of friendship for the rest of this evening, the school has thrown open its doors."

But with the lights on, people were leaving. When they emerged, they moved through a courtyard already empty. The owner of the funeral home strolled across the flattened grass, folding chairs and leaning them along the flaking chapel walls.

Inside, the boy who had run the slide projector walked up to the screen, folded it, put it under his arm, and left, his feet clumping noisily down the aisle. The principal had disappeared, though this was unheard of for him. Mr. Whitelaw spoke, looking first to his right, to Sol and Kathy and Tracie and their family, then to his left, to Jerry and Wynn, and at the back, to Whitney's birth-father, with what must be his own new wife.

"There's nothing left but the reception at the school. See you all there in about twenty minutes." Then he too hunched his head between his shoulders and headed out, as those in the congregation who chose to filed by the coffins and out the side.

Jerry saw all this. He saw it from above. He had trained himself to do it. He glanced behind him as Whitney's "real father" pulled himself to a standing position, propped himself against a wall, groped and rummaged in the pocket of his jacket for a cigarette, and, fingers trembling, lit up. Jerry heard his own parents whispering behind him. He saw and heard his brother-in-law speak in a low voice to Wynn, telling her to get up, it was time to go. Jerry knew, being her husband, and father to one of those who had died, that he should be the one, it was *incumbent* upon him, to pull her to her feet, take her out behind the coffins through the side door where cars were waiting. But he stayed frozen, chilled. He watched the family across from him. Sol's head pressed a polished pew. His shoulders heaved. His brothers, old men, consoled him awkwardly, their hands on his shoulders. One man patted his hair.

Jerry watched as Tracie and her mother finally stood, moved out into the narrow area in front of the noncommittal, nonsectarian altar. Kathy's face was red, splotched, wild. She held on to, was held up by, her daughter, whose arm caught her mother by the neck. As they moved slowly to the center of the sanctuary, they swayed as one person with two heads, one anguished, one controlled. Wynn got up then, and went out there by herself. Jerry saw, from above, the way he'd trained himself, that it was up to Wynn to connect with the two women; make the gesture, renew her strength. But she was alone, because Jerry didn't feel like he was going to be getting up. He saw that Wynn was out there for forgiveness. Because although she had lost two children to their one, it was her car, her Volvo, her idea, her daughter driving, her existence in the world, that had caused this. She was mistaken, maybe, but Jerry could understand how she might feel that. He saw that Wynn could only get within a foot or so of the two women. She stopped, and put out an arm to steady herself on the pulpit.

Kathy held out her arm, but hid her head in her daughter's neck. There is no counting, her body said. One or two or one million or two million. It doesn't matter. I have lost my One. Jerry knew he had to get up. But it didn't look like he was going to. He heard the voices of the two women, exchanging cold words. And because he saw everything from above, felt himself observed. His testicles drew in. His neck stiffened. He turned to Whitney's "real father," but it wasn't him. Then Jerry saw Tracie, in colors of brown, brown skirt and brown blouse, clouds of half-braided blond hair, looking at him with brown, intelligent eyes, judging him by her own standards. A region in his chest shifted. *Am I having a heart attack? Am I paying for something, I don't even know what it is, with my life?* But no. It wasn't a heart attack, only his heart breaking. He'd blown it this time.

He did what he could, though, and sidled over to where Whitney's father and stepmother braced themselves against the wall, smoked their cigarettes. "I'm not sure you know where the school is, and it's hard to find at night. You're welcome to come along with us."

■
▬▬▬▬▬▬▬
▬▬▬▬▬▬▬
▬▬▬▬▬▬▬
■

Donny and Thea

Simi Valley/
Benedict Canyon
November 17

DONNY COULDN'T KEEP to his part of the house. He came
over all the time now, using the inside door that had, in earlier,
post–World War II times, opened from the kitchen of the
home into the double garage, so that the lady of the house
might step right out there and choose a frozen leg of lamb
from her freezer — and the veteran husband, home from his
good job, might step directly from his car into his kitchen to
shout, "Honey! I'm home!"

Hadn't Thea sealed up that door when she moved in? She
was positive she had. Had Donny cut through plywood on
one of those long status-quo San Fernando Valley afternoons,
or had Thea done it herself? She'd put a refrigerator in the
garage, a little one, right over where the freezer once had been.

She didn't eat, but she'd begun to drink again. There were times when she woke up at night in her single bed, and looked at the tiger's eyes that stared down at her, and got the last-stand blind shivers. "Oh, God," she'd pray automatically, "Oh, Father, Son and Holy Ghost," or alternately, "Oh, Virgin, Kali and Kwan Yin." Usually her prayers worked like one of those second-rate telephone systems you signed up for, where they promised you the world but delivered you static. She was left in the night with panic and emptiness; she couldn't keep track of the hundreds of subplots that clogged up her brain.

A well-meaning neighbor hauled her off to church, some Protestant outfit full of good intentions where they said if you weren't saved you belonged to Satan. Thea could hardly sit through the service. If there only *was* a Satan! Someone like that Mystery Man with the eye patch who turned up in that old comic strip, "Brenda Starr, Reporter." At home one night, in Donny's living room, she watched footage of their own local serial killer on television; the Mexican boy who'd caused so much trouble in Valley homes like this one, raping with screwdrivers, and firing shots with such a bad aim. Then he tried to use Satan as his employer, to pass himself off as a middle-level executive in some imagined cartel of evil. She could only swear and change the channel. The murderer had no more real idea of who he was or what he was doing than some lizard out in their own backyard.

Because what was really going on was far more terrifying than some poor dyslexic Mexican could ever dream. What if the universe was nothing more than a billion billion billion billion personal classified ads that spread invisibly from galaxy to galaxy and beyond, and an "end" would never come until all those ads had been answered and then canceled out, taken out of the paper? Until finally the paper itself could go out of business? And she was a switchboard operator in a branch office nobody had thought of in eons, eons, eons?

That's why she put in the refrigerator. So that after she had waked up, prayed — sometimes invoking the universe only — she could get up, pour herself some syrupy, half-frozen gin, walk out to the backyard and think, or try to; put some halfhearted argument to stars that she could barely see, out beyond a dusky layer of industrial smog.

Which is why they *had* smog, couldn't anyone see that? So they wouldn't have to see the stars. Which is why she'd had the inside door unplastered and opened up again — it had to do with the possibility of earthquakes, hadn't everyone decided? But it really had to do with letting Donny into her life, to clog up her afternoons, to interfere with her appointments, to wreck her concentration, to jam her station with static. But Thea knew that Donny, in his suffering and his good nature, had a dignity, a goodness running through him that was closer to the Virgin than anything Thea would ever again run into, in her life. Donny was here to take care of her, to drive her to distraction.

This afternoon, Thea got dressed to go to a party, at some place up in Benedict Canyon — where she would fill a curious slot. The hostess had at once invited her to come as a guest, and given her a check for five hundred dollars to be "entertainment." "Tell them some of the things that you've told me, but do it, you know, as if you just *thought* of it."

This would be a fancy party. If this nervous television-wife was any indication, she didn't even have her husband's deceptions on her mind (and they were numerous). Her whole mind-set had to do with whether her husband's series would be renewed, because if it was she had nothing to worry about, and if it was canceled she had everything to worry about. Thea tried to tell her about other lives leading into this one, or that the concept of a parallel universe could be useful in your thinking even if it wasn't necessarily true in the Dan Rather sense, but this woman only wanted to know about ratings. So, dutifully as an information operator scanning an electronic phone book, Thea had predicted the husband's ratings absolutely correctly for the last four weeks running. Only once did the wife have the presence of mind to remark, "Oh, I bet you think this is the silliest information I could ever ask for." Thea answered acidly, "No, back in Australia, men used to ask me about horse races, and before that, in Brighton, someone came into my mother's place at the strand to get her dead aunt's recipe for divinity fudge."

"Is that so?" the wife queried, applying lipstick, safe and happy after her hour, ready to trot down to where her air-conditioned Mercedes waited among the parked pickup trucks. "Is that right?"

She hadn't heard a thing. But maybe it was Thea on the other wavelength, listening to static. Because here was the wife saying, "Thea, I've arranged for you to go shopping over at Jôna. It's a nice store, on the other side of the Valley. I thought you could pick up something to wear for the party. It will be my gift to you, and goodness, after what you've done for *my* life, you mustn't give it a thought."

Well, *I won't*, Thea thought. I won't give it one thought at all.

Over at Jôna on Ventura Boulevard, the girls fitted her out according to pretty specific instructions, so that she left with thirteen hundred dollars' worth of crumpled beige and gray linen, a pale gray scarf, beige linen boots, and a note the wife had left for Thea to get her hair styled "next door, on me." The guy had taken three inches off her lemon yellow hair and put on a beige rinse. He toned down her eyebrows too and, looking in the mirror, she didn't mind. What the wife didn't know was that these natural fibers messed with her mind. Thea got vivid images of sheep, and cotton plants, and even those bulrush things they found Moses in.

At first she didn't even know she was irritated. But after her shower this afternoon, as she laid out about twenty pounds of crumpled linen that she was going to have to struggle into, and as she looked at her gleaming pewter hair which made her look younger, richer, duller, dimmer, she began to do a slow burn.

Donny came in without knocking, or rather with just one cursory knock, opened her refrigerator without asking, pulled out gin and two glasses from the freezer section.

"I don't know, Thea, I've been thinking about my life as a peasant on the Hungarian plains. It seems like *no matter what I do,* I get stuck with the same boring life. I'm so happy for your company, you know what I mean? But those guys down at the White Night, some of them even told my ex-wife, and she's so *mean,* you know? *Finally,* I'm getting some sex the way I like it, but, what I'm trying to say is, when I told the boys that I might have spent some time in Hungary, one of them started doing that stupid Russian dance, with his arms folded, and his feet stuck out? Then he lost his balance and rolled around the floor. I got so sick and tired of it that I told them, *all right*! I don't think any of *your* lives are such hot bananas!"

Donny filled both their glasses up again. Ignoring him, Thea had put on her underwear, her panty hose, her linen boots, her wide skirt, and a light cotton sweater with floppy things hanging off it.

"Wow," Donny said reverently. "Where'd you get the duds? That must have cost a bundle."

Thea sat down at her dressing table and pulled out a fishing tackle box full of makeup. "I'm going to a party. They want me to dress like this so I won't scare people. Do you believe it?" She turned on the lights around her makeup mirror, thought of the television-wife. Thought of spraying a bright red streak through her hair, or Day-Gloing her whole face fire

engine red, but instead she carefully applied a light foundation. In the mirror she watched Donny.

She asked him, "If you could be anything at all that you
wanted, what would you be?"

"I honestly don't know. I *finally* have what I thought I
wanted. What I want. I have my house, and it's looking good
now, and my kids like me again, and some girlfriends, and
you. I don't know."

"I'll give you another life. But don't tell it down at the
White Night. Don't tell it to anyone." Thea applied deep dull
gray to her eyelids, then added glitter. "You were Antonia,
you had eleven children, as long as I'm into numbers this
week. You had a mole on the right side of your nose. All your
children were boys, and poor as you were, you greeted each
baby boy with a wild rush of hope. You told anyone who
would listen, '*This* boy will grow up and work hard and
honor his mother like the fourth commandment says!' But
each one of them died. Most of them never saw their first
birthday, even if you could have remembered it. You couldn't
remember your own birthday, and the face of your own
mother came to you only in dreams."

"What . . . did I do?"

"You worked as a maid, close to the shore, in a city, Rio,
no, further north, Bahia. You worked from the time you were
a girl of eight or nine. You got up in the night and you came
home after the sun had set over the mountains. You climbed
steps each night. Your feet were purple and swollen and in-
fested with worms and you were so tired. There were, I make
it out to be, two thousand steps or footholds or handholds in
the climb from the city up the hill to the room where you lived,
and you lived alone except for one boy who grew to be nine
or ten before he died. You couldn't even sell your own milk,
although you gave it away sometimes. Malaria, typhoid, dys-
entery, you had all of these things. When you slept on your

240

cot, face down, sometimes the young boys in the houses next to yours came in with candles or lamps to see the worms that crawled from your anus in the night. You did those boys a good deed, even in your sleep, because you gave them something sadder and poorer and more ugly than they." As she spoke, Thea finished her mascara, her eyeliner, pulled out her blush — a discreet shade, hardly more than a pale apricot.

"Didn't I have any . . ." Donny groped for words. "Husbands? Boyfriends? Anyone to look out for me?"

"You grew up alone, in the streets, well, they weren't even streets. Dust, mud, stepping stones, bits of concrete, some bricks. *Things,* hauled up these hills over a century or so. Your place had no windows, no door that would shut. You got the place, with a terrible quick desperation, when a man died in there from something and began to stink. You went in there, maybe you were twelve and already pregnant. You pulled him, that man, by his feet. His skin came off in your hands, you wiped his skin away on a skirt, a green skirt, hiked up and held with stolen pins — and arranged his body across the opening to the room. And then you stepped across and into that stinking hole. 'I'm in here,' you shouted, when anyone paused to observe that rotting body or look at the room as a place to live. 'I'm in here now, and this place is mine.' You lay down in the mud, and there was plenty of shit around too. You curled up and cried for your mother. '*Mama.*' Oh, you cried for a long time, but even when you were sick no one came to help you. You stood outside your house and fucked for food. Boys would pull out some money, or a cigar for you — you liked cigars, their smoke — and women in the neighborhood might bring a tin plate of beans, and leave it inside your door."

Thea had finished with her makeup. She stared into her mirror, a perfectly groomed matron of style. Where was her lawyer husband? Where were her two children? Not her mosquito-bitten outback Australian littlies but the self-regarding little brats that went along with this outfit? She blinked at the mirror, then picked up her eyeliner and began to draw another eye where her third eye might be.

"In some ways, Donny, you carry stupidity with you, down through these lives. You might call it a *through line*. Why would you even ask me a question like that? *Nothing happened!* Your first baby was born dead. You nearly died of fever. Then you walked down the hill to the city. You took the first job you found, cleaning in a derelict hotel. The few men who lived there had made their way down or off that hill. You swept for them and washed for them in a river thick with soot, so their shirts came back dirtier than when they put them in your hands. They rewarded you with blows, and sometimes money. They fucked you, holding their breath and cursing their luck."

"But —"

"*No.* No to everything you're going to say. Yes to only one thing. Each year on Christmas or sometime, the people of that city float candles out from the beach. Even when you were there, the sea was filthy. But on that one night these candles are placed there by the devout and the prosperous to float out to sea in homage to the Virgin. On that night, holding whatever baby you might have had at the time — you named them all Thomas or Reuben, believing, against all facts, that Thomas and Reuben would protect you in your old age . . ."

Thea peered in her case and came out with a set of false eyelashes. She picked up one arc of hair, painted its edge delicately with glue, concentrated intently and stuck it into place. "You took your baby down to the beach where young couples paraded, and chaperoned maidens batted their eyes at the bachelors of the town, and priests showed up, slogging through sand in their shiny black shoes, carrying statues of the Virgin, and banners. The sun set, and the tide went out, taking the candles with them. Lights sparkled out on the sea. Your soul, quite as large as it is now, and that's very large, Donny, followed those lights. You prayed to the Virgin for your boys to live and grow, and respect and protect you, but it was really a call to your own lost mother. 'Mama. Mama.' You'd say it. You'd stay on the beach and watch the last light float away and lie down next to a damp rock that jutted out of the sand."

"But . . ."

Thea's shoulders stiffened. Her third eye, gray-violet with delicate eyeliner and lashes a little less thick than her own, glowed in the makeup lights.

"*No!* When people saw you, they made the sign of the cross and looked away. You were vermin-infested. Rashes from every disease covered your body. Your hair was alive with lice. Your mole had grown. Your face and body were covered with scars. You held your right arm across your face, to ward off blows. That's it, Donny. That's why you know what you know."

"*What* do I know?"

"Oh, Donny." Thea got up and slung her new leather purse over her shoulder. "This is so much to wear and think about. How do they do it, day in and day out? You know *everything*. How do you like my *eye*?"

Later that night, Donny hit the White Night. He wanted to dance, he said. He wanted to get down, he said. He danced like a wild man. He drank a hundred drinks but he danced them right through his skin. He danced for every life that was not his own, every woman lying in agony, every man looking away in shame, every baby that ever drew its legs up to its cramped stomach, and then cried, and died. He even danced for the worms! Talk about living in an asshole! He danced until two o'clock and persuaded everybody there to stay, even though the bar itself had to close. He went over to fat Valley women sitting at the bar watching him in resentment, and made them dance. He yanked railway men out onto the floor. No one gave a flying fuck for anyone who lived out here in Simi Valley, next to factories, and railroad tracks, in houses where nobody knew them, where they broiled in the summer and shivered in the winter. You could kid yourself that sex might help, but what it really meant was embarrassment and loneliness and shame. That wasn't the answer and neither were big houses or pickup trucks — only dancing. They danced all night at the White Night. The regulars would talk about it for years, when Donny lost his kinks, and started his new life, and everybody had a blowout time.

When Donny got home he went out back. It was close to six in the morning; there was a little ground fog waiting to burn off. He rested his elbows where Thea sometimes rested hers and told him that if he wanted to, he could look two ways. But he didn't look out at the view. He looked instead at the fence his arms were resting on, wood that still — at some level — lived. "Mama?" A whisper. "Mother?" He didn't think of an answer or a question, but watched the splintered, shivering wood awhile, wondering absently where it had been. Then in the fresh morning he went inside, took a long, great shower, and fell across his king-size bed, face down.

Earlier that evening, a well-dressed woman with three eyes drove in a borrowed car through unmarked suburbs like Van Nuys and Sherman Oaks and finally Encino, getting herself lost, feeling her way, thinking, Fine! What good are your psychic powers to you now? Passing 7-Elevens and Golden Arches and K-marts and Wendys and whole blocks where the signs were in Spanish or Thai or some other language. When the sun went down there was no way of telling where she was. Just scrubby hills (like outback hills) looming darkly up on the other side of the Valley, with a crawling worm of lights she figured had to be the San Diego Freeway.

She held her map in her left hand and steered with her

right. She found the canyon, finally, and drove up to its rim, worlds away from the place where she lived her quiet life. Her palms began to sweat, from the pure fear of driving, of accidents, of death. Once past the summit, where these mountains divided the San Fernando Valley from the cities of Hollywood and Los Angeles, the narrow road curved out over a great empty chasm. Maybe this is a bad idea, she thought. I haven't got it right. I'm lost.

But she found street signs, turned right and left, going always farther up into dry chaparral where scrubby little cabins jammed up against concrete mansions lit from the outside, so that each concrete pillar could plainly be made out. Even on these almost one-lane roads, sport cars roared past her at seventy miles an hour. This was too hard for her! She wasn't getting any younger! And her disposition had never been particularly fine.

When she found the place, she had the presence of mind to inch her way farther up to a cul-de-sac, turn her car around, and park pointing downhill. She knew that she'd find good customers tonight. She knew she'd be a smash. So why didn't she want to do it?

She sat in her parked car for a minute or two, fingering the eyelashes on her third eye. Two or three swabs with a Kleenex and it would all be gone; she'd come in with a smudge and say she'd been in a fender bender, hit the glass — go into the bathroom and come out a normal person.

But she climbed down onto the loose gravel of this hill and went into the party the way she was. A chunky girl at the door handed out camellias to the women and racing forms to the men — but they weren't racing forms. What they really were was some kind of claptrap about television shows and their ratings, with silly handicap information: "This one loves children," "Good for a rainy night," and even "Sex-sizzling cutie." The wife who had invited her had been right about the clothes — she'd never seen so much wrinkled linen in her life. So far, not one person had mentioned — or even looked at — her carefully made-up third eye.

"I hear you're the one to tell me." A fiftyish man offered to hand her a Perrier but she plucked a champagne off a passing tray and gulped it. *HIV positive* was all she got from him. "My wife says you know everything." His gray curly hair was false and washed over his tired forehead to bushy gray eyebrows of real gray hair. The hair in his ears was gray. *HIV positive.*

"Yes. I know."

Fear blew across his poor face like wind across rye grass, but he kept a smile pasted on. "I've got a Movie of the Week coming out in about six weeks. Science fiction. Everybody thinks this guy's normal, then he drinks some milk out of a carton late at night and he's alone and his eyes turn green."

"I told you. I *know.*"

"So . . . my wife told you?" *Positive.* "She *would.* What do you think? What do you see?"

"Don't sleep with your wife," she said. "Pretend something. Say that you . . . have prostate trouble."

"That's what I told her!"

"She knows, but she doesn't know. Let her leave it at that for now. She'll do the best she can for you."

"No one knows. No one else knows."

"Who owns this house?" she asked him brightly. "It seems like a boat more than anything else. What an incredible view. I don't think I've ever seen so many lights." She placed her empty glass on another tray, took a full one, drained it.

A beautiful woman took the man's arm. "I'm the one who told my husband to come over here. You have to forgive him if he was rude. He doesn't believe in the supernatural!"

"I'm not supernatural and I don't like to work in the present. I think that the present *is* a present. We should unwrap it, and we should be surprised. No matter what we think, we should try to be polite." She felt a small circle of people, young, gathering behind her. "Be that as it may," she said, "I'm into numbers tonight, and I see a twenty-eight share for that movie of yours. But some people will be switching channels in the last half hour unless you work on the next to last act."

"Anyone could say that," a voice whispered behind her, and Thea answered, without turning her head, "*Any*one wouldn't be right." Somebody handed her another glass.

She saw under it all. That the women were desperate and loveless. She saw disease all around her. She saw sweet boys, their renal glands ulcerating. She saw green patches on their livers, saw their souls panicking, preparing for flight. Their souls knew, but most of their bodies didn't. But they *did* know, too. They remembered, or barely remembered, nights when they'd done something they shouldn't.

Three kids in their very early twenties eyed her from the perimeter: one of them, a serious girl who had to work hard to keep up with her partners, and got no love from them, because they loved each other, murmured, quoting from an old movie, "Get out of the road! Get out of the way."

Thea answered back, "Have you no room in your carriage for a dying man?"

And the three, on the brink of short, sweet success, looking early death and great grief right in the face, answered smartly, "Hunh . . . Ack as though dey won de war!"

"I *told* you she was wonderful," Thea's hostess said. "She knows everything. She's a *delight.*"

For the next hour Thea recited movie lines with the new generation. They had the good sense not to bug her for concrete answers. They didn't want to know if their pilot would be picked up, or what ratings share some dreadful show of theirs might garner. Or if they might finally get to direct instead of write, or work on staff or be story editor. They were in their short lives for the fun, and the fun only.

Thea saw a greedy young man, an agent, whose disbelief came off him like green ink. Finally she drifted away from her circle of doomed, joyous children. She'd had enough to drink to suggest to him, "Yes, you will make all the money you ever wanted and more. But no one will ever like you, not your wife or your children or your clients. They have already stopped liking you. By the time you die, you will be everybody's bad joke. Evil men will console themselves by saying, 'At least I'm not as bad as *he* is.'" She turned to his stricken wife and said, "You will marry three times and travel widely. Your soul is so sweet that you will never speak ill of your first husband."

She felt a strong hand on her elbow and said to the hand's owner, "Well, I guess I've done murder. Oh, I won't think about that now. I'll think about that tomorrow."

"Come on outside. Get some fresh air." She followed a big man out onto the redwood deck, noticing that he wasn't trying to sober her up — he held two glasses in his hand. Behind her, she felt the agent's eyes glittering with hate. What had been the point of telling him? What could he do about it? How could he change it? It was his errand in life to be evil and to ruin lives. It wasn't her business.

Out on the deck the dry air carried gum tree smells.

"Australia," she sighed to the big man who stood by her, half leaning on a redwood table, "this place is so much like Australia." She gave him the once-over — how could she not? And saw a human body like an old Cadillac, big, roomy, in excellent running condition.

"So, did you memorize *Gone With the Wind*?"

"No, I didn't." She dabbed at her eyes, her real ones that saw this world.

"There's no point in making an enemy of Max. He remembers everything. He'll make it hard for you in this town."

"I don't live in this town." Her shoulders shook. She couldn't help it. "I don't like to work in the present."

He draped an arm across her shoulders and gave her a handkerchief. After she'd blown her nose and wiped her eyes, he folded the handkerchief once again and harshly wiped her third eye away. "You shouldn't go outside in that getup."

She sobbed into his shirt.

"Listen. I'm leaving. I've got one stop to make, right on this street. We can walk there. Then we can go back to my house. You've worn out your welcome here."

He took her hand and led her back though the party, past their hostess, past the frightened fifty-year-old. "*Remember,*" she called to him, but the man she was with now tightened his grip and pulled her away.

Outside, a moon brushed dusty sumac, and the smell of gum trees was strong. Animals — coyotes? raccoons? — rustled in dead leaves at either side of the road. Houses perched and clung everywhere she looked, some light, some with windows dark, but *everywhere,* as crowded as the tract in Simi Valley where she lived. This place crawled with humans, but another world lived here too, languages she didn't know, perceptions she couldn't tune into. Voles, for God's sake, digging. Shrews. Cats eating shrews, tossing their heads and twitching their whiskers to get rid of that sour shrew taste. Lizards in perpetual terror, always losing their tails over this and that. Deer, farther up on these slopes, extremely dumb, their whole lives something about climbing and hiding.

The man who held her arm was tuned to getting rich, but there was kindness, like a big kidney, embedded in the middle of his trunk. She couldn't really see his mind; what a relief. But he didn't have *positive* written in blood and sperm all over his body, all under his skin.

"What'd you say your name was?"

"Irving."

"Irving what?"

He looked over his shoulder, vaguely amused. "You're telling me you don't know?"

"Irving *what*?"

"Careful where you walk. Snakes love places like this, in this weather."

Just jump then, take a dive! Go for it! No pain, no gain! Take a dive, go for it! How do you think Rome was built? People who lie at home in bed are going to feel like shit that they weren't out here on this St. Crispin's day, dashing themselves down, taking a risk, making history, shining like the Sun of God!

The voice crackled at her from somewhere, along with the voles and the deer.

This is it, she thought wearily. I really am going to get out of this line of work. Get a lobotomy. My wiring's shot.

Her companion knocked on a door and an older man in shirtsleeves opened it. The entry hall and living room were brightly lit. "Irving! We've been waiting. Afraid you might not make it."

Irving took her into the dining room where four Americans and two Japanese were pulled up to the table brooding over telephones and faxes and contracts. Their mood was glum.

"We've just come from a party. This is my new friend . . ."

But they were plainly as bored by the prospect of an introduction as she was. "Don't bother," she said, in her most British voice. "Don't bother getting up." None of them had made a move to do anything of the sort. "I'll wait for Irving out on the trellis." (But didn't she mean balcony?) One of them, a somber redhead, watched her leave the room. Did she know him from somewhere?

She used her so-called powers coupled with what was left of her common sense to find where they had hidden a wet bar

250

in this house. She was forgetting more than she remembered. People were coming up to thank her for crucial advice she couldn't recall giving them. More than that, sadder than that, you could tell somebody something, and it wouldn't mean beans, it would roll right off. She knew for a fact, for instance, that the fifty-year-old man back at the other party would have sex with his wife tonight; knew that his wife would collude in his effort, despite her own darkest suspicions, and that in two years, five years, they'd both be *goners* — what an American word! — goners, gone back to the Holding Center, having proved *what*?

And these *men,* in the other room, going to their graves with yet another piece of property in their possession. For *what*? Was that second sight she was having, or just common sense? She went out on the balcony and sat down on a lounge chair. She heard, hidden by the trees, the sounds of another party she would have liked to have gone to, and was struck by a bolt of drunken gloom: voices across this dry little wash just having fun! She finished her gin, found an owl to look at on a television antenna a few houses over, and passed out.

Irving shook her awake and common sense told her he must have had second thoughts about it. He could have left her here, but he took her hand and led her through the rooms again. In the dining room the men were still at it. Would the deal go *through*? (Like she gave a tumble!) On the street it was darker, the moon had gone down, more humans slept. More animals were out and about.

They strolled down to Irving's dark house. He must have a flock of ex-wives out there somewhere, but there wasn't a trace here. A smell of leather: two new couches, probably with the price tags still on them. Still holding her hand, he took her into his bedroom, and still the quiet prevailed; only the sound of that owl on the TV antenna, and another one, answering back, close to here. He began to undress and she did the same.

Here's a man as tired as I am, she thought, and rolled over onto sheets so new they hadn't yet seen water or a laundry.

He preferred the missionary position and she did too. He was heavy, and clean, and wonderfully thoughtless; his mind washed clean. When he finished he fell immediately asleep on top of her. She locked her arms around his neck and pushed her face directly into his chest. Only blackness. Only silence. Only quiet. Only life, without the complications. Surprising herself she wept some tears — for her crazy mother on the English pier, for her Australian husband and her kids. The whole point was that you were supposed to see life, and love it too. She was afraid she wasn't going to be able to do it, not in this life. She wasn't going to be strong enough. That wasn't the kind of strength you got by body building or meditation or praying or asking or practicing. You had it or you didn't. You fought to a draw.

The next morning he'd rolled off her and lay on his back with the sheets down to his knees, snoring loudly. Even his sleep was dreamless, a quiet absence of image. It was a cloudy day. The trees, which had seemed so Australian and clean the night before, hung dully in a pall of smog. The digital clock by the bed said 5:48. She carried her linen jacket and walked barefoot to her car, her shoes and panty hose jammed in her purse.

Easy to get down off the hill, easy to get back into the Valley. Easy to head east through this flat landscape. Somewhere in Van Nuys, she spotted a McDonald's on her side of the street and pulled into the parking lot. Lots of single men, and women with kids — men reading the paper, women gossiping as they chomped into Egg McMuffins, or wiped away debris from their kids' chins. Thea ordered a large coffee, a chocolate shake, an Egg McMuffin. She chewed, swallowed, bummed a cigarette, picked up a thrown-away Los Angeles Times, and turned to the Travel section, looking for cheap fares from L.A. to Sydney. In her mind's eye, she could already see her kids.

J e r r y

**L o s   A n g e l e s / W e s t w o o d /
P a c i f i c   P a l i s a d e s
J a n u a r y   1 3**

WOMEN AT THE OFFICE eyed him anxiously, told him,
even, to see a counselor. He never answered them, except with
a contemptuous stare he'd recently picked up, knowing that
was why some men, so many men, developed that mask.
Don't say anything! Don't require me to answer! Don't make
me say anything.

What a world. What a world. Insomuch as he was able to
think, he thought that. He couldn't look at the news at all anymore — the streets in the countries where, as a matter of
course, police and soldiers poured out onto city streets to beat
their citizens. Women, in rags, wailed. Sometimes they held
dreadful parcels, dead children, offered them up to the cam-
eras, screaming, screaming. See? See? See? See? This is what

you have done! But who — what — was the *you* in it? There was no *you* in it.

He knew about it all now, when he got up in the morning, suffocating, under his eiderdown comforter (although there was no comfort, now, or ever). He got up, leaving the bed where Wynn lay far from him. How glad he was for the far distances of a king-size bed. He left Wynn flat on her back, giving off a strong acrid smell, as though she too had died. She lay on her back, or on her side, her eyes opened or closed, her pillow soaked with tears and sweat.

In the three and a half months since Josh and Whitney had died — through Halloween, Christmas, New Year's — his wife had been wearing Whitney's nightgowns, and when those ran out, her blouses, her T-shirts. Wynn would take one and wear it for ten days or so, then throw it out — he had seen them stuffed in bathroom wastebaskets. (And he had seen them, rescued, washed and folded, on the foot of Carmela's bed, or in the torn, roughed-up back seat of Carmela's old car.) Once they were washed, they were Whitney's no longer. Wynn would take another one to wear. Sometimes, in the night, he would wake, hear her muffled sobs, her strangled gasps. Once, on a night with a full moon, he had seen her profile against their bedroom window. She was still on her back, but she had kicked off her part of the comforter. He saw her bare legs, not young anymore. He saw that she'd taken the hem of Whitney's nightgown and stuffed it into her mouth. She was eating the nightgown, and rubbing the rest of it on her face, grinding it into her eyes and across her cheeks. He saw that she wasn't really crying at all. Her long, desperate sniffs were really inhalations; she was trying to inhale Whitney back into her being. And he saw, sometimes, at the far side of the bed, the same three toys that, from the beginning of his life, Josh had taken to bed with him, and that, during the day, had stayed lined up in a row against his Ghostbuster pillowcases. A cloth bear named Squarey, a lion named Lioney, another bear that had no name. Jerry knew that when Wynn turned away from him and lay on her side and stretched Whitney's nightgown a certain way, that she had arranged Squarey, Lioney and that other one against her stomach. She pulled the nightgown down over them, trying to give birth again, to Josh.

For Jerry, it was horrible. The first night, after the funeral, after Wynn's mother, his mother and father, and Whitney's father and stepmother had left the house and the hotels and motels around and about — peeling back, with evident relief, to the distractions of their own lives — he had tried to put his body against his wife's, put an arm around her as they sat on a couch together, moved conscientiously toward her in their huge bed. But he couldn't.

He kept thinking. He could lie down with death. But he couldn't fuck it. He couldn't even touch it.

Really, the nights were not so bad. Looking at it from his own point of view, he came home late, as he always did anyway. He got home about nine-thirty every night, bringing a videotape. There was always a fresh, full, opened bottle of Chivas Regal waiting in the cupboard in the breakfast room. He would have worked hard, and he'd be tired. He would have picked up six o'clock sandwiches with Loring, with Mac and Gus (and how great those guys were), cloaking everything in the cool and numbing solace of work, killing time with him: Potomac Electric Power, what did it think *it* was doing with its two-thousand-plus shares on the Tokyo Stock Exchange, the one for foreigners only? Was General Motors living in a *dream* world then? And Du Pont? *Please!* Mac and Gus spent hours going over the figures of the *real* Tokyo Stock Exchange with him, never extending, except at the funeral, any sympathy at all. At the funeral they had come, all the Japanese, in one rigid, dark-suited group, and — not trusting their second language at such a time? — had limited themselves to bows, to him and to Wynn, and going by the closed coffins, stopped the friends and acquaintances who had lined up to say goodbye to Whitney, to Josh, to the baby, by bowing, three times each to the baby, the little boy, three times to the once beautiful girl.

But now, at the office, the subject of family misfortunes never passed their lips. No more stories about avenging Japanese wives. Now it was all club sandwiches and coffee and talking on the telephone, and even language tutors — teaching assistants hired directly from UCLA — to instruct the Japanese in English from eight-thirty to eleven in the mornings, and to teach the Americans Japanese.

It was necessary to stay late at work, wasn't it? Around seven or eight at night was when the heaviest trading on the TSE usually occurred. If you were going to put through calls to Tokyo, or Hong Kong, or Sydney, or Jakarta, seven at night was the time to do it. Those phone calls were taxing — conference calls, so many of them. Mike Bartch and Loring Freed and Mac and Gus listened intently to a disembodied voice flying across the Pacific to them, and Mac might pass Jerry a note: Is this a scam? A scam they try? Because now, they really were all in this together, heavily invested, had a lot riding on everything, were working from the same side. Once you started to think globally, the world really did open up.

So it was nine or ten before he got home. Carmela would have made a dinner and cleaned up the kitchen to an impersonal spotlessness. Tina would be bathed and fed and put to bed. He knew this because when he picked up the scotch bottle to take it into the den, before he settled down, he went upstairs. He'd open Tina's room and she'd be asleep, her scrawny fingers clenched against her chest. Like she was praying. On the one hand he hoped Carmela wasn't teaching her any of that stuff. On the other he hoped maybe she was. After

256

looking in on Tina he'd quietly walk the halls to his own room, where the light would be on. Wynn, propped up on pillows, would be watching television with her eyes closed, a Sue Grafton novel turned upside down on her stomach. She had her bottle too. Cinzano or Dubonnet. Sweet, sickening things. Her eyes would be glued shut.

So he would go downstairs and watch his videotape in the darkened den and drink his bottle of scotch, and feel some kind of peace. Here was the room. There was the screen. The taste of the scotch. You breathed, you saw, you swallowed. You laughed, sometimes, in the dark room, when something funny happened on the screen. You watched the fights. You watched the Lakers.

When the bottle was gone it was usually eleven. He used to watch Arsenio, but he couldn't now. And he needed his sleep. By twelve or one he'd go up the stairs again, not even unsteadily, so careful was he with how he paced himself. His pain worked the way cancer did with morphine, it soaked the scotch up. He didn't want to get drunk, wasn't looking for that. Just dosing himself and watching a video to relax.

If he felt like shit in the morning, that was a hangover. He knew from college that you could work out a hangover. Instead of rowing five miles in the morning he rowed fifteen. Instead of biking twenty minutes, he took it to a half hour. He walked another ten miles on his treadmill, holding hand weights, watching the "Today" show, listening through earphones, though he could hear, sometimes, floating up the stairs, the low Spanish growls of Carmela, the terrified high squeak of his little girl.

He was denied his peace at breakfast, where, cleansed inside and out, he sat at his customary place at the table and watched his perfect garden explode with early bougainvillea and late chrysanthemums, orange and lemon banks of them. Sitting opposite him, looking at a Lego waffle in a little pond of syrup, Tina took up a place in his vision. Carmela's decision, he was sure of it: her mother can't do it, so you have to, señor! Do your duty! Take your place as head of this family. If this *is* a family. If you *are* its head. The body of the family is like the body of Christ, so do it, *manso,* coward! Do what you must.

With the heavy, all-seeing presence of the big Mexican maid behind him, he would look across to Tina, whose head would be haloed by all the customary scenery he was so used to; the hummingbirds, the Anna's and the occasional Rufous with the wonderful-looking black chins, and swarms of Audubon's warblers just tuning up for their winter plumage. But in the middle, like a thumbprint on a perfect dashboard, the blot of his daughter's face.

Her hair was blond, like her mother's, and it was clean, of course, but raggedy. Her eyes were pink and blurry, as though they'd been gashed and hadn't begun to heal. Her lips were thin and bluish, her teeth looked like bat's teeth. She sat, her chin close to the tabletop, looking miserably down at the sweet mushy stuff she was supposed to eat.

"So . . . how's school, Teen?" My God. He *had* to do better than that. She wasn't even in kindergarten yet!

"OK."

"What's your favorite subject?"

"Nothing."

"Wouldn't you like to take a bite of that waffle? That's your favorite, honey."

She wouldn't like to take a bite of the waffle.

"Aren't you going to get hungry later on, in school?"

No.

"What's your least favorite? Tina? What's your least favorite?"

"Nap time, I guess."

"Need some help? I can give you some help on that."

Liar! Sinvergüenza! Shameless fool! All these vibes came

from behind him, where Carmela spread peanut butter on wheat bread for Tina's lunch.

"So, honey! Would you like to go to a movie on Saturday?"

"I . . . guess so," the answer dragging out of her, both of them knowing it would never come, that Saturday.

Then it would be time for Tina to go to school. Carmela would come around the table with a damp washcloth to scrub the grayish skin around Tina's mouth, and gently clean the syrup away from each of her brittle little fingers.

"Honey, I can give you a ride to school on my way to work, OK?"

But she shrank from him, pushing her whole skinny body into Carmela, hiding her face from him entirely. Every morning he'd put a good face on it, saying, "OK, then, I'll see you tonight," even though she would have been asleep at least an hour when he got home.

All the time this was happening, every morning, from the moment he came, freshly dressed, into the breakfast room, another whole voice gabbled along inside of him: You can't let things go on like this. The responsibility falls on you. You certainly can't take care of it, you haven't got the capacity, so what you need here is professional help. Grief counseling. Support groups. Parents of children killed unexpectedly. School counseling. You have to talk to Tina's teachers. Your wife can't do it. She can't do anything. She has to have some counseling. She's in trouble. You can't do anything about it. You haven't got the capacity. You've got to get some help. Help from somewhere. Read the want ads. Talk to your doctor. Find a minister. Give somebody a call. Because you can't go on like this. You've got to think of Tina.

But he thought of Josh. He would have known what to say to Josh. He could have talked to Josh. He was absolutely sure of it. He missed Josh, missed him, missed him!

And another vicious, terrible voice would whisper: If a

person has to lose two out of four of the most important people in his life, shouldn't he at least have a choice over which two it's going to be? And perfectly formed in every detail, an alternative life would swing up in his mind, as limited and perfect as any videotape he watched at night in the safe darkness of his den. If Wynn had died, if Tina had died, then he would have had the sweet comfort of Whitney's hair and face and (admittedly muted) laughter. He would still have Josh, his son, who would be as sad as Tina was now, but they could go to ball games on Saturdays, the three of them, they could walk down to the beach on Sunday evenings. He and Josh could throw a ball, the three of them could throw a ball . . .

You see? the first voice would interrupt, *that's* why you need to get some help. A support group. Someone to get Wynn out of bed. A doctor. A peer group. A teacher. A shrink. A minister. Because you have lost it entirely. And you're the head of the house. You've got to do something.

And a third voice, as fitful and tired as Tina's own, would pipe up: Why does it have to be me? Wynn is the strong one. I've lost my only son. And I have to go to *work*. Don't I? Don't I? Don't I? Don't I?

Well, the first voice would reply, you'd better do something. Pretty Quick. On the Double. ASAP. PDQ. Because things aren't getting any better over here.

He would stand up, ducking into the downstairs bathroom to brush his teeth so he wouldn't have to go upstairs and disturb his wife. He'd pass by Carmela, who'd just be picking up the car keys to her dented Ford. Every morning it would come to him as the same kind of ferocious surprise: the kid feels better with the maid than with me, and he'd muss up Tina's hair again. She'd move her head irritably away from the palm of his hand. He'd say, "Adios, Carmela. Muchas gracias para todos."

And he'd be out, fucking blessedly out of the house, heading toward the ocean on the same track that crazy divorcée had taken, covering the exact same ground, except that when he came to the street that bordered the strand of green at the top of the palisades, he turned left, went south, avoiding the spectacular Pacific view that unrolled along his passenger window — those palms, those graceful waves, the clear morning sky. He kept his eyes on the road until he got to Colorado Boulevard, turned inland four blocks, past the shopping mall on his left (the best one in L.A., Wynn used to tell him when she still went out) and Sears Roebuck on his right — the poor still went there. Then right, left, a quick jog, and he barreled onto the Santa Monica Freeway, heading east, downtown. He put on the cassette for his Japanese lessons. He'd be OK, until tomorrow morning.

Because the irony was, now that he'd had his mind taken off it, it looked like everything he'd thought he wanted was going to come to pass. The Pacific Rim venture had become a reality in the first weeks after his terrible loss, even though his consortium was still looking for the right property, the right country. The Japanese investors had come to see (he *guessed*) what he'd seen all along: that the safest investments now were not in products, but in whole lives. Now was the time to make this "innovative move," with Europe and the Middle East squirming like a can full of maggots. The Pacific Rim provided an alternative view, another way of looking at life. A visiting expert from the Rand Corporation had taken up two hours of their valuable time explaining that modern thought, East and West thought, left and right thought, had sprung from the fact that man had a left hand and a right hand, and enjoyed opposing them. (But the guy didn't know what to say at all about the Middle East.)

It was worth everything, if you took life second by second which was what he was trying to do right now, to watch the expression on Gus's face, on Mac's face, that morning, as their hard-won, hard-studied English finally filtered what they were hearing through their percolating brains. Is *this* what they'd been missing all this time, stuck on Japanese islands of hard work, spending hours on their phones putting together deals? Mornings like this? Theories like *this*? No wonder America was falling behind. How had it ever gotten ahead in the first place?

Nevertheless: subsidiary deals had been made, with Bartch, Bridges, Freed as the principal American coordinator, Irving Rossman as principal American investor, and Mac and Gus's outfit signing on for Japan. The project would remain in a developing stage for seven to ten years, using skilled labor from America and Japan, and unskilled labor from islands and communities around and in the South Pacific. They would build an artificial community, a unit defined by economics and (even ethical) values as much as nationalistic considerations. Even in his deepest grief, this thought heartened Jerry. *Imagine,* John Lennon had suggested. A world — if everything went well — where workers were treated fairly, tourist money poured in, and the diversified economy spun along like a self-winding watch.

Their miniature country would be a Hong Kong, but without the congestion; a Singapore, but without the fascism; a Catalina, but with meaningful work attached to it; a Bali, but without the hard-eyed peddlers. A better world. A meaning behind the glib cliché, Pacific Rim. And any saltwater crocodiles would be caught and repatriated onto the southern beaches of New Guinea, where (somebody finally admitted) the natives caught and ate them.

Eight A.M. Jerry turned into the basement parking lot of Bartch, Bridges, Freed, locked his car, set the alarm, hurtled up in the elevator. At the twenty-sixth floor, his ears still cracked. They would *always* do that, no matter who died, or what money was made, or how civilization improved.

As he walked in, for a millionth of a second, his eye processed all the windows in Los Angeles, every one of the thousands of microchips between his office and the blue strip of sea, picked out the one, went on around again, in close focus; took in his offices, his messages. Patty had his schedule typed up for him. Eight to nine: Japanese conversation with a tutor. Nine to ten: conversation with Japanese visitors and interns. Eleven to twelve: a lecture from someone in the State Department on why what they were doing now wasn't like Drexel Burnham Lambert, only the title wasn't that.

Lunch in-house. Ordered from Rex. That was an idea they *had* taken from Drexel — eat inside, get the work done. Eat the best, you *do* the best. Architects would be presenting alternative plans for a series of light-industry complexes during lunch.

Two to three: tea with the Australian consul, a cultivated man who'd spent most of his postings in Europe and came out of a distinguished career with a mildly Belgian accent. He'd have Aussie businessmen with him. The consul had repeatedly reminded them in the past six months that Australians had taken in more Asian refugees, even more Central and South Americans, in proportion to their population, than any other country in the world, many more than America. So they should be included in this upcoming project.

Three to five: early phone calls to the Orient; conference calls to their brokers on the Tokyo exchange. The American partners would place orders, trade, *do business* in Japanese under the watchful, amused eyes of their Asian partners, their young mentors. These were grueling hours. Bartch said once, "Every Jap joke I ever made when I was a kid? I'm paying for it now." And he was right. But the numbers came over the fax and on the ticker tape, reassuring in their lack of feeling. The only feelings the Americans got to have were embarrassment, stress, shame at making mistakes, elation at getting a transaction right, occasional bursts of uncontrollable laughter at the difficulty of it. But, Gus and Mac assured them, Bartch,

Bridges, Freed was the only, *almost* the only firm on the West Coast — and that meant America — making this kind of aggressive push to meet the Asians on their own ground, their own terms. The world was a maze now. But they were flying out of the problem.

Six P.M.: drinks with developers at the Regency Club in Westwood. Spouses *dis*couraged. Then a late dinner, up in the Malibu colony, given by a former contractor who had once built twenty-seven thousand houses in New Jersey after World War II and wanted, now, to build twenty-seven thousand more, dotting some unspecified island with stucco boxes and little green lawns. Jerry hated the proposition, but he knew that workers had to live somewhere. Houses like that, coupled with money from the GI Bill, had made it possible for people like Jerry's own father to succeed. So: the party was on. Spouses *en*couraged. Mrs. Bridges was a *no,* Patty noted, but she'd check Mrs. B. again at four P.M., just to be sure.

So. OK. A day. A good day.

Why was it that only the Japanese knew how to talk to him, when Loring couldn't meet his eyes? Loring took it worse than *he* did, for Christ's sake. When Patty had talked to him for two months now in a voice an octave above what usually came out of her throat, a *pert* voice: would it go on like that forever? He didn't think he could stand it. But she was the one who checked in with Wynn four or five times a day with one meaningless question or another. He didn't think he could stand that either.

Gus and Mac, in their dark suits, got him through. The boys went drinking with him, silently watching sports events in downtown bars. They allowed long times to pass without anyone saying anything. And like a burn victim who can bear anything except to be touched, Jerry cherished the silence. Young as they were, they took what happened and ran with it, somehow, beyond sorrow. They knew how to joke. But it was more than that. They knew why to joke.

The guys lived in a Bunker Hill condo. They could walk home. Jerry would sometimes spend the night at the Biltmore. All he had to do was register, take the elevator. Crash and wake up. (Because there were nights, in that first couple of weeks, he couldn't go home.)

Gus might say, "Rams by three. I'm giving you points. Is that right?"

Silence, broken only by what was most trivial, was what he craved. If he didn't move, he could get through.

Before lunch, energy dipped around the office. That was why they scheduled "notable speakers" in this spot.

"To be sure," said their speaker today, that man from the State Department, "actions may speak louder than words — but sometimes with a stupefying ambiguity, and sometimes deafening overstatement."

Grief rushed Jerry, kicked him silly, the way it did several times a day. It hit him like a punch. Or worse. Like a nurse. A terrible nurse, coming to rip away the scabs, the dead tissue, the only protection he had.

"Most talking is not glamorous. Often it is tedious. It can be excruciating and exhausting."

The speaker got a round of laughs then, and didn't quite know why. But he smiled along with his audience.

"Talking can also tame conflict, lift the human condition and lift us closer to the ideal of peace."

Jerry went inward, created a swirling pool in his mind. Now was a time to rest. To sleep with his eyes open. That last blast of grief? Just a stab. Just a prick.

But then, out of a fog of words in the somnolent morning, Jerry woke up again to hear, "The United States, unlike other nations, is not identified by common ethnic traits or cultural traditions. Instead, the United States, uniquely, is organized around an idea — principally, a reverence for the inherent worth and the dignity of each human being."

Jerry got up, reaching in his pocket for his key. He hit the men's room at a trot. Slammed the door behind him. Found the far basin and laid his head down sideways in it. Turned on the faucet, the cold water. Let it squirt on his face. If he was ever going to cry about this, and he wasn't, it wouldn't be from an eleven o'clock *talk*. That would be . . .

He kept his eyes shut, then opened them, watching water wash over his eyes. Watching the side of the basin, the white impersonal porcelain. OK. He straightened up. Reached for the cloth towels. Scrubbed at his face. Blotted his collar. Pulled off his wet tie, flung it in the wastebasket. Saw that Mac had followed him in and was standing with his back to the door so nobody else could get in. They eyed each other in the mirror. Mac loosened his tie, unbuttoned his own top shirt button, held out the tie. Jerry took it, put it on.

He traded in the afternoon, made several hundred thousand dollars in yen. Fun.

Just after five, he drove west to the Regency Club. How *torn* he was, between home, business, strangers; tomb of home, claustrophobia of work, and, here, the hideous intrusion of strangers. He was known now, on the West Side; he was a myth. He was like the parents of those poor kids who'd turned left on San Vicente and rammed into the tree trunk in the middle of the street. His life, now, was an exemplum, far worse, he thought, than if Josh had grown up to die of AIDS. Jerry still looked like himself, looked, on the outside, even *more* like himself. His arm muscles — biceps, triceps, flexors, extensors — filled out the sleeves of his suit. His face kept the tan that came from running and tennis on the weekends. His eyes, he swore it to himself, still looked the same. He didn't carry the death the way Wynn did, he didn't show the outward bruises Tina wore. He looked OK! But as he got off the elevator and walked along the shining hardwood floors of the club, as he bent to sign the guest book for tonight's event, he felt the shrinking of human beings away from him. He stepped into the room where the reception was, where it seemed as if all the Southern California developers and bankers and suppliers and glaziers had gathered in one big room. All their faces, some greedy, some kind, some amazingly vacant considering how successful they'd become on this gold coast, arranged themselves into either pity or fear. Without planning for it, Jerry had become their lightning rod — all disaster had come down on him.

Then Ernie, a man who'd glassed in the Bonaventure Hotel, a man in his sixties whose wife had died a few years back, started on over to him. And from another corner of the room, a tall slim city councilwoman with perfectly coiffed black hair whose husband had cornered cardboard in this part of the country. ("I'd never consider going into plastics," Rick had said to him once, "because when you go into a warehouse full of cardboard, and especially paper bags, you can hear it breathing. Really! No shit!") Salli walked toward him from the southwest corner of the room. She and Ernie got to Jerry at the same time.

Salli took his arm. "We're all so glad to see you here! We're praying for you." The three of them headed to the bar. Ernie handed him a scotch. His poor old face had cracked in so many places. And he had a couple of those raw pink patches where he'd had skin cancers removed. *Life's a bitch and then you die*. Jerry had always hated that T-shirt, that message. He understood it now.

Ernie handed him another scotch. They pushed together toward the west window, to watch the sun go down. Dark clouds clustered near the horizon. Automatically, reflexively, Jerry's eyes scanned the coast for one window. He was fifteen miles closer to it, but he couldn't find it. Of course, the light would be out.

"Feeling rocky?"

"Yes."

Ernie shook his head. Looked out the window. "Nothing to say. Pray for it to lift, a little."

But what Jerry wanted to know was: How had this happened? How had he been wrenched into this antiworld, this dark world? How had he been pushed into this place, *which had been here all the time*? He looked at his watch. "I've got to get out of here. Listen! Are you up for some big-time South Pacific glazing?"

Ernie drew back. Jerry knew he'd blundered. Pushed away a human being. "Give me a call," he muttered. "At the office tomorrow." The scotch hit him, not with a buzz but a heavy blow. He turned, focused his eyes on the way out, and walked in that direction. By now no one noticed him, so deep were they in their own conversations and lives. They'd already lost interest in him. Soon, other kids would die of cancer, some would get AIDS. There would be other terrible accidents.

He chose to drive the freeway, the Santa Monica, heading west. Insofar as he could look forward to anything he looked forward to tonight in Malibu. Meet some new people. Make the deals. Put together more configurations to change the world. Make conversation in different languages. Stay out late.

In the opposite lanes of the Santa Monica Freeway, people going downtown had come to a total halt. Their headlights came on in the January dark. He faced a string of strong white light. It looked good, he had to admit. A great spot of water spread out across his dusty windshield. That happened sometimes on the freeway. A few cars up, some joker had decided to wash his windshield, but he was driving so fast that water came down on the shield behind him, or the one behind that. So somebody eventually got a clean windshield.

There was something perfect about a crowded freeway with everyone going a close sixty-five; like flying in formation. He checked out the cars around him, everything cool. Everybody zoned out. Another splash caught on his windshield, spread itself out, thinning at the edges. Jerry looked at the sky.

Was this going to be the first rain of the season? Dully, he remembered oil slick — that the season's first rain brought out the oil on every highway. He could die tonight, if he didn't slow down. Dozens of drivers did every year, in the first rain of the season, skidding on greased highways.

Then, as he flew past the Cloverfield turnoff and the Centinela turnoff, and Twenty-sixth Street, only twenty-six blocks from the ocean, he remembered, with a shudder that made the palms of his hands slick on the steering wheel, that he would have to get off, quick. He would have to get off at the last cluster of exits, Lincoln, Fifth, Fourth, because if he didn't, if he didn't, he'd . . .

He'd go swooping down through the McClure Tunnel where the freeway ended. He'd be out on the Pacific Coast Highway, driving past where the Cirque du Soleil held its autumn season, and the Santa Monica pier. To his left would be the ocean. To his right would be the palisades. He'd pass the California Incline, that carefully engineered road that drew a diagonal paved line up steep cliffs to the beautiful streets and the sorry house where he and his wife and his last, lonely daughter lived. (But you had to approach the Incline driving south, you couldn't make that sharp right turn going north. He could only suppose that Whitney and Tracie would have driven that extra mile north, to turn up Santa Monica Canyon to get home.) He hadn't driven that stretch of highway since the accident. He had promised himself he would never drive it again in his life. But he realized, he *knew,* that the big semis traveling west in lane two, lane three of the Santa Monica Freeway would never give him a chance to take the Lincoln off-ramp. Even as he thought that, he passed Fifth and Fourth and zoomed toward the short tunnel that separated freeway from highway, land from sea. He thought, in anguish, that it was just as well. He couldn't avoid driving over where Whitney and Josh had died forever. Pull off the scab again! Pull it off! Because, why not! The torn flesh was there, the gaping wound was there. Nothing could cover it. Nothing ever would.

"Oh God, Whitney," he said out loud, in the car, as he flashed out of the tunnel, remembered the four flags and the brave white lights that had lit up the little tented circus. "Why didn't you turn *right* out of the parking lot? Why didn't you go up by the Rand Corporation and go home on top of the cliffs? You *could* have! You were supposed to. It would have been just as easy. *Easier* in fact!"

The traffic slowed. Jerry's motor began to heat. He turned off his wipers. I can sneak right past here, he thought. I can roll right over this. I can go right under this. I can drive through the past and on up to Malibu. I can find a tall blond young woman. I can take an airplane, Northwest Airlines, straight to Hong Kong. I can buy an apartment on the Kowloon side. I can buy two Porsches and put them in a double garage. And those Porsches will be our children. And they will never break down. And they will never get hurt.

Then he started to cry, grinding his forehead along the steering wheel's rough skin.

"Oh God, Whitney! How could you do it? How could you do it to Josh? How could you do it to me?"

Well, hell, Jerry, I didn't do it!

A horn honked behind him. He raised his head, saw blurred taillights move out in front of him. He put the car into first. He sniffed, wiped his nose on a french cuff. The cufflinks had been a Father's Day present from Whitney. He scraped his upper lip, scratched his cheek, went on crying.

Far across the city, Donny finished his evening walk down through the cluttered streets of Simi Valley, found the White Night bar already lit up, crowded in the pleasant threat of rain. He pushed through the swinging doors and smiled appreciatively at all the junk on the walls he'd persuaded them to put up during the last months, the grass skirts, the travel posters, these great-looking guys with bright red and blue faces, looking so grim, but dressed up too: "We're so scary! Stand back, world! We're acomin'!" The bartender gave him a happy wave. Business was great these days. Donny took some credit for it. He liked the crowd. He liked the music. Thea was responsible for that, of course. No new-age crap. No country western. And not too much left from the islands either. Just a jukebox full of Van the Man. "Best music in the world," she'd assured Donny months ago.

Forget everybody else. Forget romance. All that broken-heart stuff. Just play Van. And dance.

Donny ordered champagne tonight, some local kerosene they bottled down the street and called Chateau Simi. He felt like partying, celebrating his new life. The end of his loneliness and grief. He poured some from the bottle, smiled and toasted the others at the bar. "That'll take the enamel right off your teeth, buckaroo," but Donny waved at them and punched up J23 on the box. "No Guru, No Method, No Teacher." He liked it. (Although Thea, the night before she caught her plane home, had told him she'd been putting him on about everything. There *were* no other lives, she said, just this one stupid little life, and Van Morrison was the sweet-and-sour pork of spiritualism. But so many things had changed by then that Donny'd given her a hug and helped put in her steam curlers. Because she wanted to be sure to look good for Randy and Brad and Bob when she got home.)

After a while, Donny moved out to dance, in the middle of the worn-down floor. The White Night rattled, the way it always did when a train went by.

> "Well, here it comes!
> Here comes the night!"

He'd gained some weight. He took to the floor alone, rocking out.

"Donny's going for it now," one old bar-bat said. She poured some of his kerosene champagne and watched him with tenderness. He didn't move his feet tonight, just shifted his body, and moved his arms in arcs, waving to the rest of them, inviting them to join in. A few of them did. By the end of the night, they'd all get around to it.

The traffic going north out on Pacific Coast Highway came to a halt. Jerry Bridges held the steering wheel now, hard enough to break it; held it for all the times he'd forgotten to hold Josh, for all the times he couldn't hold Whitney. He cried like a kid, and did what Ernie, the glazier, said. Prayed for it, *please,* to lift a little.

The traffic moved again, inching north, in oil slick and rain.

Robin

Pacific Palisades

IF YOU EVER SAW dumb grief, that was dumb grief, ignorant grief, sad grief. I for one was glad when the traffic loosened and her stepdad's car could start up again. Turn on your wipers, asshole, I called out to him. You want to end up like we are, heh heh heh?

But Whitney, in air, gave me a reproving glance. Jerry turned on his wipers. They made those radical, temporarily clean double arcs across his streaming windshield. He was crying like a kid, more easily now that he'd got started, and like any kid who's crying, you could get his attention. Part of it got caught by the rims that his windshield wipers made, the lovely arcing yellow light against the dark rain. The car was moving again, a steady forty-five, and I watched closely because I was about to find out what was going to happen. Whitney moved away from me, a little. I'm watching you every second of your life, she told him. You're such a good man. You know the right thing to do.

The traffic had broken up pretty well. The city was moving again. You could see bright lights all the way east over the Cajon Pass out to the dark of the Mojave Desert, and airplane-strings across the Pacific to big cities in the Orient. And that one Highlander down in Irian Jaya, still looking in the airport window, all dressed up, waiting for the man or woman of *his* dreams.

I heard Whitney speaking then to her mother, that gray mound of soggy tears, speaking as sensibly as noontime: There are good men everywhere, but you have to keep your eyes open! I bet one's coming home now. Hold out your arms to him, Ma! Don't be a lameshit *all* your life!

And then all my attention went down to the light on the road, and the first rain of winter, and all those windshield wipers, as the rain cleaned everything. Boy!

Boy was it pretty! And what I was supposed to do was make all of it the absolute most beautiful world at that moment, so that everyone within my sphere would be happy to be alive. And I did. And they were. I pride myself on it.

Whitney separated herself from me and went down to perch on the back of his neck. *I knew how to do that! This love will surely last forever! This love will surely last all ways!* I lit up *everything,* as far as I could see. Tina came out of the den where she'd been watching TV. She went into the dark bedroom where her mother was crying, and patted her hair. Her mother gave her a kiss, a dim one, but still a kiss.

Up at the corner of Topanga Canyon and Pacific Coast Highway there's a traffic light. It turned red, on my demand. I'd always liked this intersection. I thought I'd pull out some leftover Indians from up in that dark canyon. Jerry opened his right window for some rain-swept breeze and they blew down and in. This is a beautiful world just the way it is, they breathed, waving their waterproof baskets. Don't worry too much about it. You don't have to fix it up *too* much!

Jerry's ribs rattled, his heart opened. Whitney jumped right in. And there, *wow,* I thought *I* was an ace driver! Jerry's car broke right out into the intersection in a beautiful perfect arc, making a gorgeous, perfectly safe-but-daring U. Without thinking at all about it, he headed back south to his wife and his home, where in ten minutes he would drive up the California Incline, because good men did that, made those wonderful, short, straight moves that held everything in the world together, that kept life going in the world. (But sometimes you had to remind them.) I looked around for Kali, her birth part, not her destruction part, as Wynn — for no reason she could think of — got up off her bed and splashed cold water on her face and combed her hair. And went down to the den with Tina, the first time she'd done that in months. And turned on the lights.

Of course, *looking,* I saw several gold arms reaching, pulling across the sky, stretched out from land to sea and back again. Weary, and caring. Holding it together. Keeping it going. I never knew that about Her. Goodbye, I called to Whitney, but she was gone, safely locked away in a heart that would love her forever. I considered helping a comedian bombing at the Comedy Store out on Sunset but then thought, I've *had* it with good deeds, and decided to head out, looking for Amy Ming, that beautiful, neglected star in the heavens.

But first, I couldn't help it, I stopped for a last turn or two on the beach. Found an empty potato chip bag and cartwheeled around in it, along the damp sand, in fresh, rainy wind. I was the total last straw for some stern girl who'd been lured out here to the beach on a double date and was trying hard to keep her good manners even as the water came pelting down. She reached out and grabbed her girlfriend's hand but that hand got snatched away. I took that crackling bag in for another pass and the girl sat up, at her wit's end: "Come *on*, you guys! Come *on*, you guys! Will you cut that out? We've got to get *started*. We've got to go home!"

For some reason, that tickled me. Made me laugh! I laughed, and bounced on the sand a couple of times. Did two broken cartwheels, exquisitely beautiful in their execution. And whizzed on out.